THE LOVE Detective

THE LOVE
DETECTIVE

ANGELA DYSON

Matador
9 Priory Business Park,
Wistow Road, Kibworth Beauchamp,
Leicestershire. LE8 0RX
Tel: 0116 279 2299
Email: books@troubador.co.uk
Web: www.troubador.co.uk/matador
Twitter: @matadorbooks

ISBN 978 1789010 282

British Library Cataloguing in Publication Data.
A catalogue record for this book is available from the British Library.

Printed and bound by CPI Group (UK) Ltd, Croydon, CR0 4YY
Typeset in 11pt Minion Pro by Troubador Publishing Ltd, Leicester, UK

Matador is an imprint of Troubador Publishing Ltd

The Love Detective is dedicated to the wonderful, strong, and charismatic women of my family:

My sister Claire
My aunts Frankie and Lillie
And in loving memory of my mother, Ann and my grandmother, Mary Bridget.

CHAPTER ONE

It hadn't been a good night. Table six had sent back the chicken, table eight had slapped her boyfriend around the face before flouncing out of the restaurant, and table seventeen had just disappeared in the direction of the loos looking in rather a hurry. At eleven thirty I'd started mouthing polite we're closing soon noises, but now, at past midnight, tables two and nine were asking for yet more coffee. Behind the bar, Dave was playing Adele for the third time in a row and Tara, my fellow waitress of the evening was bleating on about the pros and cons of a carb-free diet. I'm about ready to slit my throat. Tuning her out I positioned myself at the service station and resignedly scooped up another handful of cutlery to polish and allowed my gaze to wander over the room.

Standing apart from the trendy bars and restaurants lining the high street of Wimbledon Village, Abbe's Brasserie is a curiously old-fashioned place but somehow very charming. The décor's a bit tatty but the glow from the masses of candles dripping from wall sconces and flickering upon the tables, hide the worst of the wear and tear, and give it an intimate, inviting appeal. The food's good too. There's no nouvelle cuisine at Abbe's. We serve classic dishes in generous portions. It would be, I decided spitting at a particularly stubborn water stain on a fish knife, just the type of restaurant I'd like to own one day, if I had any ambitions in that direction. I sighed and rubbed hard at the knife with a tea towel trying to distract my mind from the familiar but uncomfortable thought that by now, at twenty-six years old, I should at least be nurturing an ambition to do *something*.

I have four or five shifts a week at Abbe's but this couldn't, even by the most generous and supportive of my friends, be described as a proper career. And yes, there were occasional temping jobs, but they didn't really count. I knew that no matter how much I wanted to put it off, sometime soon I was going to have to make some decisions. I couldn't be a waitress all my life. Believe me it's not all big tippers and interesting ways with leftover lobster. Tonight, my ankles were swollen, my cheek muscles ached from all those welcoming smiles, and the bra I'd bought to do justice to my white uniform shirt was a size too small and digging painfully into my sternum.

Later as I peeled it off and crawled under the duvet, I speculated on the jobs out there that I could possibly be fit for but soon gave way to sleep. In my dreams, I folded thousands of tiny white napkins into the shape of water lilies.

You can tell a lot about a person by the way they eat a pizza. Some attack it savagely from various angles; others dissect it neatly into mathematically precise portions and some, like Laura, start from the middle and work their way out to the crust. It was one o'clock on the following day and we were in the aggressively cool new pizzeria down on the Broadway. It was busy and very noisy, the buzz of conversation bouncing off hard bright surfaces. I shifted uncomfortably on my over-designed ironwork stool, as Laura started at the heart of the matter and worked her way out to the details. "It's not that I doubt him, it's just that…" she began.

And immediately memories of countless he-done-me-wrong tales sat down to join us. Laura is unbelievably unfortunate with men. Is it that she just happens to be particularly unlucky? Or, is it that she's way too trusting? This, she considers rich coming from me. Perhaps she has a point. This is how it goes. She meets what she describes as the Perfect Man. The sex is mind-blowing. They have a real connection. It's absolute heaven. Then three weeks later, he disappears off to a commune to *find himself* or goes back to his oil rig/country of origin/wife. This last one crops up with wearying regularity. Now, I've nothing against affairs with married men. After all a girl has not matured until she has had at least one regrettable hair straightening experience and has been lied to by at least two misunderstood husbands. These things happen and later we laugh and we cry about them over many bottles of rosé with our friends, but Laura, wonderful warm-hearted Laura, is always knocked sideways with surprise and disappointment. Now she was telling me about her latest.

"He's attractive, he's successful, and he's charming. And yes Clarry, before you ask, I did remember to check this time, he's single. There is definitely no wife in the background. He's great, he really is. It's just… well it's probably nothing."

I rolled my eyes at her. "What? Come on. Spill."

She rested her elbows on the table. "It's just that he's asking a lot of questions about my work."

"So? That's a good thing isn't it? A man who's interested in your life and not just his own, that's rare in my experience."

She took a swig of wine "True. But no matter what we start talking about, he always seems to steer the conversation back to the business I'm doing."

She shook her head and picked up her knife and fork. "Forget it, I'm probably imagining it."

"Back up. Start at the beginning."

She took a deep breath, her eyes shining. She wore a look that I know of old. Oh dear, I thought, she's got it bad this time.

"OK. He's Simon Napier. I met him at the Local Luncheon Club two weeks ago."

"God. What's that?"

"It's just this boring monthly lunch that I have to attend. Lots of solicitors go and other business people as well. The food's always terrible and I usually end up sitting next to some old chap from a building society rabbiting on about interest rates and the credit crunch." She flicked back her long brown hair and took another slug of her wine. "Anyway, there I am looking at my place card and suddenly there *he* is. Simon Napier, newly appointed manager of Dunstan Stead estate agents. Over six-feet tall, blonde hair, totally fit, bloody gorgeous in fact and he's sitting next to me at lunch."

She'd got my attention. "So, what happened?"

"We've been out for drinks and dinner twice and it's great. He's funny, he's bright, we have a lot in common, and he's unbelievably sexy but…" Her voice trailed off and her shoulders slumped.

"But what?"

She shrugged. "I suppose that I just want to be sure that it's me he's really interested in. That he doesn't just see me as a source of business for his firm."

"And are you?" I asked picking up my glass.

She nodded. "Remember I told you that I'm heading up the conveyancing division and handling all the probate sales? I gave Simon two quite large houses to sell sole agency. He got offers on them straightaway and the buyers wanted a really quick exchange, which was great. And I've just instructed him on another one, a huge old place off Wimbledon Hill."

I thought for a moment. "Did he get good prices for the houses?"

"Well actually no. But you know what the market is these days and a quick sale is always what the beneficiaries want anyway, especially if there are a lot of them. Some nephews and nieces scattered all over the country for example, all wanting their share of the profits of some rundown old house, most of them never having visited Great Aunt Dolly or whomever for years. They don't care if she's dead, they just want the money."

"Charming. So, have you slept with him yet?"

"Not quite, but the rev-up's been fun." She took a bite of her pizza.

"I bet. Look you probably don't have anything to worry about, but we both know that it never does any harm to keep your eyes wide open."

She beamed at me. "I'm so glad you feel like that because that's just where you come in Clarry."

I shot her a look, not liking where this was going. "Come in where?"

She pushed aside the last of her food. "Look, you're not doing much and I thought…"

"Hold up, I'm waitress extraordinaire remember?"

She ignored me and finally got down to what I now realised the whole of this lunch had been leading up to. "I thought you could nose about a bit. Ask a few questions."

"No," I said flatly. "No way."

"Clarry please, I really do want to be sure about him before I get too involved. You've said it yourself that I'm too gullible. This time it's going to be different but I can't do it myself. What if he turns out to be The One and I blow it by being too suspicious and pushy? That's why it's got to be you."

"For starters, I'm not sure I believe in the concept of The One. It sounds rather limiting and secondly, what do you mean by *asking a few questions?*"

She leaned eagerly over the table and topped up our glasses. "Couldn't you pretend to be looking for a house or something?"

"No, I could not! I've never even bought a house and I wouldn't know where to start. It's ridiculous."

"Or how about a property developer? It shouldn't be that difficult."

"Laura, this is crazy. I haven't any experience with this kind of thing."

"You were always good at drama at school. Especially improvisation."

"That was a million years ago," I snapped. "And besides, a few creative workshops acting out teenage angst with Sister Granger isn't exactly the perfect grounding to pretend to be a property… whatever… type person."

"But you can. I know you can. It'll be just like being a…" She thought for a moment and then, as if throwing down a trump card, said breezily, "It will be like being a private detective."

"Hardly."

She looked down at her plate. "I need you Clarry."

And that was that. When your oldest and best friend in the world asks for help, then you give it, if you can.

"And what's more…"

She was triumphant now knowing full well that I'd never had a choice in the matter. "I'm going to pay you."

"If I do it at all, I'll do it for nothing."

"Don't be silly. I'm doing pretty well at the moment and you're flat broke."

As she disappeared upstairs in search of the ladies, I considered the seventy pounds in my purse that I'd earnt last night being on my feet for six hours at Abbe's. She's right, I thought, I can't afford principles.

Laura filled me in on some details, insisted on paying for lunch and leaving me with a swift hug, disappeared in the direction of the tube before I could come up with any further objections.

CHAPTER TWO

No 12 Hillside. My home. This tiny, two-bedroom cottage had been left to me by Grandma P., my father's mother. Every time I put my key in the lock, I offer up a grateful prayer of thanks to her memory for the independence it gives me. She had been a remarkable woman and I had loved her. With a tongue abrasive sometimes to the point of rudeness and a determined self-reliance that could make her a difficult person to really know, she had been a major influence on my life. She had died three years ago, but here in this house where she had lived for nearly fifty years, I still felt the comfort of her presence.

As an only child I suppose I could have felt lonely, but with much of my school holidays spent with Grandma P., somehow, I never was. She taught me so much. I may never have her light hand with pastry, but I do know how to build a well-constructed compost heap and make up a bed with proper hospital corners. You'd think that those talents alone would guarantee me an exciting and glamorous career, now wouldn't you? From the usual childhood tantrums, through to the dramatic door slamming days of self-centred adolescence, Grandma P. had always been there, with solid but unemotional comfort and advice. When I wept in self-pity over some party I hadn't been invited to or over some imagined slight from a classmate, she would put everything back in perspective.

"Clarry there is nothing that you can feel that you need ever be ashamed of. You are suffering now I know, but take it as a sign that you are alive and part of the world. We are here such a short time, so isn't it a shame to waste any of it by being unhappy?"

In the first year after her death, I hadn't had the heart to change anything and so had lived with her 1970's décor in the colours of a condiment tray. The shades of mustard, ketchup, and vinegar had weighed down on me until I finally understood that my redecorating didn't represent a betrayal of her memory. She would have wanted me to breathe my own brand of life into the house and so slowly I had transformed every room. With paintwork in duck-egg blue, sage, and tea rose, the cottage was, even on the darkest of days, full of light and warmth.

The only area I hadn't properly tackled yet was the hall. It was papered with a stubborn Anaglypta in hideous ochre. Now, on Sunday evening, as I regarded the three-square feet it had taken me two hours to scrape off, my thoughts turned to Laura's request. Sipping thoughtfully on a glass of Pinot Grigio, I tried to imagine myself in the role of private detective. Attracted as I am by the idea of being just like Angelina Jolie in "Mr. and Mrs. Smith", cool, sexy, and tough, I knew realistically that I could never pull it off. I'd never get *into* a rubber corset dress, let alone *out* of one. I didn't have any high-tech gadgets. I knew nothing about surveillance and I'm definitely not brave. The Miss Marple approach it would have to be.

It was with thoughts of Miss Marple and her twinsets that I surveyed the contents of my wardrobe the following morning. I'm particularly sensitive to the influence of clothing. In a satin slip dress, I'm sweet and just a little coy. Actually, I'm not sure how much longer I can pull off coy. In a tailored suit I strut purposefully, looking for the entire world like I have something important to do, which is rarely true. Mostly however, I'm a jeans girl. They can be dressed up or dressed down and go with everything. I have a considerable collection of white shirts, some sexy with a masculine cut, others cut low at the neck, feminine and sheer. I love them all. They freshen up the complexion, they don't look like I'm trying too hard, and they wash well. Whatever works?

Munching toast, I finally settled on a pair of black skinny jeans and a white T-shirt, a structured black jacket giving the casual look a self-assured edge. Tying back my hair and rooting around for an oversized pair of sunglasses, I felt dressed for the part, which is half way to feeling confident I'm told.

I picked up the phone. "Simon Napier?" I pitched my voice to register several octaves lower than usual. "You don't know me; my name is Gemma Buchanan." I've always liked the name Gemma. And it's as good a name as any. "Word is," I continued huskily, "You're a man I should meet."

"Really Ms. Buchanan? And why should that be?" His cultured drawl was tempered with impatience.

"Because I understand that you have an eye when it comes to development properties in the area. The consortium

I represent would be *grateful* for any leads." I weighed the word with what I hoped was a subtle emphasis.

"I see," he replied, but wasn't picking up the bait. "Well if you'd like to come in and register, we'll put you on our files." And there was that… I'm a very busy person and I'm ringing off now note… to his voice. I interrupted hastily.

"I'm not sure that you understand me Mr. Napier. I'm not interested in registering, only in getting the right deal. Alwyn Road for example."

"Alwyn Road? How do you know…?" he broke off.

"Are you available this morning?" I asked not giving him time to reply. "How about eleven o'clock? I'll drop by your office, shall I?"

He blustered but I sensed a tinge of hesitation in his tone. "I'm not sure I'm free at eleven. And no, not at the office. I'll be… out."

"Fine. At the property then and we'll make it half past. I'll see you there."

I put down the receiver, my hands sweating. Of course he probably wouldn't turn up. Why should he just drop everything on the say-so of a total stranger? But I was relying on a combination of curiosity, unease, and my assumed breathy purr to send him popping into his BMW.

Deciding that my battered old Renault wouldn't hold up under scrutiny, I parked a street away from Alwyn Road. Walking down the quiet residential street in the watery sunshine of early April, I thought about what Laura had told me. She was handling the estate of the late Miss Davenport, of which No 29 Alwyn Road comprised the major part. It had recently gone on the market through Simon's agency, and so far, apparently there had been several viewings but no real interest.

As I reached the house a car pulled up. I was right about the BMW and Laura was right about his looks. Smooth but not flashy, tall with floppy blonde hair, regular features, and sporting a slight tan, he was a bit conventional for my taste but handsome enough. And it was my job now to convince him that I was who I claimed to be. Having totally failed to concoct any kind of a plan, I would just have to wing it.

"Ms. Buchanan, how do you do." His handshake was firm.

I nodded my head in acknowledgement, suddenly feeling nervous and out of my depth. Suppressing an urge to turn and run back to the car as fast as my heels would carry me, I forced myself to smile. "Good morning Mr. Napier."

"Shall we?" he asked and opened the front gate.

I followed him up a black and white tessellated path to the front door. Turning the key in the lock, he then gave the door a good shove as a large pile of mail blocked our entry. As he leant down to clear them aside, the seat of his pinstripe trousers stretched tautly across his butt.

The house turned out to be a dream, although it did need quite a lot of work. Early Victorian, double-fronted with six bedrooms, it clearly hadn't been touched in decades, but was chock-full of original fireplaces and fancy ceilings. We exchanged only a few words as we toured the empty rooms, Simon pointing out various features and I concentrating on looking quietly knowledgeable. A look, I fear that I'm going to have to work on.

As we came back out into the fresh air he remarked, "Not much interest in such big houses these days, too expensive to maintain."

I had to hide my surprise. Wimbledon is an affluent area and I would have thought that there would be plenty of comfortably off families who'd jump at the opportunity to buy a place like this. The huge garden, the masses of space, its proximity to the tube, everything screamed desirable.

"So Ms. Buchanan," he continued. "What is this consortium that you represent and how do you happen to know about this house?"

This was a question I was not ready to answer and so I went on the offensive. "Why shouldn't I know?" I batted back at him. "It's on the market, isn't it?"

"Of course," his pale blue eyes narrowed. "It's just that you don't appear to be registered with us. There's no For Sale board, for security reasons you understand and it's not yet on our website."

"One hears these things," I trialled the idea. "Perhaps one of your staff?"

"Properties such as these are only dealt with by me, as I'm the manager."

For a guy who could only be in his mid-thirties, his manner was pretty pompous. Not a characteristic I find particularly attractive in a man. Perhaps Laura hadn't spotted it in him yet.

"Properties such as these?" I allowed a slight edge of enquiry to creep into my tone. I would like to have raised one eyebrow for added emphasis, but I can't do so without making myself practically cross-eyed, so I resisted the temptation. He answered stiffly.

"It isn't normal practice to leave houses of this size in the hands of junior staff."

Pompous *and* prickly. It was time for me to be gone. Thankfully we had now reached the front gate and so I stuck out my hand. "I'm grateful for your time Mr. Napier."

He shook it and immediately I turned to walk away. "But I don't know how to contact you," he protested.

I looked back over my shoulder. "Oh, I'll be in touch."

As I passed the BMW I took a quick look at the car registration number and committed it to memory. Once I was around the corner and well out of sight I broke into a jog, let myself in to the Renault, and made a note of the number. It was only when I started up the engine that I realised that I hadn't asked him the price of the house. I thumped the palm of my hand down hard upon the steering wheel. I was such an idiot. I'd been so busy trying to look cool and in control, the kind of woman who brokers deals every day and is at ease in the world of money and property that I'd completely missed the most obvious point. Then suddenly a thought struck me. Why hadn't *he* told me the price?

Any nerve-wracking situation invariably makes me hungry. What I wanted was cake. I would nip back up to the village, to Bayley and Sage, our local swanky delicatessen and pick up two pieces of lemon sponge. No I wasn't being greedy (though I am often guilty of this); I was going to pop in on Flan.

Auntie Flan isn't my real aunt but she had been Grandma P.'s best friend and near neighbour for over thirty years and that had earned her honorary status. Whilst Grandma P. had schooled me in practical matters, Flan had introduced me to the feminine world of clothes and cosmetics.

At eight years old I had sat beside her at her dressing table, avidly watching as she applied lipstick to her Cupid's bow mouth and sweeps of rouge to her high cheekbones. I had yearned to look like her, like a film star. Now at seventy, she is still undeniably glamorous, with dark eyes bright with energy and enthusiasm, and hair originally chestnut but now cunningly low-lit with honey and caramel.

"Darling, I shall never allow myself to go grey, it's so unbecoming." She had a long lean frame to which age only lends elegance. I adore her.

She greeted me at the door dressed in loose purple trousers and a flowing, lilac silk shirt. "Clarry darling, how lovely. Come in."

Fully made-up – I had never seen her otherwise – she looks marvellous and can still turn heads. She had never married but there is always a man in her life. Currently, she was enjoying the attentions of Mr. Harold Babcock, a retired undertaker and of Mr. George Huxton, a retired joiner and keen horticulturist. Between these two charming old gentlemen (I had met them both); there was a keen rivalry as Flan kept them in a permanent state of lovesick fervour fanned by the flames of jealousy.

Proffering my cheek for a kiss and the white cardboard cake box for inspection, I padded down the hall after her towards the kitchen.

"The kettle is already on. Now sit down and tell me all your news." She busied herself taking the familiar blue Spode mugs and plates from the dresser and the milk jug from the fridge. She was of the generation that would never dream of pouring it direct from the carton. When the tea was ready and we had both taken our first mouthful of the moist lemony cake, I began my story to which she listened intently.

"I could tell straightaway darling that you were keyed up about something. You get a certain look in your eyes."

This was interesting. Was I really so transparent? I guess I'll never make a poker player. "What kind of a look?"

She ignored me. "So, you say he seemed unsettled by you?"

My mouth full, it took me a moment to answer. "Well not necessarily *by* me, more by the fact of me. He was very keen to know how I knew about the house." I broke off and put down my fork. "Something has just occurred to me. Something I didn't register at the time. If other people have been shown around, other would-be purchasers, then why was there so much post blocking the door? Surely that much couldn't have accumulated since it was last viewed? There was tons of it."

"Yes, that does seem odd but I don't see what that has to do with his feelings for Laura."

I sat back in my chair. "I don't know. Maybe nothing, but let's think about it. If there *is* something funny going on with the house then that means… that means what?"

Flan crossed one purple clad leg over the other. "Who knows at this point? But that's where we need to start, with the house. Because it's all we have to go on."

I paused with my mug half way to my mouth. "What do you mean *we*? Flan, you are not getting involved in this."

She held up a placatory hand. "Clarry, someone needs to go into that estate agents and find out if the house is genuinely on the market and that person cannot be you, or Simon will recognise you. So who else can it be?"

She eyed me speculatively. I opened my mouth to protest and then closed it again.

CHAPTER THREE

Having spent some time checking the immediate side streets for any sign of Simon's car, we pulled up on Wimbledon Hill just a little way up from the offices of Dunstan Stead. I hoped that he was still out, but it was possible that the BMW was a pool car, which meant it was now over to Flan.

I put a warning hand on her arm as she opened the car door to get out. "Now Flan, don't overdo it. Act casual."

She sketched a mock salute, then glided down the street and disappeared. I hate waiting at the best of times. I don't do queues. No club, restaurant, or sale is ever that good. I fidgeted and inspected my face in the rear-view mirror, adjusting it to get a better look at my hair. Hmm, not bad, but a bit flat on top. I needed a trim and my highlights were beginning to look a little faded, but could last another week or two.

At last after nearly half an hour when I'd exhausted the contents of the glove compartment and earnestly studied an ancient A to Z to find out exactly where I lived, Flan reappeared. She looked very pleased with herself as she rapped on the window.

"Went like a dream Clarry. Such a nice young man and he had lovely teeth."

"Who Napier?"

"No I asked for the manager but was told he was on appointments. I was looked after by a young man called Stephen Oakley. It's rather a swish office dear, with flowers on the tables and even a couple of armchairs. Anyway, he sat me down to register me officially and then he tapped things into his computer about my requirements. I told him that I was only interested in houses in Woodside, Alwyn, or Compton Road, that I was very particular about it."

"And," I interrupted eagerly. "What did he say?"

But Flan, it was clear, wasn't going to be rushed. She settled herself more comfortably in the passenger seat and continued, "I explained how it had to be big enough to accommodate me, my son and daughter-in-law and my three young grandchildren. I couldn't remember how big you said the house was, but I thought that a woman of my age would want somewhere large enough to get away from all the noise children make. And not to mention toys left all over the place. There would probably be bicycles in the hallway and on the stairs where I could trip over and it simply doesn't do to risk a fall at…"

"Flan!" I cut in urgently. "You don't *have* any grandchildren, with or without bicycles!"

"That's as maybe, but to be convincing it is imperative to believe in the story you are telling." She looked at me reprovingly. "If you are going to take up this line of work you will do well to remember that Clarry. Do you know I'm sure that I would have made an awfully good detective? Is it too late for me to take it up now do you think? I wouldn't have thought it was a job you would need a degree or to have passed exams for. It takes a clear head, a keen eye, and just the right amount of daring." She broke off thoughtfully.

I put my head in my hands and groaned.

"So, I explained to the young man with the teeth that the cost was of no importance as my son is a very important man in the City. That he'd always been ambitious even as a small boy. That he'd worked hard at school, had handed in his homework on time…"

I now started to bang my head against the steering wheel, but she didn't miss a beat.

"I told him that we didn't mind whether the property needed redecorating, it's the exact location we want. *And…*" she paused and as I looked up holding my breath, she flashed me a raffish smile. "And they definitely do *not* have anything in those three roads currently on the market!"

I exhaled loudly.

"He was most apologetic and promised that the minute something comes up he'll be in touch. So obliging. He even offered me a cup of coffee but I explained how I never drink it as it's so bad for the skin."

Sparing a thought for poor Stephen Oakley, I kicked the engine into life and shot out into the lunchtime traffic to a trumpet of blaring car horns, as I all but collided with a black cab turning out from the station. Damn. I hadn't returned the rear-view mirror back into position.

Flan, ignoring the bellows of abuse from the taxi driver buckled up her seat belt. "Perhaps I should have taken up the stage? When it comes to lying I'm a natural."

After dropping her back to Lauriston Road, I headed for home. I needed to think. I'd sit down with a cup of tea and decide what to do next. Letting myself in, I pulled off my jacket and kicked off my heels. I filled the kettle and checked my mobile for messages. There were two; one from Dave, the manager at Abbe's, confirming my shift for Wednesday evening and the other from Laura.

"I couldn't sleep last night for wondering if this plan was just completely crazy. Actually I couldn't work out who was the most deranged, me for coming up with it or you for agreeing to it?" She laughed a little breathlessly but excitement was there in her tone. "But Clarry, I woke up this morning certain in my mind that I was doing the right thing. I'm sure Simon's motives are genuine and that you will find out only good things about him." Her message ended with, "Bye love and thanks. You know I'm counting on you."

Great. No pressure then. Trying to calm my thoughts, I made tea and sipped it at the kitchen table but it was no good, my mind was spinning. Should I phone her now and tell her what I know? But what did I know? Nothing really. I got up, too wired to sit still, and opened the back door to the garden. Still barefoot I stepped out on to the narrow path that skirts the edge of my small rectangular lawn.

The late afternoon sun shone brightly and the sight of a small cluster of primroses peeping shyly up through the grass to meet its gaze filled me with a sense of optimism and purpose. I realised that I hadn't been out here for a few days and in that time there had been changes. The crocuses had faded out. The pink and blue hyacinths had died off; their long bitter green leaves flailing now that the heavy scented flower heads had dried. Daffodils still raised their sunny faces to the sky and the first of the forget-me-nots straggled their way along the raised beds and jostled for room with early budding wallflowers.

Grandma P. had loved this garden. She could be found out here at any time of the year, leaning over to pull up any stray weed that dared to force its way through her carefully tended beds. In summer, she wore a battered straw hat on her head and in winter, she wrapped herself up in an ancient brown overcoat with sleeves so long that they had to be rolled up. I think it had originally belonged to my grandfather.

Some of my earliest memories are of helping to deadhead the roses that clambered over the back fence and of watching her raking up scattered leaves from the lawn. I did my best to keep up with the garden because I loved it too. Every time I snip off a few flower stems to arrange in one of her old glass vases, I can almost feel her smiling.

I looked down at the splash of pale yellow primroses; their velvet petals and furry leaves so precious because there were so few, and decided to leave them undisturbed. The forget-me-knots however, were going to get it. I snapped off a handful and headed back inside for the pale blue jug I keep under the sink. The quiet of the garden and the soothing action of arranging the spindly fragile stems had cleared my mind. I grabbed my keys, snagged an old sweatshirt from the coat rack, thrust my feet into a pair of trainers, and headed out the door. So what if I didn't have a clue what I was doing? I would just have to make it up as I went along.

CHAPTER FOUR

Pulling the Renault into a space a few doors up from Dunstan Stead, I stuffed my hair up into an old baseball cap that had lain abandoned along the back window for months and hunkered down a little in my seat. I could see the BMW parked in a slip road next to the library. It was after five thirty; surely they'd be closing up sometime soon?

An hour later and I was beginning to wonder if they were ever going to shut up shop, when a middle-aged woman in a shirtwaist dress, came out to retrieve the open/closed board. Five minutes later, she and a young guy, possibly Stephen Oakley but I wasn't near enough to catch a glimpse of his teeth, left together in the direction of the station. They hadn't locked up so presumably someone was still in there. I didn't have to wait long. Lights were turned out and there he was. Simon Napier. After performing some complicated operation with a large bunch of keys, he let himself into his car and drove off.

Allowing a couple of cars to get in front of me, I eased out into the traffic behind him. Now I've seen it in films and on TV of course, but actually following another car without drawing attention to oneself is no easy thing. There's a lot of weaving in and out. The driver of a silver Toyota whose passenger side door I narrowly missed colliding with, probably thought that I was driving under the influence of drugs, alcohol, or mental impairment. This last may be close to the truth.

Simon was an aggressive driver. Sweating under my cap, I concentrated on keeping the BMW in sight and wondered what on earth I was doing. What was I expecting to discover? Fighting down a growing sense of the ridiculous, I followed him along the Broadway, past South Wimbledon Tube and out on to Merton High Street. Where was he going? Probably off to the gym or just home. A sudden thought occurred to me and I nearly veered off the road as the extent of my own stupidity hit me. I hadn't thought to ask Laura for something as basic as Simon's address. I groaned aloud (I seemed to have done that a lot today) and mentally beat myself up. I just knew I'd be crap at this. And I was surprised at how disappointed I was with myself. OK, so I could turn around, go home, phone Laura and tell her that it was no good, she'd just have to abandon the whole insane idea, or, I could for once, finish what I'd started.

Now is probably the time to admit to a whopping character flaw: I have a history of giving up. Yes I know it's a sign of immaturity and I'm not in the least proud of it. The thing is, I'm always madly keen at the start of things; a new job, new relationship, classes in this or that, but when the first flash of enthusiasm has waned and determination, self-discipline and… well, courage, are needed to go on, then I have nearly always taken the easy way out and quit. Not good. So it's taken me a while to face up to the fact that I am not exactly the queen of the *follow through*. Somewhere inside me I have a suspicion that this is the real reason Grandma P. left me the house. She knew I needed its security. I felt a prickling of shame and then looked anxiously ahead for Simon. There was the BMW, five or six cars ahead now. Keeping a tight grip on the steering wheel, I followed him as he indicated right and pulled out on to Tooting High Street. Without conscious thought my mind, it would seem, had made the decision without me.

The light was beginning to fade and it was getting harder to keep Simon's car in sight but doggedly I followed him, crawling through the traffic along Upper Tooting Road, until finally he swung off on to the forecourt of a pub car park. I almost pulled in after him but realised just in time that it would be better to drive past and then double back. Nearly ten minutes later and I'd practically given up all hope of coming across a side street that one could actually drive through. The local market was in the process of closing down for the night. Traders were humping boxes into vans, vast wooden trolleys were being wheeled across the rat-run roads, and commuters were adding to the chaos as they poured out of Tooting Bec tube.

Finally, I found my way back down the hill and drove into the car park. I scanned the dozen or so cars and located the BMW by the rubbish bins. I parked carefully, away from the street light but with a good view of both his car and the pub door.

The Falcon was not a pub I knew. It was bit shabby and not the kind of place I would have expected to find Simon. A few people entered; office workers by the look of them, eager to end their day with a few drinks and a few laughs before heading home. As I waited, an impressive looking dark blue car pulled up. It looked expensive, as did the man who got out of it. He was of medium height but thickset and powerful, wearing a dark suit and was in his early forties I guessed, with a strong profile and dark hair. There was an air of quiet self-confidence in the way he walked that was attractive. Idly I watched him step over a stray cabbage leaf that had blown across from the market and then enter the pub.

I now understand why, in films, it is mostly men that carry out surveillance: bladder control. I had resisted the thought for as long as I could but was now getting desperate. It's OK for a man, he just has to hop behind a lamppost, or up against a wall… I had no choice. I would have to risk going into the pub. Pulling my cap down low over my eyes, I sidled in and found myself in a small outer foyer. Thank God, the loos were located there and not inside the main body of the bar. Almost whimpering with relief, I locked myself into a cubicle, ripped down my jeans, and finally plonked myself down on the cold wooden seat. Washing my hands and taking a hasty look at myself in the mirror, I felt my confidence return. Now I was here, I might as well see what Simon was up to.

Exiting back out into the foyer, I turned to a large pair of double doors, the entrance to the bar. In each door there was a murky pane of oval shaped glass and through which, feeling rather foolish, I peered furtively. I couldn't see him at first. My gaze took in a long central counter where a big-boned girl with a topknot was pulling pints and a guy in a heavy metal T-shirt was polishing glasses. A few customers stood waiting their turn to be served, but Simon was not amongst them.

I craned my neck to get a better look and squinted through at the clutches of drinkers sitting at the tables that edged the room, but still couldn't see him. Perhaps I'd missed him when I was in the loo? Looking anxiously over my shoulder, it then struck me that to someone coming in from outside I probably looked like a recovering alcoholic slavering at the door, desperate for a drink but not trusting myself to go in. Flexing my neck muscles, I once more raked the room and finally spotted him at a small table in the far corner deep in conversation with a man. It was the guy in the dark suit from the car park. Casting one more glance behind me, I studied them.

Simon appeared to be explaining something. Even from this distance I noted much shaking of the head and hand gestures that were mostly palm-upwards. The Suit, in contrast, didn't seem to be saying much. Legs crossed and his body still and relaxed, he rarely looked at the younger man and hardly seemed to be paying attention. That was about as far as my limited knowledge of body language could get me. What they were talking about I couldn't begin to guess at and what their relationship was I had no idea, but it didn't look to me like they were just a couple of friends having a quiet drink together.

After another five minutes, it appeared that their conversation was coming to a close because Simon got up and held out his hand to The Suit, which was my signal to get the hell out of there. I scooted back to the Renault and panting a little with adrenalin and nerves, I hit the throttle and headed for home.

A vodka shot and a bubble bath helped a little with the nerves. Then I thought about supper. I am not one of these girls that only have half a lemon, a pot of cottage cheese, and some wilting salad in the fridge. I love to eat and cooking relaxes me. So I knocked up one of my favourite pasta dishes, mushroom and tarragon fusilli, poured myself a glass of red wine, and took both into the sitting room to enjoy on the sofa.

When I was done I reached for my mobile. "Hi Laura, it's me."

There was a beat of expectation in her tone. "Clarry! I've been dying to speak to you all day. Have you found out anything yet?"

I cut across her. "No not yet, these things take time. Just wanted to check something with you, for my research. What is Simon's address?"

She sounded disappointed. "Sorry I didn't mean to rush you, it's just… well, you know… "

I did and I felt for her, but I wasn't telling her anything yet. Grabbing a pen, I jotted down the street number and name. "So, when are you next seeing him?"

"Tomorrow night. He's booked a table at The Lighthouse."

"Have a great time love. I'll phone in a couple of days for a proper chat." I rang off hastily before she could quiz me.

Stretching back against the cushions I took a thoughtful sip of wine. I was due back at Abbe's on Wednesday evening, so that meant I would have to make full use of tomorrow. I put down my glass and dialled Flan's number.

CHAPTER FiVE

I woke at seven o'clock and, before I could talk myself out of the idea, reached for my trainers and headed off to the Common. I am not, repeat not, a fitness freak (I'm very happy being a curvy girl), but I do need something to work off my highly indulgent diet. So, dutifully I thunder down the bridle paths and through the thickets of Wimbledon Common four or five times a week and this means that I can continue to spread peanut butter on my toast so thickly that I leave teeth marks and still fit into a pair of size 14 jeans.

It was a beautiful morning and the usual dog walkers were out. Mostly mature sturdy ladies in waxed jackets with ringing voices, they cut across the greetings of their fellow early risers to admonish their Labradors and retrievers with "Jasper!" or "Lillie *No!* Put that down, put it down!"

It all seemed rather comfortable and clubby, a safe and certain world where retired people enjoy small reassuring routines. Some days I envy them and stop for a chat, but this morning I struck out into the woods following a small stream from Caesar's Well that leads down towards Beverly Brook. I hadn't run this path for a month or so. The hawthorn and hazel that had been stripped and bare were now thick with buds. Small brown birds darted through the briars and I could hear the insistent hammering of a woodpecker high up in the trees.

As I plunged through the undergrowth I felt fresh and alert, building up a rhythm and concentrating on my breathing. My mind was clear. I knew what I was going to do next and when I got home I'd make some calls to put the first stage of my plan into action. The second part of the plan however, the part I had concocted with Flan last night, I was not so certain of.

I pounded along a winding track overgrown with ivy and thought over our conversation. Stephen Oakley had told Flan that they had nothing for sale in Alwyn Road. This could mean that the house was already under offer, but then why would Simon have shown it to me? And what about all that junk mail? And the fact that he'd been most insistent that he was handling the sale personally bothered me. Did his colleagues even know about the property? If they didn't then the details, and there must be some sort of paperwork even in this digital age, were unlikely to be kept in the office. In the bright light of day, the second part of the plan seemed shadowy, insubstantial, and downright crazy. Of course we couldn't go ahead with it. Could we?

After a shower and a bowl of cereal, I was ready for stage one.

"Dunstan Stead," a chirpy female voice at the other end of the line greeted me.

"Mr. Napier please." I injected as much crisp professionalism in my tone as I could muster.

"Certainly, and whom should I say is calling?"

"Gemma Buchanan."

I was put on hold and listened without pleasure to a ghastly instrumental version of 'The way you look tonight'. Just when I was regretting that Elton John had ever sat down at a piano, Simon picked up.

"Simon Napier speaking, good morn…"

I didn't give him time to continue and cut in with, "We want to make an offer on Alwyn Road. Shall I meet you on-site or at your office?"

There was a pause. "I see. How much are you…?"

Again I interrupted him. "I think these things are done so much better face to face, don't you? How about twelve o'clock?"

Another pause and a longer one this time, but when he did respond he was brisk. "I'll meet you at the property and it will have to be half past twelve." And with that he disconnected the line.

Time to get on with my research. Armed with a large mug of coffee and a notepad, I looked up the numbers of various local estate agents.

"Hi, my name's Lucy Frost from *Village Life*. Oh, you have not heard of the magazine? Well… um… we're new. Anyway, we're doing a feature on quality homes for the larger family, six, seven, bedrooms. We will be approaching your firm next week to give you the opportunity of advertising with us, but in the short term I'm just making some preliminary enquiries on price. For example, houses of that size in… say… Alwyn Road, or on Woodside or Compton?"

The agents I spoke to were uniformly helpful and all told pretty much the same story.

"I see; it can range from three to six million. Wow, and that, I take it, would be for properties in good condition? Right, thank you very much. Our advertising department will be in touch."

I didn't have time to start approaching local builders for a rough estimate on doing up a house of that size, but whatever it cost; Alwyn Road was worth a whole heap of money. And I was going to pretend to be making an offer. No, not me, I remembered, but the consortium I represent. That makes all the difference then. I dressed with care, in a white pencil skirt and pale pink blouse, all the while trying but failing to compose a suitable profile for this bogus consortium.

Again, I parked a street away and this time Simon, looking sharp in a navy single-breasted suit, was waiting for me as I approached the house.

"Mr. Napier, I'm glad you could find the time this morning."

His pale blue eyes looked me slowly up and down and his gaze lingered a little too long on my chest. I became conscious that something in him had subtly changed. He was more confident. Yesterday I had wrong-footed him, but today he was very much in control. Why confidence in men so often displays itself with a sexual edge, I don't know. Women instinctively recognise it and the suggestion of threat that can lie beneath its surface.

Leaning back slightly, allowing one hand to rest on the rusting metal of the front gate, he asked, "Would you like me to show you around the house again?"

Something about his stance and the self-satisfaction of his manner got under my skin, and in that spurt of irritation, I felt my nerves abate. I smiled coolly up at him. "That won't be necessary. We are ready to make an offer in the region of five million."

His eyes flashed with surprise. Whatever price he had been expecting, I am sure it wasn't as much as this. I'd hoped, rather than calculated, that at this price he had to take the offer seriously. "I see. Well I'll put it to the vendor of course and I'll get back to you in a couple of days, but I should warn you that there is a possibility of the property being withdrawn from the market."

I stared at him. "Really and why's that?"

"I can't divulge that information Ms. Buchanan."

Whatever does Laura see in this guy I thought, but asked, "Is there another offer on the house?"

He folded his arms across his chest and gave me a frigid smile. "I can't discuss that with you. However," he said as he took a pace towards me, "I do need some details about *you* Ms. Buchanan. What exactly is this consortium? I would need that information in order to qualify your offer."

I felt suddenly charged with energy and resolution. I didn't like this man and I sure as hell wasn't going to be bullied by him. Shooting him a dazzling smile, I shrugged my shoulders. "Well as we don't even know if the house is actually for sale it's hardly relevant is it?" Stepping away from him, I added, "A couple of days you said? Right then I'll be in touch on Friday. Goodbye."

As I walked swiftly away I could feel his eyes on me.

Slowly I drove the Renault back around the corner and spotted him, still outside the house, squawking earnestly into his mobile. After a minute or so he rang off and got into his car. At a discreet distance, I followed him out on to Wimbledon Hill but away from the direction of his office. Snaking around the back of the Village and down behind the Tennis Club we joined the A3 and filtered into the Wandsworth one-way-system.

Adrenaline was pumping through me as we headed for Clapham North and towards Kennington. Where was he off to now? Maintaining a space of at least two cars between us, I threaded my way behind him through the lunchtime traffic into Camberwell Green, keeping well back as he drew up outside, of all things, a *barbers*. Perhaps in times of stress he nips in for a quick short back and sides?

I managed to park almost opposite Nikko's the barbers and reached for the baseball hat to tuck my hair into. Nikko's was a small shop with an old-fashioned faded look to it. It had the traditional red and white striped pole above the awning and a clear glass front allowing a good view of its interior. There were only three customers, each sitting in oversized dentist-style chairs that presumably could be raised down to the level of the low china basins that edged the far wall.

Simon was standing talking to someone who sat with his back to the window and who was being shaved by a short man in a white jacket. That was as much as I could see and for nearly ten minutes I waited with mounting impatience, until Simon finally walked towards the door. The other man, shave apparently complete, then stood up taking a towel from around his shoulders and dismissing Napier with a nod. I could see him quite plainly and even at this distance his presence had impact. It was The Suit – the man from the pub. Who is he I wondered and does he have anything to do with the sale of Alwyn Road? I didn't know. I didn't know anything except that something felt off.

As I followed the BMW back towards Wimbledon, I realised that if something *was* wrong, if there was something shady about Simon and the sale, then Laura, by default as the one who instructed him, could get into trouble. So, it wasn't just her love life she should be worried about, but perhaps her professional life as well? I pulled over and dialled Flan.

"It's me. We're on for tonight."

CHAPTER SIX

Elborough Street is a quiet residential road in Southfields. Thankfully, at nearly nine o'clock, there were very few people about. We could see lights on in the house to the left of Simon's, the semi-detached side, but the one to the right was in darkness, as was his. The BMW was parked outside, so I presumed he'd caught a cab to the restaurant.

Carefully we had scanned the Edwardian bay windowed exterior for signs of an alarm system, but unless it was cunningly positioned at the back where we couldn't get to it, then we were in luck. Mr. Huxton, Flan's seventy-two-year-old admirer, had been adamant on this point. An alarm meant that we would simply have to abandon the whole idea.

I was amazed that Flan had talked him into helping us at all, but had clearly underestimated her powers of persuasion. What was it about her that made her still so irresistible to men? I checked myself; my mind was wandering again, which it has a habit of doing when I'm nervous. Right, I told myself, here we go.

Mr. H. stood there, clutching a huge bunch of keys and picklocks. These, he had unearthed from a dusty old suitcase stashed away in his loft, remnants from his working days as a carpenter joiner. "I don't like to throw things out," he had told me when I had picked him and Flan up earlier. "You just never know when they might come in handy." How right he was. Flan at his side was practically dancing up and down on the spot in excitement and typically, had dressed up for the occasion. In an outfit apparently inspired by Honor Blackman in the 1960's TV show The Avengers, she wore black trousers, a black roll-neck, and a black scarf to keep her hair back.

We were ready. I took one more look around. All was quiet and even though an occasional car drove by, we still had some protection from a squat overgrown hedge that fronted the property.

"Right Mr. H.," I whispered. "It's over to you. Are you sure you want to do this?"

He gulped and wiped a nervous hand over his forehead. "I just hope I haven't lost my touch. A lot of years have gone by since my working days."

Tentatively he inserted a key into the central security lock. "We have to get through this one first," he explained wriggling the key back and forth and then gently withdrawing it. "The Yale will be a doddle after that." He shook his head. "No this one's no good." With trembling fingers and muttering quietly to himself, "Steady, George, steady, you can do it," he painstakingly tried key after key. At intervals Flan patted his arm offering soothing words of encouragement.

Trying desperately to control my impatience, I crept towards the hedge and scanned the street again. There was no one around. So far so good. Turning back to the front door I nearly jumped out of my skin on finding Flan at my elbow.

"This is such a lark Clarry! I'm so glad that you've taken up this line of work. It really is great fun," her voice upped to a dramatic decibel.

"Shut *up*," I hissed, shooting an anxious glance at the house next door. "We could get arrested for this and carted off to jail and have to spend the rest of our lives trying to beat off the attentions of…"

My own voice had taken on a distinctly manic edge and at the mention of the word *jail* Mr. H. promptly lost his nerve and dropped the key bunch.

The noise was appalling. We froze as if some invisible presence had called a sudden halt to a particularly rowdy game of musical chairs. Minutes passed. Nothing happened. Slowly we breathed again. After patting his chest with a weak hand, Mr. H. then stooped down to retrieve his tools and got doggedly back to work. Flan and I waited in chastened silence; until finally after what seemed an age, we were in.

"Thank God," I breathed as we stumbled in the darkness across the threshold. "Well done Mr. H. you're a marvel. Now we will just have to risk putting on the lights. I wish I'd thought to bring a torch."

Sliding my hand across the wall, I groped my way until my fingers found a switch. We all blinked at the sudden brightness. I looked about me. We were in a narrow hallway with a staircase directly ahead of us. "OK," I said softly, putting my car keys down on a small table behind Simon's telephone. "We need to be out of here as quick as we can."

"What's the hurry dear?" piped up Flan. "You checked with the restaurant and know that their reservation was at eight thirty, so we should have plenty of time."

I had indeed checked with the Lighthouse restaurant, pretending to be Simon's secretary, and had timed our spot of breaking and entering for when I hoped he and Laura would be having their first drink and studying their menus. I had decided not to let Laura in on what we were doing, reflecting that she might consider my actions as going just a teeny-weeny bit too far, and who would blame her? I'd been having palpitations all afternoon, at the very thought of it. What I was doing was illegal, morally reprehensible, and just plain outrageous. Not only that, I'd induced a couple of old age pensioners to help me.

"Right, I want to go quickly from room to room and take a good look around."

"What exactly are we looking for?" asked Mr. H. puffing up his chest like a pigeon, his fears of being arrested having apparently given way to a sense of pride in his dexterity with the picklocks.

Before I could respond, Flan answered, in a loud stage whisper, "Clues, George darling, clues!" and strode off down the hall flinging open the nearest door and bustling into Simon's sitting room.

We followed. Almost impossibly neat and ordered, it was hard to believe that someone actually lived here. It looked more like a particularly unimaginative stage-set or a show home, with its spotless cream walls, an oversized black leather sofa, groupings of architectural prints in black frames on the wall and a state-of-the-art plasma TV. On a low glass table in the centre of the room, GQ magazine, Men's Health and copies of The Estates Gazette were fanned out in perfect symmetry. His DVDs and CDs, stacked in a glass fronted shelving unit that took up most of one wall, were arranged in alphabetical order. There wasn't a thing out of place, not a cushion, not a furled-up newspaper, nor an empty coffee mug. It was all so unwelcoming; everything about it screamed uptight control freak. Once again, I seriously wondered what Laura saw in him. Stepping across to a pale wood sideboard to the left of a tiled fireplace, I opened a drawer. In it I found a pile of brown linen napkins, which looked like they had never been used and a box of after-dinner mints (unopened). Flan joined me as I stooped to open the base cupboards and whistled appreciatively at the sight of Simon's well-stocked drinks cabinet. She gazed longingly at the nearly full bottle of Bombay Sapphire and gave Mr. H. an exaggerated wink. I shook my head warningly. That was all I needed, a couple of inebriated septuagenarians on my hands in a house where we had absolutely no business to be in the first place. Leaving George looking through Simon's very limited bookcase of mostly thrillers, Flan and I explored the kitchen.

Now that I'd seen his sitting room, the kitchen came as no surprise. A display of shiny steel pans on clean white surfaces, it had all the warmth and charm of a surgical operating room. By the look of the hob, it was quite clear that no one ever cooked here. Raking through his cupboards we found tins of low salt this and low-sugar that, and every vitamin tablet from ginseng to zinc. Where was the ketchup?

Where was the Marmite? And it was the same story with the fridge. No cold beers, no wine, just Flora and skimmed milk and bottled water.

As we opened and closed cupboard doors and drawers I realised that I hadn't answered Mr. Huxton's question for a very good reason: I had no idea myself what we were looking for. What was I expecting to find? A file marked *Alwyn Road – Top Secret?*

"Flan, you keep a look out down here and I'll have a go at the bedrooms."

The usual Edwardian layout: master bedroom, guest bedroom, box room, and bathroom all off a square landing. I whizzed through the guest room first and quickly dismissed it. All it revealed was that Simon probably never *had* a guest to stay. His bedroom disclosed little more. Just like the sitting room it was neat and uncluttered, even the bed had been made which may just mean that he was planning to skip desert at the Lighthouse to come back and enjoy Laura under his navy checked duvet but still, there was something so sterile about the room.

A couple of mounted photos loomed down from the wall above the bed showing Simon in various sporting poses; on a golf course leaning self-consciously on his club and in another brandishing a badminton racket. That was it for photographs and I realised belatedly that there hadn't been any downstairs: none of his parents or friends, not even of a boozed up stag or rugby weekend. Nothing that gave any clue to his personality or, now I came to think of it… his life.

The pine dressing table yielded several pairs of expensive looking cufflinks, a gold tie-pin, a hairbrush, and bottles of aftershave. Raking through a large pine wardrobe I found suits: lots of. Shirts: racks of and ties: a multitude of. Obviously, a bit of a peacock in that department, he favoured pale silks made by Armani and Yves Saint Laurent. Everything looked sleek, even his casual clothes were not exactly what I'd call causal. Did this guy ever relax and just slob out? Apparently not.

I turned to the bedside cabinet. Surely there, if nowhere else, I'd find something that truly revealed the man. There could be porn but probably he'd just look at it online. I allowed myself a few seconds to speculate on what his *thing* might be and decided that if I had to guess it would be… spanking. Uptight men are so often into being punished, I'm told. Not my thing at all. If a guy wants me to whack him, wallop him, or whip him, I'm out of there. But that's just me. Perhaps Laura was different?

I slid open the drawer expectantly and peered in: an opened packet of condoms with only one remaining (disappointing for Laura), some headache pills, and a Nick Hornby novel. That was it. So much for the secrets of his sexual psyche.

I sighed and moved on. Just one more room to try and I hoped it would be a home office. It was. The tiny box room housed an unmade up single bed and a small metal desk and chair. I settled myself down in front of his computer and powered it up. The screen came to life and demanded a username and password. Swearing softly but imaginatively under my breath, I instantly shut it down. No way was I going to muck about trying to guess what the password could be. There was probably some security device installed that would cut in and he would know that someone had tried to access his files.

I turned my attention to the contents of his desk where there was a copy of today's Telegraph opened to the crossword and besides it an old-fashioned fountain pen. I gazed thoughtfully at the pen, remembering the tie-pin. There was something incongruous about them. But maybe he was what's called a Young-Fogey or perhaps they were simply presents from his parents?

I lifted a pile of papers from the corner of the desk and, being very careful not to get them out of order, I inspected each one in turn. There were a few utility bills all on direct debit, a reminder from his dentist that his six-monthly check-up was due, and a letter about his pension plan. Well it certainly looked like he had a secure retirement to look forward to. If the annual figure he expected could be relied upon, he'd have no worries about his old age. Continuing to rake through, I came across an invitation to someone called Isobel's housewarming party on the 21st and notification of a gala dinner at his golf club at the end of the month.

Then, finally I found something that caught my interest. A letter from a company called Lehman Black Investments detailing his first year's dividend from his initial investment of £200,000. That's a lot of money. Hunting on the desk for some paper and finding a Dunstan and Stead message pad, I jotted down the company's name, tore off the page, and stuffed it in my breast pocket.

Getting up from the desk I realised that I'd missed something. On the floor near the bed was a leather-bound Filofax. Again, old fashioned. Did I have time to go through it? I looked at my watch, Christ! It was nearly eleven o'clock.

I ran out on to the landing and hailed Flan and Mr. H. who were having a nice little sit down at the bottom of the stairs. "I'll only be two more minutes. Make sure we've left everything as we found it, doors, lights, everything."

I dashed back and picked up the Filofax. I started with the address section but there was nothing listed under B for *Baddie* or C for *Criminal,* which I found disappointing. I did learn however, that he knew a lot of people with names like Roland and Felix. I flipped to the diary part and looked up the entry for yesterday – "The Falcon" 7pm but he hadn't written in a name, which meant that for me, "The Suit" was still anonymous. I flicked through the pages; his dinner date tonight with Laura was there, he was having a squash game tomorrow night with Barney and on Thursday night he was going to somewhere called "The Vine" in Camberwell at six thirty and again, there was no name. Camberwell – that was twice in one week. Was it with "The Suit" again?

No time to think about it now. Hastily I ran down the stairs to find that Mr. H. had the front door open a crack and was peering anxiously out.

"Coast looks clear," he whispered.

Killing the hall light Flan and I followed him out of the house and then took cover behind the hedge, whilst he fumbled with the locks again. We were just in time. As we made our way briskly down the street and around the corner towards the main road where I'd left the Renault, we heard a black cab ticking its way slowly up the opposite side of the street. I nudged Flan and dropped swiftly down on to one knee as if to tie my shoelace making sure to keep my face averted. As the cab bowled past I risked a glance up and could distinctly make out Simon's profile. He was alone. Strange, where was Laura? Perhaps they'd had a row? I made a mental note to call her tomorrow.

As the taxi disappeared around the bend, I straightened up grinning triumphantly, "We did it!" Laughing and exultant, we linked arms, all the pent-up tension of the last few hours spilling out so that we're talking over each other in wild relief.

"Fan-bloody-tastic!" Flan enthused. "I haven't enjoyed myself so much in years."

"Didn't think my old ticker would take it at one point," chortled Mr. H. "But I have to say that I wouldn't have missed it for the world. What an exciting life you do lead young lady."

"Not usually," I confessed beaming happily at him. "This is rather a departure for me but thank you, thank you both." Turning to hug Flan, I said, "I couldn't have done it without either of you."

We continued to make for the car, swapping notes and congratulating ourselves on our cleverness.

"And you George darling," purred Flan. "You are simply the best, the most marvellous man in the…" But her voice trailed off as she realised that I'd come to an abrupt halt in front of the Renault. "What *is* it Clarry? What on earth's the matter?"

I didn't answer, only shook my head. I couldn't speak, couldn't get the words out. My legs buckled as fear gripped and threatened to swallow me completely. Flan and Mr. H.

gazed on in agonised silence as frantically I began to pat myself down, desperately turning out my pockets, but it was useless, I knew they weren't there. I did not have my *keys* – my bloody fucking car keys. I knew exactly where they were and I could see them quite clearly in my mind's eye. They were just where I'd left them… behind the phone on Simon's hall table.

CHAPTER SEVEN

I looked at Flan. "What on earth are we going to do?" My voice came out cracked and hoarse.

"We've got to think, Clarry, think!"

"I *am* bloody thinking!"

Mr. H. had turned very pale and was leaning back against the bonnet of the car. I felt a stab of guilt as I thought of the ordeal I'd put him through and tried furiously to steady my nerves and clear the crippling fog of panic from my brain. "OK. Right," I gulped. "Uh… the thing to do… is… we've just got to…"

I broke off my pointless ramblings as Flan squared her shoulders and said slowly and deliberately, "There's only one thing for it. We have got to get back inside."

"How?" I cried. "Simon's in there. I can't just march up to his house, knock on the door and say, 'Hi, it's me. I was just burglarising your house and appear to have forgotten my keys, silly of me I know, very careless. Would you be a real sweetie and get them for me?'" My words spiralled out into the night but Flan held her ground.

"He doesn't recognise *me*. I'll get them."

It was Mr. H.'s turn to cut in, his voice thick with anxiety. "But how Flan? How? Whatever excuse could you come up with?"

She laughed, with some of her old spirit returning, and immediately I felt hope revive. "Leave it to me darlings, just leave it to me." And with that she pulled off her scarf so that her hair fell in a soft cloud about her face. Mr. H. and I looked on in wonder as she then wiped off her red lipstick onto the back of her hand. Suddenly she looked years older. "No time for explanations," she commanded. "Follow me but be sure to stay well back when I get near the house."

Mutely, Mr. H. and I did as we were told and ducked behind a parked car on the opposite side of the road. We couldn't see much as the presence of the hedge that had distinctly worked to our advantage earlier that evening, now effectively blocked our view, but we watched as Flan slumped her shoulders, stooped a little at the waist, and disappeared through the front gate, her left leg limping a little. Straining, we could hear the echo of voices and the sound of the front door closing.

"She's in, she's in," breathed Mr. H. who had been clutching my arm so tightly I was beginning to lose all feeling in it. The wait was excruciating as we crouched in the shadows. Poor Mr. H. kept shifting his weight from leg to leg muttering ruefully, "My knees aren't what they were you know."

Five minutes passed, then ten. What was going on in there? And whatever it was why was it taking so bloody long? It was no good; I was going to have to do something, but what? I started to get to my feet, no clear idea in my mind of what to do when we heard Simon's front door open again. Instantly I bobbed back down, scuttling crab-like in besides Mr. H. We looked at each other and held our breath.

Flan was coming down the path, this time with her right leg limping, calling over her shoulder in a frail weak voice, totally unlike her own.

"No thank you, I'll be fine now. Yes, I'm quite sure. Thanks again for your great kindness. I feel so much better now. Bye Bye." She waved, repeating her thanks and made her way slowly towards the main road.

We let her go a few yards, and then as soon as I was sure that Simon was back in the house and not watching from a window, I sprinted after her with Mr. H. following a close second.

With a theatrical bow and smiling beatifically, she flourished the car keys in my face. "I got them darlings."

We hugged her ecstatically, besieging her with questions and demands as to how she'd managed it.

"No," she laughingly shrugged us off. "Come on, let's go home. I think what we most need now is a drink. I'll tell you all about it when we get back."

Fifteen minutes later we were lounging in her sitting room, Flan and I with large glasses of Merlot and Mr. H. with a hefty tumbler of whiskey.

"After what we've been through tonight, a drop of the hard stuff is required," he grunted taking a generous swallow. "Now, Flan my dear, do please tell us…"

"Yes," I interrupted having already downed half my wine. "How the hell did you manage it?"

"It was simple really," Flan returned airily. "When he answered the door I apologised for disturbing him but explained that I was taking my evening constitutional later than usual and had suddenly come over quite faint."

Her voice dropped to a tremulous register. "If I could just trouble you for a glass of water young man?" she mimicked, sounding very Miss Havisham. "He asked if I wanted him to call someone or could he get me a cab but I said no, I just needed to sit down a moment and catch my breath."

"And he bought it?" I asked incredulously.

She looked hurt. "Darling, why shouldn't he?" her eyes twinkled dangerously. "And you know I really am frightfully good at this sort of thing; I've told you before that I should have been an actress…"

"So, what happened then?"

"Well he led me into the kitchen and sat me down with some water. Really Clarry, are you sure he's up to no good? He seemed rather a nice young man."

"Appearances can be deceiving," I muttered darkly. "And so… the keys?"

Flan sat back on the sofa, nestling into Mr. H.'s shoulder and clearly enjoying being the centre of attention. "Well, as he led me out towards the front door, I *stealthily* scooped them up from behind the phone and *noiselessly* slipped them in my pocket. Easy!"

I grinned. Flan could have her moment of glory; she certainly deserved it. Without her… well… I didn't like to think where we'd be now. I stretched and yawned, suddenly exhausted. Had the risk even been worth it? I couldn't work it out. I was just too tired to think straight. Home and bed that was all I was fit for now. Home and bed.

CHAPTER EIGHT

We're told that the sleep of the just, of the innocent, is the soundest. Not true. I slept so heavily and so deeply that I woke up with a sleep hangover, woolly in the head and heavy in the legs. A run wasn't going to do it. I needed to swim. Grumbling because I still hadn't got around to renewing my gym membership, I thought of the public pool down on the Broadway.

Eleven o'clock on a Wednesday meant that it wasn't busy and so I was able to get in twenty lengths without being elbowed in the ribs or kicked in the crotch. Go to a public pool at peak times and you can come out black and blue, from the flailing limbs of the madly keen as they plough aggressively through the water perfecting their backstroke.

Coming up for air and leaning my elbows on the side, I watched two young mums over in the shallow end dunking their squidgy gurgling babies in and out of the water. Their voices echoed off the white tiled walls and I could hear them complaining about sleepless nights, endless nappies, and the alarming plummet of their libidos. But, it was clear by the look on their faces that the feeling of those happy crowing infants in their arms was compensation enough. Lucky them. Time to go. If I stayed there any longer I'd probably disappear into some hormonal hyperspace and I was so not ready for any of that.

A quick scoot around the supermarket and I was back home. I made a huge sandwich from a stone-baked baguette and a wedge of creamy brie I'd got at the deli counter and then chucked in a few salad leaves, to make up the green content and to distract myself from the amount of fats and carbohydrates I was about to wolf down. Sitting at the kitchen table with this and a mug of tea, I felt, at last, able to reflect over last night's doings.

All morning I'd been trying to push aside my mixed emotions. At the start, it had been such a rush. It had felt dangerous and badass and then… near disaster. The fear I'd felt, the risk I'd put all three of us in, and my total lack of any coherent idea of how to get us out of the situation, even now made my face flush and my skin crawl, but I didn't want to dwell on this conflict of reactions. It was too disturbing. Still chewing I got up and went into the sitting room to find my notebook, then returned to the kitchen table and sat staring at a blank white page.

After everything we'd risked; what had I learnt? That Simon was a neat freak and boringly careful about his diet didn't seem enough somehow. I thought about the papers I'd gone through. He was clearly financially comfortable. That much was obvious. The big fat pension plan and the £200,000 investment and dividend from… what was the name of that company? I got up and took the stairs at a jog to retrieve the shirt I had worn last night from the washing basket. Yes, there was the note I'd made: Lehman Black

Investments. They were probably some flash money-moving house in the City but then again their address in The Seven Sisters Road didn't sound particularly impressive. However, it was easy enough to find out.

My spare room is thankfully nothing like Simon's in that guests *do* stay in it occasionally. It doesn't double as an office, but is big enough to have Grandma P.'s old roll-top desk against one wall where I keep my computer.

As I sat down, I glanced at the piles of old bills and receipts that I kept meaning to file and then chucked them into the wastebasket by my feet. Much better. I should come in here more often.

I looked up Lehman Black Investments. Nothing. I found companies with similar names, mostly big players, American firms whose home pages were punchy with details about investment strategy and solid expertise, but after half an hour when my eyes were beginning to bug, I still hadn't found anything on Lehman Black.

I gave up. I'm just not patient enough for this kind of research. I sighed and looked at my watch. It was after three o'clock and I was due at the restaurant at six. I'd promised to phone Laura today and was surprised that by this time she hadn't called me.

I called her office and got put through to her secretary, Mandy, a motherly lady in her forties with tiger-striped highlights and a six-month-old bulldog puppy called Hastings, whose framed photograph she kept on her desk. She told me that Laura had unexpectedly had to go to Norwich for a few days to handle a particularly complicated will.

"She said you might phone and that I was to give you her hotel number, but you might be lucky and get her on her mobile if she's between meetings."

I thanked her, hung up, and dialled Laura's mobile.

"Hi love, how was last night?"

"Clarry hi, I've only got a minute as I'm dashing off to meet a client, but thanks it was great. Lovely place the Lighthouse."

"And Simon?"

"Oh," her voice softened. "I'm getting more and more in to him. And I really like the fact that he didn't automatically assume that at the end of the evening, we'd have sex. You know, the way guys always do."

I grunted. I knew.

"Not that I wouldn't have been up for it last night," she sighed. "But this trip was a last-minute thing and I had to get up at five o'clock. Anyway, how are you getting on? What have you managed to find out? Quick, tell me because I've got to go."

"Not much yet, I'll tell you when I see you, but there is one thing that would be helpful. What were the other houses he sold and who were the buyers?"

There was a silence and then her voice low and unsettled down the line,

"Clarry, what's going on?"

"Nothing sinister, I promise," I crossed my fingers. "I just need to get at the facts and…"

"OK, OK. I haven't got time now. I'll get Mandy to call you back with the details. Look I've got to go. Bye, take care."

"When are you coming back?" I asked, but found that I was talking to myself.

Whilst I waited for Mandy to get in touch, I made another mug of tea and thought about Simon's diary – The Vine, tomorrow night at six thirty in Camberwell again. I looked it up. The Vine was a Greek restaurant, on Camberwell New Road. Could Camberwell be The Suit's turf? Perhaps he was Greek? Well whatever nationality he was, I wanted to know what his connection was to Simon and it just so happens that I really like those little pastry triangles stuffed with cheese and spinach.

My mobile rang.

"Hi Clarry, I've got the information you wanted. How are you by the way?"

"Fine thanks Mandy and you? How's Hastings?"

"Not very well behaved. He insists on sleeping on our bed and Stuart gets cross with him because of the snoring and tells him to get off, but when he looks at me with those big brown eyes and starts drooling, I can't resist him and…"

"Who… Stuart?" I asked, rapidly losing the thread of this doggie inspired stream of consciousness.

"No Hastings. You should see him Clarry. He's got so big and his paws are…"

"That's cute Mandy, it really is. But about those houses…"

She gave me the addresses. "And the buyers?" I asked.

"The one in South Park Road was purchased through Dunstan Stead by Cornett Developments Ltd."

"A development company? Laura didn't mention that."

"Well it bought it right enough. I've got its address. Do you want to make a note of it?"

I jotted it down and she continued.

"And the one in Bathgate Road by Marble Developments Ltd."

"Another developer?"

"Well yes, but that's quite common you know."

"Oh, OK. I just didn't know that, and the address is?" I made a note of it and started to say my goodbyes.

"And Cutler Farrow solicitors acted for both purchasers. Is there anything else Clarry? I need to finish a letter before I head home," Mandy added.

"No thanks, you've been really kind thanks." I thought a moment and asked, "What address do you have for the firm of solicitors?"

She read off an address in Nunhead and rang off.

I looked down at my notes: lots of information that meant absolutely nothing to me. I glanced at my watch. It was nearly five o'clock and I had some serious work to do on myself before I was fit to be seen by the public.

The whole of the basement had been booked for an office do by one of the claims division from a local insurance company. It would be a table of twenty. Stephanie, my fellow waitress for the evening, arrived just after me and gave me a hand shifting the tables from individual twos and fours into an L-shape with, we reckoned, just enough room for me to squeeze around the chairs if I sucked in my stomach.

"Anyway," she said. "The director says to me… who are your inspirations? Your theatrical role models? So, I had to think a moment and then told him that Kristen Stewart had been a big influence on me in Twilight."

"Good answer."

She wiped the rim of a glass on her apron. "He didn't seem to think so. Said I was too lightweight."

I circled the table with a small white side plate looking for where I'd missed its spot. "What was the part?"

"A cat food commercial."

Upstairs the kitchen was gearing up for a heavy night. Midweek we normally manage with two chefs and Jose the kitchen porter, but because of the party there were three on tonight and the place was buzzing with a controlled energy.

Alec, the thin wiry sous-chef was julienning spring onions and cucumber for miniature duck spring rolls that were to be one of the starter specials.

"Hey Clarry, this duck won't keep until tomorrow, it needs shifting. How about a deal? Whichever of you..." he gestured with his Sabatier to include Steph, "flogs the most; gets to take me home and perform wild sex acts on me."

Steph and I – a united front and very used to his suggestions – folded our arms and regarded him with raised eyebrows.

"Darling Alec," Steph drawled. "We'd like to, we really would but we've met your lovely wife and she doesn't look to us like the understanding sort. But, promise to save us each a portion of the cherry cheesecake and we'll see what we can do."

He grinned and then shooed us away. "Laurence has got one of his moods on so keep out of his way," he warned just as the bellowing of Laurence, the head chef, could be heard from deep within the walk-in fridge.

It was something about why the fuck had Tim, the gentle but hapless commis chef, only thought fit to prep a handful of artichokes when even an idiot on his first day at catering school knows that veal medallions with *artichoke* demanded a fuck of a lot more than that? Tim's stammering excuses were lost on us as Steph and I fled the kitchen. Rule number one for waiting staff: never get under the feet of a chef in a temper – they carry knives.

During the early lull, I gossiped with Dave about the problem of finding an experienced bar person who wasn't a drunk and didn't have his hands in the till and commiserated with Steph about the lack of a leotard wearing opportunity in a production of The Merchant of Venice set in a 1980's City Trading floor that she had recently auditioned for.

"I think you were just lucky with *Mustard Seed* Steph." Being one of Titania's fairy retinue last year in A Midsummer's Night's Dream at Regents Park and wearing only a flesh coloured body stocking for the whole summer had, apparently, quite ruined her for modern dress.

Now it was nearly ten o'clock and the party was deteriorating before my eyes. So far, twenty people had consumed, between them, over forty bottles of wine and these combined with a round of beers and gin and tonics at the start of the evening, were taking their toll on the party spirit. A bread roll fight had broken out between a couple of claim handlers, and there'd just been a suggestion of a round of tequila body slammers.

Whilst doing my best to avoid high-flying baguettes

and trying to restrain myself from kicking the testicles of a belligerent salesman in a joke-tie who kept pinching my bum, I brought in their puddings, took orders for more drinks, and offered coffees, which no one was ready for.

The evening limped on, but finally just after midnight we managed to oust them. The senior manager was so drunk he slipped me three £10 notes on top of the 12 per cent service charge on the bill. As he tried to squeeze his not inconsiderable bulk into someone else's suit jacket, clearly the property of a much smaller man, he was practically crossed-eyed from the strain and from trying to sneak one more look down my cleavage.

With relief I watched him gingerly negotiate his way up the stairs and then with a sigh, I turned resolutely to start clearing the wrecked tables. At least I had the cherry cheesecake to look forward to.

CHAPTER NINE

Cornett Developments had its registered address in Maida Vale and the company directors were a Mr. C. Lianthos and a Mr. S. Zakiat. There was also a set of abbreviated accounts. I made a note of the names but the figures meant nothing to me. Marble Developments was registered in Catford and this time there was only one director, Mr. C. Lianthos again. Interesting. I considered the name. Could it be Greek? I fished out my mobile.

"Flan? Hi it's me. Fancy going out to dinner tonight? Great. It'll be an early one; I'll pick you up at six."

What to wear? The look this season was apparently classy, provocative, but untouchable. Try translating that into a wearable outfit. Eventually I settled on a black suit with a short skirt and a curvy jacket.

We parked a little up the street from The Vine at about six forty five. We had spotted Simon's car parked just around the corner in County Grove, had positioned ourselves carefully, and at ten minutes past seven had watched him leave the restaurant and drive off.

"Now let's just play this one by ear shall we Flan?"

"I am so relieved that you have decided to use your real

name after all. I'd have definitely called you Clarry at some point and blown your cover."

"Blown my cover. Where are you getting these expressions?"

She laughed, wrapping a long turquoise silk scarf around her throat. "I've been watching those American cop shows with all the initials but I switch channels whenever there are any dead bodies. So, tell me, what's the plan?" "Oh, I see," she said when I didn't reply. "We are going out to dine in a restaurant located in the back of beyond, in the hope of scraping an acquaintance with a man that may not even be there and about whom you know nothing, except that he is rather good-looking in a Mediterranean kind of way and that he appears to have dealings of some kind with Simon Whatshisname?"

"That's pretty much it," I replied.

"And if he *is* there and we *do* get talking to him, how exactly are you going to ascertain if he does know Simon and indeed what the exact nature of their relationship is?"

"I am planning to… to *ascertain*…"

She waited and drew out a patient, "*Yessss?*"

"Oh, I don't know!" I retorted. "Something's bound to occur to me. Come on let's do this."

"By the way," she flicked an appraising gaze over my suit as I locked the car. "You look very grown up tonight darling."

"I am grown up."

"Oh, I know, I know, it's just that you usually appear more… more…"

"More what? Scruffy, is that what you mean?"

"Casual," she brought out the word decisively. "I know that's how you young people dress nowadays, but it's nice to see you looking sophisticated for a change."

I waved the compliment away but was secretly rather pleased and then slipped my arm through hers. "And you Flan look fabulous as always."

And she did. Dressed in flowing black trousers and a long discreetly beaded black tunic, she was elegant and understated.

I took in the restaurant with a waitress's eye. Small, only about forty covers with the tables set not too close together. The walls were washed in a soft pink with a stencilling of vine leaves in intricate fronds, weaving their way up to a low ceiling. To the muted strains of traditional music we were politely ushered to a table by a young waiter in an immaculate white shirt and a pair of black trousers that were shiny with wear. Allowing Flan to lead the way, I covertly checked out the other diners. A few couples and what looked like a family group at a table for six and… yes, there he was… The Suit.

Sitting alone at a large corner table with his back to the wall, he had some papers in front of him, a half-empty glass, and a bottle of wine in an ice bucket. He had looked up at the bustle generated by our arrival and I saw him register me in the way a man always notices any moderately attractive woman in his line of vision. Actually, and big headed as it sounds, I knew tonight that I was looking perhaps a little more than just moderately attractive. It had taken work I admit. I have all the usual features in all the usual order: Two eyes of a rather nondescript pale blue above a straight-ish nose and a mouth that allows food in and expletives out – so that works – but there is no doubt that make-up improves my face significantly. I should always wear it, but I don't. I'm told that my best features are my cheekbones and my legs, that my breasts are comforting (whatever that means) and that I have surprisingly large hands for a woman.

I risked a direct look at The Suit. Not handsome exactly but strong looking. Large nose, dark slightly hooded eyes, square shoulders in a dark suit with a white shirt open at the throat. There was a kind of stillness about him and a confidence that I now remembered noticing from my first view of him. The overall effect was very… what? It took me a minute to recognise a quality that we naturally take for granted in a man, but is so often missing. The Suit was masculine.

I kept my gaze averted but slowed my movements down as I lowered myself into a chair. Our table gave me a sideways view of him, but I made sure for the first fifteen minutes or so to keep my eyes firmly on Flan and on the menu and not betray any undue interest. We decided upon a bottle of house wine, which turned out to be surprisingly good. It was ice cold and dry without that heavy aftertaste of resin that I recalled from the last time I had eaten at a Greek restaurant in Charlotte Street: a drunken hen night where we had all crashed plates, danced on the table to bouzouki music and, to the sullen disapproval of her new sister-in-law, the bride-to-be had ended up passionately snogging one of the waiters.

"Is he here?" Flan hissed in a stage whisper.

"Yes. Act natural."

"Where?"

"Behind you. No! Don't look round." This said as she started to twist in her chair.

"Oh yes of course," she complied and recovering herself she then groped in her handbag and brought out her silver compact. I watched as she brought it up to her face trying to get a good view of him in its small, magnified mirror.

"Stop that. He'll see you."

"You're right," she sighed shutting the compact with a snap. "It's not as easy as it looks in the films."

In actual fact, it's considerably more difficult than you'd imagine keeping up an animated conversation in a natural manner, when most of your attention is on something or someone else, but I had forgotten Flan's inevitable ability to make me laugh.

Mr. Babcock the retired undertaker and rival to Mr. H. for her affections, jealous over the amount of time she'd been spending with Mr. H. lately, had upped his efforts in the wooing department. That morning, he'd given her a great bunch of pale pink carnations, which she'd very much appreciated until from something he'd let slip, she realised that they had probably been lifted off a headstone in the local cemetery. Apparently he still liked to take his morning walk there amongst the vaults and shrines as a reminder of his former trade. "I knew he could be a little close-handed but really, grave robbing!"

We ordered the meze platter to start and, whilst the other tables filled up around us, I managed a few sideways glances at The Suit. After a while a much older man came out from the kitchen bearing a plate of olives, dips, and bread and sat down with him. Whilst they appeared familiar with each other, The Suit seemed quietly in control and I wondered if this was in fact his restaurant. From time to time his gaze flicked over me, the cool speculative gaze of a successful man used to attracting women. Such appraising scrutiny I usually find too full on, too predatory, but in him it was oddly magnetic. Only once did I allow myself to lock eyes with him, keeping my face impassive. All my instincts told me that maintaining an aloof distance was the way to play it. A man like this wouldn't respond to an obvious flirt. Thankfully Flan appeared to have forgotten all about him and seemed quite content just to enjoy the evening.

After our main course, I needed to go the loo and rose to my feet. A sign pointed to the back of the restaurant meaning that I'd practically have to walk right past him. I took it slowly. I didn't want to trip over my own feet or cannon into a waiter loaded with plates. I felt his eyes upon me but didn't look at him.

After washing my hands, I checked my hair, reapplied my lip gloss, checked that the hem of my skirt wasn't caught up in my knickers, and opened the door back out into the restaurant. I felt ready to trust to the inspiration of the moment.

My eyes sought his table but... it was empty. Damn. He'd gone and I'd blown my chance. I looked across at Flan and then looked again. She wasn't alone. The Suit was sitting at our table. Now that was impressive. I should have remembered never to underestimate Flan's ability to ensnare a man, of any age.

He got to his feet as I approached them, but Flan gave him no time for explanations.

"Clarry darling, this very nice man has just offered, as we are newcomers here, to buy us a drink but I positively *insisted* that the only way we would accept is if he'd sit down and join us."

"With your permission?" the voice was low with a discernible accent.

I smiled but said nothing, not to be mysterious and distant but simply because I couldn't think of anything to say. Flan more than made up for my silence.

"Now tell me," she smiled brightly at him. "Are you the proprietor of this lovely restaurant where we have had such a delicious meal?"

He shook his head. "No but I am connected to Thanos the owner. I am Chris, Chris Lianthos." He turned to me, "And you are?"

I barely heard him, my brain was buzzing. Lianthos. Mr. C. Lianthos... Chris. Both Cornett and Marble Developments had a director by that name. It had to be the one and the same man. Simon had sold him the two previous houses and was possibly planning to sell him Alwyn Road. Well, this was what I had come here to find out and it had been so much easier than I imagined. His name said it all.

"I'm Clarry and this is Flan and... oh thank you..." this as the young waiter brought some more wine.

Chris poured and lifted his glass to clink with ours. "Yamas." His eyes met mine. Up close, the quiet confidence and powerful aura of alpha male was reinforced.

"Yamas?" asked Flan.

He laughed softly. "It means cheers in Greek. So, you have enjoyed your dinner?"

She nodded. "I particularly liked all the little tasty starters."

"Ah then you are probably a Mediterranean at heart. We Greeks like to eat slowly, to linger over our food. Meze is designed to stimulate conversation and to relax the body and mind."

"What a perfectly civilised idea," rejoined Flan. "The English simply shovel their food down and don't talk to one another. No wonder the average Englishman is as stolid as the jam roly-poly he eats."

"Roly-poly? I am not familiar with this."

Flan opened her mouth and I knew that a blow-by-blow account of exactly how it was made would be immediately forthcoming and so decided to cut across her.

"It's rather a dull old-fashioned pudding."

"Which you loved when you were a little girl," said Flan.

"I'm quite sure Chris doesn't want to hear about..."

"Oh, but I do," Chris replied. "I'm trying to picture you as a little girl."

The glance he flicked over my body was charged with intent.

"Well what I can tell you is that she was a very stubborn child," continued Flan.

"And are you still?" asked Chris, this time looking directly into my eyes.

"When I have to be."

His smile was slow and languorous as he picked up his wine glass. "I admire strong-minded women."

67

I had absolutely nothing to say to that. And this was the time to ask something intelligent and yet cunning that would draw him in to disclosing the full extent of his dealings with Simon, but what I found myself looking at were his hands. He had strong square hands with very clean nails. "We should be going," I said and turning from him I flagged down the waiter.

"Must you?"

The waiter appeared with the bill and I settled up. Flan who, breaking the habit of a lifetime, had remained unobtrusively in the background for the last few minutes, now took command of the situation. "Well it's been lovely meeting you Chris." Her smile was brilliant as she drew her turquoise scarf around her neck and gathered herself up to leave.

He acknowledged and returned the compliment, but it was evident that he was making his mind up about something.

"Ladies it is Thanos's sixtieth birthday on Sunday and in the evening the restaurant is closed to the public. We are having a little party to celebrate…" He paused and whilst he glanced at both of us, it was me that his eyes lingered upon. "I would be delighted if you would attend as my guests."

"Oh how nice," Flan's tone was genuinely regretful. "I would have loved to, but I'm afraid Sunday is… is… my poker night and I *never* miss it."

I bit back a laugh. She'd never played anything more adventurous than seven-card whist in her life.

"Clarry, you're free aren't you?"

"I'm not sure… I'm…"

He turned to me. "Please come." And just for a second his hand grazed mine.

There was no reason whatsoever to accept the invitation. No reason to meet him again, because although I didn't know all the details, I knew enough to be sure that he and Simon were involved. And, whilst I had no idea if what they were up to was illegal, Laura certainly would. It was her that I had to think of now. I would just call her and tell her what I'd found out and leave it at that. But then again, I argued with myself, if I did go I might discover some pertinent facts and fill in some of the blanks. Isn't that what a real detective would do?

"I'll try," I said and stood up.

"I will be here from eight o'clock," he said and turning to Flan continued, "And I promise to look after her."

"I don't doubt it!" her eyes glittered as she held out her hand and we said our goodbyes.

Flan and I didn't exchange a word until I had started up the car and she was pulling on her seat belt, then she said, "Heaven's darling. What a dish! But rather a dangerous one and I would tell you to be careful of him, but I don't suppose you'd listen, would you?"

"Probably not," I agreed.

CHAPTER TEN

The first thing that struck me as I opened my eyes bright and early the following morning was that I was due to phone Simon about the offer on the house. I lay on my back, instantly feeling wide awake and stared up at the ceiling. What was I going to do? Was there any point in going any further with the offer? I stretched out under the duvet and considered the facts I had learnt and as I tried to place them in coherent order, I realised that somehow, in all the intrigue and excitement of the last five days, I had again allowed myself to wander away from Laura's original brief.

Heaving myself out of bed and trotting through to the bathroom, I thought back over the conversation we'd had at the pizzeria. It was simple. All she had wanted me to find out was if Simon saw her merely as a source of business or if he was genuinely interested in her for herself. I scowled at my refection in the mirror. It was more than possible that he was using her but did that necessarily preclude the fact that he may have developed genuine feelings for her? Even if it had started as a deliberate attempt to win her business it might be that he had been unwittingly drawn to her. The truth was that I had absolutely no way of knowing what

Simon felt about Laura and no remote possibility of finding out, short of asking him.

As I stood now under the shower, I toyed with, but then dismissed, the idea of coming on to him. Always a good test of your man's true level of commitment is to set the classic honey trap. After all, if faithfulness is just a question of opportunity is it of any value?

Then I mentally replayed last night's meeting with Chris. There was something about him, a brooding sense of power. Should I go to the party at The Vine on Sunday? No time to think about that now. I had to be at Abbe's for my shift at six and before that I had things to do.

Simon picked up the phone himself this time.

"Good morning Mr. Napier, Gemma Buchanan here." I rode over his less than enthusiastic greeting and ploughed straight on. "Now what's the situation with Alwyn Road?"

There was a pause and then he said, "It's as I thought; the house is no longer available. Ah… that's my other line going so I'll have to ring off now."

I cut across him. "Why? Why is it no longer for sale? Have you had a better offer or what?" I didn't trouble to disguise the edge of accusation in my tone.

"I've told you all you need to know and so there is no point in continuing this conversation."

"Oh, but there's every point… I'll be in your office in an hour to discuss the matter further."

"I'll be out on viewings."

"No problem," I said nastily. "I can wait."

There was silence.

"I'm not going to go away Simon. You can either meet me this morning or I'll just sit in your office until I get the answers I want."

A long pause and then he snapped, "I'll see you at the house, in half an hour." And he actually hung up on me.

Temper, temper, I thought, but my hand was trembling slightly as I put down the receiver.

I was waiting for him as the BMW drew up. We didn't bother to exchange pleasantries.

Simon headed off down the path with an abrupt, "We might as well talk inside." But, he suddenly stopped short and turned uncertainly towards me, his voice low, "The door's open."

I looked past him and sure enough the door was slightly ajar.

"As far as I know only me, the executors, and the solicitors have keys," he said. "They would normally have told me if…" He trailed off as suddenly the door was flung open and a scary looking thickset bloke somewhere in his late twenties stood glaring at us. His doughy face was studded with piercings and a riot of inky blue tattoos crept up his neck. Not a solicitor I was guessing. We stared at him.

"What the fuck do you want?" he growled.

Simon hesitated and then demanded, "Who are you? What are you doing on these premises?"

Scary Bloke leant back on his heels with a slight rocking movement in a pantomime of exaggerated indifference and looked Simon over carefully. Then scratching his mousy cropped hair asked, "And who wants to know?"

"I've been instructed to sell this house and as far as I'm concerned you have absolutely no business being here and I assure you that…" Simon was forced to break off at this point as Scary Bloke suddenly barged threateningly forward, snarling.

"Do yourself a favour mate and fuck off out of here cos I ain't got time to mess around." He thought for a moment and then continued in a quieter almost conversational tone. "You see today's a Friday and I'm not always in the best of moods on a Friday. Never figured out why that is, what with the weekend coming up and all, but here it is; that's just me. Call it a personality disorder if you like." He turned his hands palms upwards as if in genuine wonder at the complexity of his own temperament.

Simon and I exchanged looks. This guy was obviously a total nutjob. I was ready to beat a hasty retreat, but Simon, to his credit, held his ground although he'd gone awfully red in the face. "I demand to know who you are and what you're doing here."

"You are seriously starting to get on my nerves," said Scary Bloke. "Now I'll tell you what's going to happen."

There was a pause and I held my breath.

"You two are going to sod off right now and not come back. Got it? Because if you don't…" He left the sentence unfinished but took a step towards us. Simon and I instinctively pulled back and he laughed. As he turned to go back inside he looked me over. "You can stay if you like darling. I like blondes. And not just on Fridays. I like them any day of the week." With that, he disappeared into the house, slamming the door behind him with a bang.

I only just beat Simon back down the path. "Not an offer I'll be taking up," I said. "Look, it's way too early for a drink which is probably what we both need." I smiled at him conspiratorially hoping that what we had both just gone through would have created enough of a bond to induce him to confide in me. "But let's go and have a coffee, shall we?"

For a moment, I thought he'd refuse, but maybe I was right about the bonding experience. "Where are you parked?" he asked.

"Oh, I didn't bring my car," I lied. I certainly didn't want him clocking the Renault. "Isn't there a place on the Hill we could walk to?"

He nodded and casting one more glance at the house, set off towards the main road. We walked in silence, which we didn't break until we were sitting opposite each other at a small table hedged in by the pushchairs and strollers of a posse of Yummy Mummies who had monopolised all the sofas. At the counter I had instinctively offered to pay for our lattes and he had accepted. I've never liked mean men.

"So, what's going on Simon?"

"What do you mean?" his voice was flat, his habitual pomposity all but evaporated. He looked a little peaky under his tan. I leant forward across the narrow table and gazed into his eyes. They were the kind of pale blue that in some lights appear to be grey and I suppose many women would have found them attractive. I didn't.

"Simon, listen to me please. I, or I should say the consortium I represent, want that house. The offer we've made is a good one and..."

He made as if to interrupt but I deflected. "Yes, I know you've said that it's no longer available…" I put a teasing stress on the words and smiled warmly, hoping to take some of the sting out of what I was about to say. "I think the real situation is that you've had an offer from another party who have made it worth your while to carry the deal through."

He said nothing but abruptly pushed back his chair and made as if to get up.

"Relax, why don't you?" I soothed, leisurely lifting my latte for another sip. He hesitated and I ploughed on making sure to keep my voice low and caressing. "You're clearly an ambitious man Simon. I saw that the minute I met you. Here's a guy, I thought to myself, who thinks big. He won't be content to stay managing a small agent like Dunstan Stead for long. He's got the talent and the drive to branch out. Perhaps set up his own agency or become a developer?"

I took a breath wondering if I was laying it on too thick, but as a look of dawning complacency lit up his features, I knew I had him. Never underestimate the male ego I thought. "And I can see by the way that you dress that you like to live large, to play hard." Visions of his rack of designer shirts flashed across my mind. "And that takes money, doesn't it?" I had his full attention now. "And it's sweeteners that make the business world go around, wouldn't you agree?"

He gave a slight nod of acknowledgement.

"So, the question is; how big a sweetener are we talking?"

I leant back in my seat regarding him. I'd done. He would either take the bait or he wouldn't.

He looked down at his cup and then up in to the middle distance and then back down to his cup. I curbed my impatience, reining in the desire to reach out my foot under the table and kick him hard in the shins until, at last, it was clear that he had reached a decision. A look of calculation flickered across his face.

"To be able to secure your bid I would need a cash deposit of £25,000 and then the balance of £25,000 when the deal's done."

I had to force myself from reacting. I had no idea we were talking about so much money. I thought of the £200,000 investment he'd made through Lehman Black and wondered how many similar deals he'd done to put aside that kind of money. This man had to be stopped I decided. And it wasn't just about Laura. I had no idea how I was going to do this but I had to try. Play it out I told myself and see what develops.

"And if we agree?" I asked. "What guarantee would there be after the initial payment?"

He flashed me a broad frank smile. "My word of course."

Right, I thought. That's a real clincher. Really, I couldn't work out which one of us was lying to better effect.

"But of course." I allowed myself a slight laugh. "I'm sure that we can come to an agreement on this Simon. I'll get back to you soon. Give me your mobile number."

He did so and I rose from my chair holding out my hand to him, although the contact made me want to recoil.

"Looking forward to hearing from you Gemma." His grip was firm. "Oh, one other thing... all deals are off if that thug isn't removed from the premises."

I blinked in surprise. "What?" I stammered. "What do you mean?"

"What I say," he replied coolly. "Get rid of him and then we can do business."

"But how on earth?"

"That's up to you and your client to arrange. Got to rush, I have another appointment." And with that he backed out from the table, edged past the baby strollers and headed for the door. I sat back down heavily in my seat.

CHAPTER ELEVEN

Twenty minutes later I walked back up the hill and turned into Alwyn Road.

"Change your mind then didja Blondie?"

"I… um… was wondering if I could talk to you?"

Scary Bloke regarded me impassively and then shrugged. "Glad to see you dumped the Stiff." He held the door open for me "After you then love."

I hesitated, but steeled myself and walked on into the house. I crossed the hall into the main sitting room and immediately spotted signs of occupation: a couple of bulging bin liners, bundles of clothes, and two shabby looking sleeping bags on the floor. Stepping over towards the French windows at the far end of the room where I noted that a piece of cardboard had been tacked up at a broken glass pane, I found that Scary Bloke had followed close on my heels.

I cleared my throat thinking that it would be safer to get him talking but nothing came out. The words seemed to have clotted in my throat. Scary Bloke was getting impatient.

"So, whatcha want?"

"Well… I'm… I'm interested in buying this house. That

was the estate agent you met earlier and he was just about to show me round again when…"

This got a reaction. Folding his arms which I noted were curiously too short for his overall size, he laughed in my face. "Forget about it. You won't want it at any price by the time we've finished with it."

"Why? What do you mean?"

He thrust his face a little nearer to mine, presumably never having received the memo about invading another's personal space, and glared at me suspiciously. "I got a little set up here and I ain't looking for no interference, right?"

"Right," I nodded emphatically. "Yes of course. Absolutely."

Unfolding his arms again and visibly relaxing at my show of respectful attention, he looked me up and down appraisingly. "The thing is, I'm kind of a businessman, see?"

I nodded again, although I didn't see at all.

Just as in our earlier encounter, he had adopted an oddly confiding tone and the change in style and pace was unnerving. Shifting his weight more comfortably, he now had his back to the main door and was effectively blocking me in. I forced myself to smile encouragingly. "I make things happen, I'm what you might call a fixer. The thing is I…"

Whilst concentrating on displaying a sincere and rapt interest, I risked a quick glance behind him, scanning the room for any means of escape. It seemed an awfully long way to the hall. Suddenly, out of the corner of my eye, I spotted a slight movement. A pale girl with a mass of long dark hair was peeping around the door and listening intently to the conversation. Our eyes met and then she disappeared back into the gloom of the hall. Anxiously I brought my gaze back to Scary Bloke but he appeared to have noticed nothing and was becoming expansive in his volubility.

"Yeah, this is part of what I call my going concern," he explained. "I haven't got an office or nothing but I'm still what you might call an *onton*preneur."

"Right," I said. "Like Richard Branson."

"Exactly. Richard Branson. I organise accommodation, deluxe accommodation." He sniggered and looked at the sleeping bags.

"You mean like an agency?"

He actually took the question seriously and cocked his head to one side as he carefully considered his answer. He appeared to be enjoying the exchange. Perhaps he rarely had a chance to dazzle a woman with his achievements.

"Well Blondie, not exactly." He gave the stud in his tongue a thoughtful twist, and he was, regrettably, still close enough for me to notice that flossing was not part of his morning routine. "I find an empty place and arrange tenants."

Now I was getting it. "And you charge them rent?"

"Like I said, I'm a businessman."

"But this house isn't yours," I said without thinking "You can't just…"

I'd gone too far. All the danger signs were back. His eyes narrowed, his posture changed.

"I can do anything I want. And I think you'd better clear off now." His voice was low. "I'm beginning to wonder about you."

"Fine. Yes," I squeaked. "I'll just be going. Right now is good for me."

He was still blocking me in and so cautiously I edged around him and backed slowly and deliberately away, all the while being very careful to maintain eye contact. Each step felt like a mile but at last I reached the hallway. Turning, I wrenched open the front door and then with an absurdly bright, "Bye then," I catapulted my way out of the building.

I made my way unsteadily to the car, locked myself in, rested my head back against the seat, and patted my chest. It felt like a troupe of out-of-sync flamenco dancers were practising that foot stamping thing they do, against my rib cage. Christ, I thought, I'm having some kind of seizure. It took some minutes before I could think clearly.

What was going on at that house? If I'd ever stopped to think about it I guessed that I'd sympathise with squatters presuming that they had no other choice available to them. Perhaps they, for any number of reasons, had run away from home or couldn't afford to rent and so they took over a long abandoned property? It would beat living on the streets. But I had no idea that there were people out there who actually made a profit from the practice.

Was the girl with the dark hair working with Scary Bloke or was she one of his tenants? My thoughts tumbled over themselves. And how did Scary Bloke happen on this particular house? How did he know it was empty? Perhaps he simply kept a look out in the area and was ready to take over at short notice any property where there was no sign of life? But somehow that just didn't sound likely.

I moved the car to a few doors up from the house and

settled down to wait. I wanted to talk to that girl and there was no way I could do that with Scary Bloke on hand. I would just sit here and keep my eyes open. One of them was bound to come out at some time or other. If it was the girl then I'd give chase and catch up with her in the street and if it was Scary Bloke, I'd wait until he was out of sight and then bang on that door until she answered. A good plan I decided.

But by one o'clock there was no sign of either of them. Take it as a sign I told myself, a sign to give up, go home, and mind your own bloody business. I cast one last look at the house. Someone was opening the gate. It was the girl and she was heading out towards Wimbledon Hill. Not taking my eyes off her, I let her get a hundred yards away and then pulled the Renault out and followed at a distance. As she approached the main road, I crawled up behind her and remaining in first gear but with my foot on the clutch pedal, wound down the car window.

"Hey," I hailed her. She turned at the sound, looking about her for the disembodied voice. "It's me," I called, letting her get a good look at my face. "I just saw you in the house. I need to talk to you."

I saw the start of recognition in her eyes but she shook her head and started walking.

"I just want to ask you some…"

She was young, maybe not even eighteen and she was thin. Even in the baggy tracksuit bottoms and T-shirt she wore, I could see the fragility of her bones. Her long dark hair was heavy and unkempt and flared wildly around her face, emphasising the sharp contours of her features.

"Just leave me alone." Her voice was flat, but well-modulated and seemed at odds with her appearance.

"Look, please, give me a few minutes, will you?"

She shook her head and glared at me with obvious mistrust.

"I tell you what," I called. "I'm just going to grab a sandwich and a coffee in the village. Come and have one with me... my treat."

Even as the words came out of my mouth, I could see that she had read me completely wrong and had taken offence at what I assumed she considered a patronising attempt to ingratiate myself.

"You can't *buy* me with the offer of a sandwich," she spat.

I laughed but was a little taken aback at her hostility. I wasn't being patronising I just wanted to talk to her. What was her problem?

"Of course, not," I said. "It's obvious to me that it would take the promise of cake, or at the very least chocolate, to do that. A sandwich would never do it in a million years."

She looked at me, unsure what to make of that, but after a weighty pause as I held her gaze, she at last gave a reluctant smile.

I leant over and opened the passenger door. "Hop in quick because I'm starving."

After another brief moment of hesitation, she nodded and clambered in as I shifted the gears into second and turned right out on to Wimbledon Hill.

"I'm Clarry by the way, and best to buckle up," I advised. "I'm a lousy driver. If I told you how many times it took me to pass my test, you'd probably rather fling yourself out into oncoming traffic than venture the half mile up to the Village with me."

As if to add emphasis to my words, the driver of a white van on my right, took exception to my distracted but exuberant style of lane filtering and let out a volley of abuse from his opened window, treating us to a series of graphic and unmistakable hand gestures.

"See what I mean? What's your name?"

"Melanie," her tone was wary.

We pulled up outside a café in the centre of the village. Most lunchtimes it's almost impossible to get a table outside, but an elegant middle-aged lady in an immaculately tailored dress was just gathering up her carrier bags to depart.

"Grab it," I said and Melanie didn't stop to argue.

I parked and then joined her just as the waiter, Ahmed, came up to take our order.

"Hey Clarry. How are you? How's that machine holding up?"

"Ahmed and I are old friends," I explained, introducing him to Melanie.

"I work at Abbe's a restaurant a few doors down and Ahmed here rescued me one lunchtime recently when our icemaker went on the blink. I had a party in from the local Rotary club who threatened to beat me with the minutes of their triplicate copied agendas if I didn't supply them with perfectly chilled gin and tonics."

Melanie laughed and as she did so her thin face lit up.

"So, what are you having?" asked Ahmed waving menus at us.

"The Middle Eastern salad with chicken, please," I answered, handing him back the menu unread. "And that special iced tea you do."

"That sounds good," said Melanie "Is that OK? What you said about treating me?"

"Of course," I responded with all the unconcern of a woman who, this month, would only be paying the minimum amount off her credit card bill.

Our iced teas arrived and I examined her, not sure quite how to begin. "There's plenty of great cafés and bars around here, do you know the area?"

She put down her glass. "No, not really. We've only just moved here. I'm from Winchester originally."

"We?"

"Ted – my boyfriend – and me."

Although I didn't really think it could be Scary Bloke, I had to ask. "Is that the guy I just met?"

She laughed. "God no. No way. That's Gary. And I can't imagine anyone wanting to be with him."

"Nor me. Who is he then?"

"I don't know really. We met him in Brixton a week ago when we were looking for somewhere to live." She looked at me from under her eyelashes. "We needed somewhere we could afford, somewhere really cheap."

She paused and I was on the verge of jumping in with a dozen questions when I suddenly remembered watching an interrogation scene in one of those American TV cops shows Flan had talked about. The detective had allowed the suspect to tell his story at his own pace and it got results. I suppose most of us babble on a bit when confronted by the reserve of another. Those little silences can be awkward, embarrassing even and I was hoping that now, with the help of the iced tea and the chicken salad, Melanie would be feeling comfortable enough with me to talk. She was and she did.

CHAPTER TWELVE

Waitressing is hard on the feet and even tougher on illusions, especially if you have ever had a fantasy of the perfect dinner date. If only diners would follow these simple rules, they and we would have a much better experience:

*Book a table and arrive on time.

*Don't de-head the flower arrangement or pick at the candle wax.

*Don't ask and then order what the waitress recommends. You will only get leftovers or something perilously close to its use-by date.

*Don't ask for something that's not on the menu. If it's not on there, then we don't want you to have it.

*Complain, if you really must, but make sure it's in a polite manner if you'd rather not have your pudding dredged with the pastry chef's dandruff, or your piece of steak tenderised by a kick-around in the kitchen.

*Do not scream at the top of your voice and, with the violent threat of taking your custom elsewhere, if the waitress "accidentally" pours gravy in your lap. She clearly has been driven to desperate measures by your boorish over-familiarity and is longing for you to sod off and annoy her competitors down the road.

*Depart before eleven pm and always leave a good tip.

Ignore these tips and you face the threat of a severe case of food poisoning, or of being subject to an assault with flying kitchen knives from a chef upset by your request for a bottle of ketchup on the side. Follow them to the letter and you will be the perfect customer and have done virtually all you can to guarantee that you and your meal won't be sneezed upon, spat in, or otherwise interfered with.

The chap on table four tonight had clearly never heard of these instructions and was acting up.

"In France," complained Ian, my co-waiter for the evening, flapping his apron in vexation, "being a waiter is a profession. In this country, the barbarous hordes snap their fingers at us and expect us to jump like dogs."

"Woof!" I replied. "Oh, Ian that woman on table… "

He wagged a perfectly manicured finger at me. "Iris darling, Iris. That's what I'm using now, so try and remember will you?"

"Got it. But I'm not sure it suits you. It's too old-fashioned."

"*That* from a Clarissa?"

"Fair comment," I acknowledged. "It's just that I think it's a bit plain for someone as fabulous as you." I looked at his discreetly made-up face. "Especially when there are so many exotic names to choose from. Like Lola or Brigitta… Or…"

He blew me a kiss, "Sweets!" Then he took a step closer towards me with an appraising look. "You're looking a bit washed out love. Someone's been living it up. Anybody I know? Don't tell me it was Not-So-Tiny Tim, our gorgeous commis chef? He's had a soft spot for you for ages. Tell me all about it. Did you get to see his adorable…?"

"No nothing like that, I've just been busy with something that's all. And anyway, Tim's younger than me. And talking of dogs, he's like a big playful puppy. Not my style at all."

"He's old enough darling and playful can be good. I should know," he drawled and then catching a movement out of the corner of his eye, "Oh hell, table eight seems to want something. *Must* they bellow so? We're working like slaves tonight and this running about is simply murder on the legs. It brings on varicose veins you know. Look, I'm wearing a pair of support tights under my trews. Great idea don't you think?" He bent down and demurely raised a couple of inches of trouser leg flashing me a glimpse of 60 denier American Tan before whisking off with some desert menus.

Friday night is always a busy one and with a distinctly different feel from Saturday evenings, when we're mostly booked with couples and foursomes. On Fridays the after-work crowd start arriving at about seven thirty, having already downed several happy hour cocktails at the bar across the road. The atmosphere is nearly always good humoured as the staff weave their way through the packed tables dispensing plates, bottles of wine, and tactful parries or witty put-downs as they see fit.

As I headed to table seven with a bowl of olives, my mind played over what Melanie had told me earlier in the day. She and her boyfriend Ted had been staying at a hostel in Brixton, sleeping in a dormitory style room with ten strangers. Although the place was cheap and clean they hadn't liked having to share with so many people, some of whom were weird, wasted, or just plain wacko. They had bumped into Scary Bloke Gary last weekend in a local pub, got talking, and had told him they were trying to find new digs.

"Your lucky day," he'd said. "It's what I do." He'd then explained how he looked after several properties and said he could get them a decent private room in a shared house.

Melanie and Ted had listened with interest at first but had grown wary. There was something about Gary they didn't like so they'd finished their drinks, told him that they'd think about it, and said their goodbyes with no intention of meeting up with him again. However, getting back to the hostel, they were pissed off to find that someone had stolen most of Melanie's clothes. That decided them; they had to get out of there. And so, against their better judgement, they went straight back to the pub, found Gary, took him up on his offer, and yesterday afternoon had moved into Alwyn Road.

They'd paid him a fee, not a refundable deposit, using up a lot of their meagre savings and were due to pay a weekly rent from thereon. There wasn't a bed in the large upstairs room they were given, but they had sleeping bags and could make do until they could afford to buy one and some other basic bits of furniture. Last night someone else had arrived with his bags and moved in to the next room and another had been due to move in this afternoon.

That was it, all I knew, and none of it I reminded myself, really any of my concern. But then why did it feel like it was?

The evening sped by. Chef Laurence was in a good mood and didn't even bawl me out when I raised orders for only two swordfish steaks when I meant three, and working with Ian was always fun.

"Clarry," called Dave. "You're wanted."

A couple had just sat down at table three by the window. Two arty looking guys in their forties working in TV, they were earnest and amusing and helloed me enthusiastically.

"We've just been having an argument Clarry," said Jake.

"No," said Carl calmly and patting his pockets for his glasses as I handed him the menu. "*You* were arguing. *I* know I'm right so no arguments necessary."

Jake turned to me explaining, "It's about the last line from an old film, listen…"

He started to recite theatrically, "'*Don't wish for the moon when we have the stars*'. What's it from? Do you know?"

I smirked. I may have flunked all my exams but I am pretty well versed in films from the 1930s and 40s courtesy of Flan. She loves them. The drama, the glamour, and especially the clothes. We had spent many an afternoon curled up on her sofa watching Jean Harlow, Greer Garson, and Joan Crawford weave their way in and out of romantic misunderstandings and entanglements, only to fall into the comforting arms of the handsome male lead. Why can't real life be like that?

"*Now Voyager*," I replied glibly. "Bette Davis and Paul Henreid."

"See," said Carl winking at me.

"Bottle of Chablis as usual?" I asked.

Things were quietening down when Ian sidled up to me and hissed, "Fancy a vodders and tonic love?"

I nodded gratefully and he headed off into the kitchen where he and Alec the sous-chef kept a few spare bottles in the pudding fridge. Whilst we regularly have an after work lock-in with leftover bottles of wine, it's an unwritten rule that the staff don't drink whilst on duty. Tonight though, I was gagging for a drink and Dave is OK about the odd one. Besides there was no reason he had to know about it.

"Chin chin darling." Ian clinked his glass against my glass. Half hidden by the service chest situated at the back of the room but able to keep our eyes on the proceedings, we could, if Dave spotted us, instantly look busy by snatching up a cloth and polishing one of the pieces of cutlery that sat dully gleaming in a great stack before us.

"So, how's life?"

"Well Clarry since you ask," Ian puffed out his cheeks and let the air out slowly. "Frankly it's not all sweetness and light on the home front. Ray's been a bit off. I don't know what the matter is with him, really I don't. He's so sulky lately."

I was surprised. Ray, Ian's partner of several years, had always struck me as remarkably patient and down to earth, the yin to Ian's yang.

"What's up? You been playing the field again?"

Ian frowned crunching down on an ice cube. "Now, you know perfectly well that that's all in the past since I met Ray."

"Ah! But does *he* know that?"

"Well he certainly should," he retorted. "We're practically an old married couple." He flashed me a wicked grin. "But, how can I help it if other men find me irresistible and will insist on flirting with me."

"But do you flirt back?" I persisted.

"Well nothing serious. Oh crap, latecomers," he groaned and looked at his watch as the main door opened and a couple walked in.

"I'll go," I said. "No, no, you just stay there and enjoy your lovely ice-cold drink whilst I drag my…"

The newcomers came fully into the room and into the light; a tall lanky guy in his very early twenties with short dark spiky hair and a young girl, Melanie.

"Hi," I said going over to greet them. "Have you come to try us out or…?" I trailed off as it became clear, by their shuffling body language, that having a relaxed drink and meal was not the reason for their appearance.

"Hi Clarry, this is Ted." Melanie's voice was apologetic. "We're sorry to barge in but we wanted to talk to you and didn't know where else to find you." She shook her thick wild hair back from her face. "We didn't come earlier because we thought you'd be busy but…" she cast a quick look around. "I guess you still are."

She looked very young and defenceless and again I felt a yank on my sympathy chain.

"Yeah, sorry about this," said Ted. He had a nice face, angular with a long nose but gentle about the mouth and with dark intelligent eyes.

"Don't worry about it," I smiled reassuringly. "My shift's not over yet, but… look, why don't you stay and have a drink and we can have a chat later."

I saw them exchange a quick glance, and suddenly

recalling their shortage of money; I thought fast and continued, "Actually we've got some wine left over from a big table earlier, and you'd be doing us a favour if you'd help us polish it off." I grinned at them. "And I'll join you when I can."

Ted's shoulders relaxed and he smiled gratefully. "Well, if that's really OK? That would be great."

I ushered them to a quiet corner table away from the other diners. "Back in a minute," I promised.

"Friends of yours?" enquired Ian waltzing by with some dirty plates balanced expertly along his arm.

"Sort of," I agreed. "They're new friends."

"They look like a couple of stray kittens that have been left out in the rain," he remarked.

I winced. The prospect of Melanie and Ted somehow becoming my responsibility struck a warning note in my head.

Eventually at nearly midnight, the last of the customers left and we had the place to ourselves.

"Night guys," Dave pulled on his jacket. "I'm off. I promised Sal we'd do an early supermarket run tomorrow. In-laws for lunch on Sunday," he explained heading for the door. "Alec's locking up and there's five half-empty bottles of wine on the bar for you. Enjoy!"

Ian turned down the latch and grinned at me. "Time for the lunatics to take over the asylum…"

Melanie and Ted, who had remained quiet at their table whilst we had done all the final clearing away, looked across at me as Ian bustled over with the wine and some more glasses and introductions were made.

"Hungry?" he asked.

"Who? Me or them?"

He made a face. "Clarry, I have never known you not hungry." He disappeared off to the kitchen.

"Thanks for this," said Melanie lifting her glass. "It's really nice of you and…" she looked about the room. "This is such a cool place."

I took a chair gratefully. I'd been on my feet for six hours, without the benefit of support tights, and was glad to sit down. "It is, isn't it?" I agreed. "I love it. So you wanted to talk to me."

Ted nodded and as I poured myself a generous sized glass of wine, he began hesitantly. "From what you've told Melanie and from the conversation she overheard between you and Gary, we gather that we have no right to be in the house…" he corrected himself. "I mean that Gary should never have rented the room to us."

"The thing is," interrupted Melanie. "We don't want to get into any trouble." Her eyes shone with what looked suspiciously like tears. "We don't know what to do. We know we have to get out but we've given him nearly all the money we have and…" her voice wobbled and Ted wrapped a protective arm around her shoulders and again took up the thread.

"We wanted to ask you not to do anything official like calling the police or anything until we've managed to find somewhere else to stay," he finished with a rush.

"Police?" I sat up in surprise. The thought hadn't even crossed my mind. But, I mused, taking another sip of wine, it was likely that Laura when I got to tell her the whole story, would, of course, take steps to clear the house and that may well involve the police. I shook my head regretfully. "The thing is it's really not up to me. But," I hastened to add as Melanie's eyes filled, "I promise that I will do my best to help you. Look, why don't you tell me a bit about yourselves? When did you come to London and why? Are you looking for jobs or are you students or…?" I gave them my most encouraging smile and looked from one to the other.

Melanie gave a great sniff and seemed to come to a decision. "Well," she said drawing out the word. "It's not really a very long story."

I nodded thankfully (it had been a bit of a day) and waited for her to continue.

"We've been here nearly three weeks. I was at art school in Winchester where we come from," she explained. "I met Ted through some friends and we…" She looked up at Ted, her face shining now with love and not with un-spilt tears. "And we got together."

"And?" I asked wanting to move things along a bit.

"Melanie's parents didn't approve. Mostly because I'm not earning regular money," said Ted in a low voice. "I'm a musician. I play the piano, jazz mostly but whatever gigs I can get."

"And they think we're too young," interrupted Melanie. "They wanted us to stop seeing so much of each other and to put the brakes on our relationship for at least a year. So, I quit my course and… we ran away."

I put down my glass. "Don't tell me that your parents haven't a clue where you are?"

" It's OK," Ted said. "We did speak to them when we first came down and every few days since we got here. And we've spoken to mine. Honestly Clarry, we wouldn't do that to them."

"Shove over," Ian's voice broke in on us. He was bearing a basket of French bread in one hand and a huge plate of pâte in the other. "Alec and Tim are coming right out," Ian added taking a seat beside me and making a space on the table for the food.

"Now come on then you two," his eyes took in the emotion evident on Melanie's face. "Whatever the problem is, you'll feel better when you've eaten something, and besides, this pâte…" he smeared some on to a piece of bread, "looks divine."

"Save some for us." Tim and Alec appeared and pulled across a couple of chairs. Glasses were filled and we all tucked in.

"I needed this," said Alec savouring his first sip of wine.

"I suppose you're going to tell us it was a tough night," said Ian. "When from what I saw, you and Not-So-Tiny here were leaving most of the work to poor old José our much exploited kitchen porter."

Alec lazily picked up a hunk of bread and lobbed it across the table at him. "The trouble with waiters and… waitresses here," he winked at me. "Is that from some inflated view of their own importance they actually seem to think that customers come in here for anything other than the food? The food that I… and… here I feel honour bound to acknowledge the assistance of the great lug sitting to my left, lovingly prepare with supreme skill and unfailing dedication."

I laughed. "And I thought it was for a glimpse of Ian's tights."

After we had all been treated to the vision of Ian's ankles in hosiery, I asked through a mouthful of baguette, "You guys don't know of any cheap rooms, locally do you? Ted and Melanie here really need somewhere to stay in a hurry."

Alec shrugged, "No, I don't think so but I'll ask around."

Melanie smiled gratefully at him.

Tim lent back in his chair, his six-foot rugby-playing frame threatening to overwhelm its confines and pushed his floppy brown hair out of his eyes, a look of concentration on his face. It is only fair to say that Not-So-Tiny Tim isn't what you might call quick. Not in his thinking, not in his kitchen prep and, as I'm told, not on the rugby pitch, which apparently doesn't matter as he's a prop. But he's a thoroughly good guy. Polite, kind, and really very sweet. Just like a puppy in fact.

"There's an empty room at my place," he said after a few moments pause.

Melanie and Ted looked at him expectantly.

"It's not much," Tim turned to them. "But Barney my landlord is pretty cool. He's a bit of an old hippie really. I think he used to be in a band because sometimes when he's had a few beers he starts playing his saxophone, old blues stuff."

I hadn't been to his home but I knew that Tim had a room in a sprawling, tatty old house on the corner of Cottenham Park Road and that his landlord who lived on the ground floor was a good-natured and rather eccentric man in his late fifties. He and Tim rubbed along together remarkably well. On top of his modest rent, Tim would cook the occasional meal and helped keep the wilderness of the garden in some sort of check, and Barney, for his part, was totally laid-back about noise and mess and all other associated trappings of a young guy in his early twenties. In fact, from what I gathered Barney himself had much the same habits as Tim.

"Really?" said Melanie. "Do you think he might take us? Will you talk to him? Can we go and see him?"

"Hang on a minute Mel," Ted put a restraining hand out and turned to Tim. "The thing is we can't afford much. How much do you reckon he'd want?"

Tim smiled his big affable smile. "It won't be a lot I'm sure. He's not in it for the money. Just likes company about the house I think. Look why don't you come back with me now for a drink and we'll talk to him."

"But it's nearly one o'clock in the morning," Ian looked askance.

"Oh, he'll be up and sitting in the kitchen with a beer. We often have a drink together when I get back from work. How about it?" He looked from Ted to Melanie.

"Great, yes if you really think it would be OK?"

Melanie turned to me. "Will you come too Clarry?"

Before I could answer, Tim added with a grin, "I've been trying to get Clarry back to my room for months."

Ian gave me a sharp dig in the ribs but I ignored him. "Thanks for the invite but I'm beat. Long day," I yawned suddenly feeling incredibly tired.

Alec got to his feet. "Come on let's get this lot cleared away. If I'm home before half one there's a slight chance that Cheryl may still be awake and I might get some tonight!"

Ian laced the six empty wine glasses between his fingers. "Right! You know perfectly well she'll have fallen asleep over *Fifty Shades…* and you won't get a look in."

"Thanks so much Clarry," Melanie whispered as we all said our goodbyes. "You've been so kind. Is it OK to stay in touch?"

"Sure. Take my number and let me know how you get on at Tim's."

She and Ted left with Tim. Two kittens and a puppy unleashed.

"Night night love," said Ian pulling a scarf around his throat as we left the restaurant. "You should have taken Not-So-Tiny up on his offer. I know I would have." And laughing to himself he disappeared off into the night.

When I got home I checked my messages.

"Hi hun." Laura's voice was happy and relaxed. "It's after ten and I'm holed up in my hotel bedroom after a ghastly dinner with the Trustees. I'm so glad to be coming home. I'm leaving tomorrow morning and then I'm out with Simon so probably won't get a chance to speak to you until Sunday or Monday. I'll call you and we'll arrange to meet up. I don't suppose you have found anything out but can't wait to see you and catch up. Anyway, better go I suppose. I'm just about to hit the minibar. Well it's compulsory, isn't it? Bye."

CHAPTER THIRTEEN

I slept fitfully. At six o'clock, after nearly an hour of trying to get back to sleep, I gave up and stomped off to the bathroom. I splashed cold water in my face and gazed at my reflection in the mirror. Not a pretty sight. My skin looked puffy from lack of sleep and my hair looked like Godzilla had been running his big furry fingers through it. Perhaps at some point in my warped dream-landscape, he had been.

Reaching hastily for a brush, I decided on an early jog to shrug off the phantoms of the night. I could always go back to bed later if I felt like it. I'd got nothing planned today, nothing I absolutely had to do. I would tear my mind away from the whole bloody house/Simon affair and chill out. And, I resolved, as I pulled on my running gear, I would not try to contact Laura until after the weekend. Why shouldn't she enjoy a hot night with Simon without me having to put her off with the details of his nasty little moneymaking scheme? She's a grown up. It's not like going to bed with a guy commits you to a relationship.

Jog over and about to head home for a shower, I realised I was no longer tired. I was feeling buoyed up and restless, needing action and coffee. I checked my watch, only seven thirty. There'd be no harm in just driving past Simon's house I told myself, so why not? I had nothing better to do and who knows I might learn something new? I set off towards Southfields and at the next garage I spotted, nipped in for a take-out latte.

I pulled up close to the house in Elborough Street and spotted his car. Reaching for my baseball hat I realised that this surveillance business was beginning to feel natural to me and what was more, I liked it. I waited for nearly an hour. Simon would probably be going off to work soon. Estate agents were obviously open for business on Saturdays; in fact it was likely to be their best day of the week for viewings. And if he wouldn't be heading for the office, he'd be having a lie-in like any normal person.

I was almost certainly wasting my time here, I decided, when I heard voices and looked up to see Simon coming out from behind his front gate dressed in a pair of jeans and a casual shirt. He also had something draped about his arms and it wasn't a sweater. Well, well, well, I thought, hunkering down in my seat. That settles that. I had him already pegged as a con man and now I could add two-timing bastard to his rap sheet, because the girl in the micro-mini dress and with the big hair was certainly not his sister. I watched them. No, I thought, as the two of them engaged in a serious goodbye snog, she's definitely not his sister. At last they disentangled themselves. Simon then disappeared back through his garden gate and the girl sashayed off in a killer pair of follow-me-fuck-me heels to a white Fiat parked on the other side of the road and let herself into the driving seat. And me? Well I followed the Fiat of course.

I nearly lost her in the Wandsworth one-way system. She was an even worse driver than me. By the time we pulled up in a side street in the wrong end of Pimlico, my hair under my cap was matted with sweat. I looked about me. I was guessing that this was the kind of area where an MP might set up a cosy little love nest for his mistress, close enough to "The House" and far enough away from the country seat where his unsuspecting wife brought up the children and where she would, one day when the scandal hit, devotedly stand by him.

Killer Heels was now getting out of the car. I watched as she picked her way along the street, past a greengrocers, a newsagent, an internet café, and finally turned in to *Bella's Beauty Salon*. Was she a customer in for a top up to her tan? Or did she work there? There was only one way to find out. I left it five minutes, and then followed her inside.

"Good morning," I said brightly to the woman behind the counter. Heavily made-up, she was somewhere in her late fifties wearing a pale pink nursey type overall with the logo *Bella's* straining across a huge bosom, and a pair of plastic clip-on pearl earrings the size of hard boiled eggs.

"I haven't got an appointment but…" I trailed off as she minutely and with obvious amusement inspected me from top to toe. "I was hoping," I began again but she held up a restraining hand and in the gravelly voice of a forty-ciggies-a-day woman, called out behind her to the hidden recess of the shop.

"Karen, you're free, aren't you? It looks like we've got ourselves an emergency case out here!"

Killer Heels, now revealed as Karen, stood before me. She was wearing the same pale pink uniform as her colleague although several sizes smaller and she had changed her heels for the comfort of a pair of flip-flops.

"Hi, I'm Karen." Her voice was flat and with a nasal quality but was friendly enough.

"Oh Hi, I'm Clarry. Well…I was passing and I thought that I should maybe get a facial or something? What kind of treatments do you do?"

"Love, you need whatever we've got," snorted Clip-Ons.

Karen grinned. "Don't mind her. It's a quiet start this morning, so she's bored and getting a bit cheeky."

Cheeky was putting it mildly. And no wonder they're quiet I thought, taking in for the first time the tired décor with its faded paintwork, and frayed carpet. The Ladies-Who-Lunch set of neighbouring Belgravia would not find this at all to their taste. And I had a feeling that Clip-Ons' particular line in wise cracking repartee might not go down too well either.

Karen picked up a leaflet from the desk and handed it to me. It listed the various treatments and prices. I scanned it and made up my mind. Well why not, I hadn't splurged on myself for ages and maybe a bit of pampering was just what I needed.

"Right, OK yes. I think I'll go for a facial and maybe an eyebrow shape and tint."

Karen nodded. "Any waxing? Legs? Bikini line?"

I shook my head. "No thanks. I had a very bad experience once and thought it would never…"

"Oh yes?" put in a deadpan Clip-Ons. "A touch of mange in the minge? That can be very nasty."

"It *wasn't* mange. It was…" I was wasting my breath.

The telephone was ringing and Clip-Ons had picked up the receiver, ready no doubt to launch her charm offensive upon somebody else.

"Right," said Karen. "Let's take you through." She whisked me out into a distinctly shabby corridor and then ushered me into a small windowless cubicle. The pink paintwork was drastically in need of a touch-up, but some effort had been made to create a suitably calming atmosphere. On one wall were a couple of framed posters of alpine scenes and, when Karen pressed a button on a console, a bland tinkly-bell style of music started up.

"OK," said Karen picking up a robe from a stack on a shelf and handing it to me. "It's probably best to take your top off and pull down your bra straps because I'll be cleansing your neck and on to your collar bones."

She turned away as I shrugged off my sweatshirt and pulled on the robe.

"And then when you're ready hop up on to the table. Is that alright for you? Comfy?" she asked as I stretched myself flat out on the consulting bed.

"Yes, fine thanks."

"Good. Right, let's have a look at you." She clipped back my hair and proceeded to inspect my skin.

Whilst she examined the state of my pores, I took a good look at her. Up close she looked somewhere in her mid-twenties with regular features, a pair of lustreless eyes of an indeterminate green, and the too-yellow tan of a spray tan addict. She was undeniably pretty, but her hair was too light for her complexion. She'd gone for the platinum to champagne range on the colour spectrum when the honey to gold shades would have suited her more. It was very long and with what looked like extensions and was scooped into one of those sexy, half-up half-down dos that look like you've just got out of bed. Which, in fact, she just had. Not particularly tall, she had a slight frame and a pair of Double Es which may or may not have been part of the original biological hand of cards she'd been dealt. I was guessing not.

Mutual examination over she was ready to begin. "First we open the pores by steam cleaning. Not too hot or it breaks the delicate veins." This said as she applied hot cloths over my face. "And then we deep cleanse. London's a very dirty place you know." She gave the statement an air of surprise as if it was the first time that she had noticed the grime and pollution of the capital.

Still swaddled in the flannels, a nod and a grunt were the only contribution to the conversation that I was capable of.

"And now I'm going to boost the circulation."

That's when the slapping began. My eyes watered as she continued to make slicing movements to my cheeks. "Um you're hurting me."

"Ooops! Sorry," she said with a laugh. "I get carried away. So now we're ready for moisturising."

She smeared a thick film of cream over my face and neck as I asked, "Does my skin look OK?"

"Not bad," she gave a professional nod. "Your elasticity's good but you're a bit dehydrated and that can lead to the development of fine lines."

"Oh?" I said not liking the sound of this. "Anything I can do about that?"

"Drink less alcohol."

"Ah."

"And up, your water intake."

"I can do that."

As she massaged various unguents into my skin she switched to conversational mode. "So, going out tonight?"

"Yes, big date," I instantly lied because I wanted to get her onto the subject of men.

"Lucky you," she replied. "Taking you somewhere nice, is he?"

"Out to a restaurant," I improvised. "What about you? Are you out with your mates or have you got a cosy night in with your man?"

She paused in the kneading of my temples and shrugged. "I'm not seeing anyone at the moment. Well there is someone but…" I waited and she carried on. "He's not really a boyfriend more a…"

"Fuck buddy?" I suggested.

"Something like that."

"Every girl should have one," I said assuming she was referring to Simon. And then, to tease out a little more info, I remarked, "I used to have a scene like that, but I found that in the end it was always only a late-night booty call he wanted and that didn't make me feel very good about myself."

"I know what you mean about that. What did you do?"

"I dumped him."

"What did he say when you told him?"

"He didn't. I texted."

She laughed and as she gave her head a little shake one of the looped-up strands of hair disengaged itself and fell across her face. Absently she pushed it away but it was clear that our discussion was over.

"I'm going to leave this on for about five minutes or so to let you relax and to give the cream a chance to really work its way into your upper dermis."

And she left the room.

I closed my eyes. Those tinkly bells were starting to grate, but after a few more minutes Karen was back and wiping the residue of gunk off my face.

"How does it feel?"

"Great." And it did.

Next, she tweezed out a few stray eyebrows and then applied the dark dye and allowed it to develop. "OK you're done."

I raised myself up to a sitting position and looked into the magnified mirror she handed me. "Thanks, so much Karen." I swung my legs down off the bed and peeled off the robe.

"Better," observed Clip-Ons as I came out into reception to pay. "Almost human."

CHAPTER FOURTEEN

In the car, I picked up a message. It was Melanie, her voice brimming with happiness.

"It's so great. Tim's landlord Barney is really nice and he's offered us a room. It's quite big with a double bed, a proper wardrobe, and everything. It's at the back of the house on the second floor and it looks out over the garden and he said we can move in as soon as we like."

There was a pause and I could make out Ted's voice in the background. "Ted says hi. The thing is we just wanted to say thank you. We wouldn't have met Tim or Barney without you, so thanks again. We're planning to move across this afternoon. Gary does his rent rounds tonight and we'd rather not see him. We haven't got much stuff, especially now I've got hardly any clothes. Anyway Tim says that he and Barney want to throw a bit of a party to celebrate. Not sure when, probably next week some time but I'll phone you. You'll be guest of honour. Right. Got to go. Bye."

I smiled to myself. At least one good thing had come out of all this. Now for the call I dreaded. Before discovering the existence of Karen I'd decided to delay telling Laura about Simon. Now it couldn't wait. If I was in her position I'd want to know. I tried her mobile but it went straight to voicemail. She was probably on her way back from Norwich.

"Hi hun, just me. Give me a call when you can."

I shouldn't have felt relieved that I'd not got hold of her because it only put off the inevitable, but I was.

When I got home I updated Flan on my doings.

"How much?" she cried on hearing the sum demanded by Simon. "That's appalling. Well, of course it's utterly despicable whatever the price of the bribe but really, £50,000 is just too greedy. Well at least we needn't feel quite so guilty about breaking into his house I suppose." When I reached the part about Karen, she listened in silence and then said, "Dear me. Poor Laura. When are you going to tell her?"

"I've left her a message asking her to call me."

Just before she rang off she asked, "And so how does your skin feel after your facial?"

"Rehydrated. She told me to drink more water."

"And less alcohol?"

"Never mentioned a word about it," I replied crisply and hung up to the sound of her wry laughter.

Saturday night and there were places I could have been. Fun places. So, what was I doing sitting in my car opposite the Alwyn Road house waiting for Scary Bloke Gary to show up? It was mostly curiosity, and a desire to provide an answer to the question of how he had come to pick on that particular house at just that particular time. Melanie's words about Gary's rent collections had been buzzing around my head all afternoon and somewhere around six o'clock I'd realised that I wanted to witness his operations for myself.

I didn't have long to wait. Just after seven, a motorbike with a noisy exhaust rattled its way into the street and pulled up outside No 29. The figure once divested of helmet and revealing itself as Gary, made his way up the garden path and disappeared from view. He was in there for less than ten minutes and when he returned I could see from the way he kicked savagely at the gate that Melanie and Ted having done a bunk, had not gone down well. But maybe he was always in a bad temper?

Trailing a car was one thing but giving chase to a motorbike was quite another. Gary dodged and weaved his way through the evening traffic and I would have lost him almost straightaway if it hadn't been for the roar of his exhaust. As it was, with both my windows wound fully down, I just followed the fanfare.

Trailing him up Wimbledon Hill, past the Common, through Raynes Park and into New Malden I kept a distance of three or four cars behind, but was on the alert when he turned into a residential street off the Kingston Road. Then I had no choice but to drive past him as he stopped and turned off his engine. I executed a hasty U-turn at the top of the road and crawled back, spotting him as he entered a house.

No 67 looked much like its neighbours except that the garden was very overgrown and even in the fading light I could see that the curtains were hung crooked. Perhaps this was where he lived or was it another one of his *deluxe rentals*? A 1930's semi, it wasn't as large as Alwyn Road but big enough, I figured, to accommodate up to eight or ten people if the downstairs was used as bedrooms. That would bring a hefty weekly rent. I wondered how many other houses he had illegally commandeered and how many other vulnerable people he was screwing money out of. And did he work alone or was he just a small part of some larger organisation? More questions. I slid down in the seat as Gary exited the house and clambered on to his motorbike. We were on the move again.

By ten o'clock, we had made three further stops, another house in New Malden and two in Worcester Park. I dutifully made a note of each of the addresses and would give them to Laura so that her firm of solicitors could do whatever they thought best. Contact the police probably.

Laura. My thoughts kept returning to her. She hadn't phoned me back. And I thought I knew why. I didn't think she had a flat battery or had lost her mobile. My guess was that at some level she knew (and possibly from the tone of my voice in my message) that the news I had about Simon wouldn't be good and she just didn't want to hear it, or at least not yet. The thought depressed me and I felt tired. What was the point of going on with following Gary?

We were now somewhere in the backstreets of Surbiton in a rundown semi-industrial area. I'd make this the last one I decided. There were few houses but we were just passing a couple of shops: a bookies, a launderette and an auto repair shop when Gary stopped outside a small boarded up commercial unit, which I could see from the signage, had once sold parts for swimming pools. There were hardly any cars about, so I pulled up outside a 24-hour newsagent opposite, made sure that my doors were locked and watched as Gary, veering away from what once had been the main entrance, cut across a cracked concrete skirting, and took a left around the back of the building.

Rather bored with the routine by now, I sat fiddling with the radio channels trying to find something to lift my mood, when I thought I heard a shout. I flicked off the radio, wound down the window a little, and listened intently. Shouts were coming from the direction of the abandoned unit and then two men, one of whom was Gary, appeared at the front of the building. I wound down the window some more.

"You're not taking any more money from us," yelled the other guy, a tall, lean white man with long dreadlocks tied back from his face in a red and white bandana.

Gary lowered his head, his stocky body tense and ready to spring. "I want my fucking money," he snarled.

Dreadlocks took a step towards him holding up both hands in a gesture of protestation. "You put the rent up two weeks ago. We can't afford any more."

Gary laughed; an ugly sound that seemed to come from the back of his throat. "Well you'll just have to get it then won't cha?" He stabbed a finger in the direction of the door. "You got a couple of girls in there ain't you? Get them busy and bring some dosh in."

"You bastard," shouted Dreadlocks and then lunged at him with a clumsy flailing blow.

Gary sidestepped the swing and then came in with a violent punch to the stomach. I could see the pain explode in Dreadlock's body as he doubled up and then fell to the ground.

As Gary kicked him in the head I could hear the other man croak in ragged breaths, "We just don't have it."

I was half out of the car when I became aware of voices behind me and turned to see that two Asian men had come out of the newsagents and were looking on dispassionately at the proceedings.

"Shouldn't we call the police or something?" I asked.

"No no," said the elder of the two men. "These things happen all the time. You go home now and forget all about it."

But I couldn't do that. I'd make the call. I was reaching for my bag when Gary, having apparently decided that he'd made his point, walked towards his motorbike. I heard him call back over his shoulder in that weirdly conversational tone I recognised. "I'll be back for it next week. Make sure I get it." Then he sped off down the street, the blast of his exhaust booming into the night.

This time I didn't follow him. I was out of the car and jogging across the street.

"Are you all right?" I called to Dreadlocks who had now got to his feet and was staring in the direction of the disappearing motorbike.

"What? Yeah... I'm OK..." He turned and focused on me. His accent was Irish and I placed him somewhere in his mid-thirties.

"But you're not," I said. "You're bleeding."

"It probably looks worse than it is." He wiped at the blood that was running down the left-hand side of his face.

"I doubt that," I replied. "You probably should get checked out by a doctor. I could drive you to hospital if you like?"

He had the hollow-cheeked face of someone who had been ill or who does drugs and his dreadlocked hair appeared very dark against the pallor of his skin. I stood awkwardly unsure of what to do when two figures appeared from behind the building. A girl with short blonde hair wearing a huge striped jumper that reached nearly down to her knees rushed to his side.

"Oh God you're hurt!" She pulled on his arm as the other, a much older woman in a long skirt with a thick coat buttoned up to her neck, looked warily about her.

"Are you sure he's gone Dan?" He nodded and she grunted. Then, catching sight of me, she asked sharply, "Who's she?"

I was just going to try and explain myself when Dan cut in with, "She's not with that bag of shite Gary if that's what you mean Maggie."

He grinned at me and although his teeth were heavily stained the smile was warm. "She just stopped to help me."

"You did?" asked the younger girl.

"Well come along in then all of you," ordered Maggie and to Dan. "I want to get a good look at you in the light."

I hesitated a minute and then followed them, stumbling through some brambles, the thorns pulling at my jeans, around to the rear of the unit. A door with peeling paintwork and a double-glazed panel was ajar and we went through it into a large, shabby dimly lit room where office desks had been pushed together to make one big makeshift table and upon which were piles of neatly folded clothing and an odd assortment of household items.

Along two of the walls, palettes, the kind that builders use for stacking bricks on, were laid out on the floor with sleeping bags and old blankets upon them.

"I'm gasping for a cup of tea Sheena." Dan looked at the girl in the striped jumper. "Make us one eh?"

Sheena picked up an old tin kettle from the table and put it on to one of those canister gas cylinders that people take on camping trips.

Dan explained, "We don't have electricity so we've got this heater and the lanterns run on batteries."

"But at least we have water," said Sheena to me. "My last place didn't and it was a nightmare."

"We've all been in worse," agreed Maggie. She crossed to a small metal sink and ran water into a plastic bowl. "Now let's get you cleaned up Dan."

He sat down on the edge of the table and indicated that I should take the only seat, one of those old office chairs with caster wheels and whose seat was ripped and shredded. I did so. As Maggie dabbed carefully at his face he said, "That was good of you to stop for me. There are not many that would. What's your name?"

"Clarry."

"Well good to meet you Clarry. And these ladies, as you will by now have gathered are the lovely Sheena…" He made a comic half bow to her as she poured hot water into four mugs and then added milk from a carton that was open on the table. Without electricity there wouldn't be a fridge I realised.

"And herself here," Dan gestured to Maggie, "Is our esteemed Lady Margaret The Venerable, Margaret The Wise."

"Your head has taken a hell of a knock if you think that," grumbled the older woman but I thought that her ministrations with the cloth seemed gentler.

We drank our tea and sat in silence for a while. They didn't appear to question my presence and seemed completely devoid of curiosity. Perhaps they were used to people just appearing without explanation?

"How long have you lived here?" I asked shifting in my chair so that the casters spun me several inches away from the table. Pedalling myself back I laughed, "I can see this could take some getting used to."

"It does," Dan said and then with an ironic curl to his lips added, "Ah but we live like kings. I've been here about three months now. When I first arrived there were two other lads but they've since moved on. And then Maggie came and then…" He turned to Sheena. "Is it nearly a month now since you came here darlin'?" He rested his elbows on the table and through the layers of old T-shirts he wore I could see the stark lines of his bones.

"We look out for each other," said Sheena tugging at the frayed sleeves of her sweater in an oddly defenceless gesture. And something about that reminded me of Melanie.

"Well let's hope we can stay together," muttered Maggie and then to Dan, "The bleeding's stopped but we could do with something to cover the wound. It's not deep but you need to keep it clean. Are you feeling dizzy or anything?"

In answer Dan tried but failed to stifle a cough. "I'll be alright." He turned to me. "You can see what a team we are? That fecker Gary won't break us up." He coughed again and then again and I could hear the rattle of it on his chest.

As he took a sip of tea I asked, "Who was that guy?"

"He's who we pay," said Maggie flatly.

"Rent?" I pressed.

"If that's what you want to call it." She looked down into her mug as if the answers to all life's questions might be there.

"How does it work then?" I pressed but she made no reply.

"It's just how it is." Sheena's tone was matter of fact. "It's always like this."

I shook my head in incomprehension and looked again to Maggie, but something in her shuttered expression prevented me from pushing the point.

"When's he coming back?" Sheena asked in a subdued voice.

Dan sighed, "He said next week."

"When next week?" Maggie asked.

"He didn't say. But let's not worry about it now."

And that effectively brought the conversation to a full stop. There was so much more I wanted to ask, but I just couldn't bring myself to. It seemed intrusive. Bullish.

They had so little – nothing really at all in the way of belongings. It struck me that might I, like much of society, be secretly afraid not just of poverty but of The Poor? And of what they could do if they ever grew tired of being the underdogs? The thought made me feel ashamed. It was time I left.

"I should get going," I said getting to my feet. "Thanks for the tea." Maggie twisting the coat button at her throat let her fingers halt for a moment and looked at me her gaze opaque. I met her eyes and then looked away.

"And I'm glad you're OK Dan," I said and meant it.

As he stood up I could see in spite of the lines of exhaustion on his face that he must have been really quite an attractive guy before illness or drugs and hard knocks had taken their toll. I wondered just what those knocks had been.

"I'll see you out then," he said and as he ushered me to the door said to the others, "Don't worry ladies I'll be back and then I'll bolt us all in safe for the night."

We walked in silence out into the street and Dan proffered his hand.

"Good to have met you Clarry. And you know where we are if you ever want a late night cup of tea."

I smiled and shook his hand. "I do. Good night and take care of you, Sheena, and Maggie."

He made another of his comic little bows as I took my leave.

That night as I fell asleep I could still hear the sound of his coughing.

CHAPTER FIFTEEN

I'd considered asking someone to come along with me to the party at The Vine. The idea of walking in there alone made me nervous, but if I asked Steph or any of my other friends to come with me, my chances of getting anything worth knowing out of Chris might be reduced. Going solo it would have to be.

It was after seven thirty when I left the house and this turned out to be a good thing as cutting it fine left me less time to be anxious. I pulled up around the corner from The Vine, entered the restaurant, and found myself in the middle of a real family affair. Greek people, Greek music, and Greek conversation, everyone laughing and gesticulating and generally having a great time.

Some of the restaurant tables had been pushed together in the centre of the room and covered with snowy white lace cloths. A feast, obviously prepared in the restaurant kitchen, had been arranged on an assortment of blue and white china. But in and amongst these festive platters were more homely dishes that I guessed had been brought by some of the guests: earthenware bowls heaped with olives, pimentos, and green beans flecked with herbs, a wicker trug piled with fresh fruit offerings; figs, berries, and droops of purple grapes that bloomed like the misted gems of a Bulgari necklace.

There were also half a dozen long-necked narrow bottles in straw baskets with handmade labels that contained a deep blackcurrant coloured wine, which I suspected would leave a livid purple stain on the lips of anyone brave enough to drink it.

I watched amused as a clutch of elderly ladies, upholstered in their traditional black, paid special attention to a platter of sticky honey pastries. Although I couldn't understand their language, from their avid and yet conspiratorial manner, I suspected them of an absorbing interest in their own and each other's ailments. As their liver-spotted hands brushed distractedly at the slivers of almonds and threads of marzipan that had spilt upon their corseted bosoms, I assumed they were comparing case notes on everything from bunions to sciatica. And these ladies could certainly eat. They managed simultaneously to graze, keep up a steady stream of conversation, and maintain a watchful eye on a band of rollicking old men decked out in their Sunday best that were grouped around a backgammon table.

There the low hum of masculine conversation was punctuated at intervals with encouraging exclamations as one of their number executed a bit of fancy dice work. Some of the men fidgeted unceasingly with the little loops of amber or coloured worry beads, but all their faces were animated. Somehow, they still, despite their advanced years, appeared to be full of life and vigour and I wondered if they were living proof of the well-publicised virtues of the Mediterranean diet, another reason to sample the delights of the buffet table.

Children darted to and fro getting under foot. With overexcited yelps they chased each other about the room, pinching food from plates, hiding under tables, and crawling around ankles. They were all splendidly dressed; little boys in frilly shirts and the girls in frothy bridesmaid-type frocks in pink and apricot. Occasionally, a young mother would softly call a restraining *Yani* or *Eleni* to calm their boisterous spirits and protect their clothes from being ripped or smeared with ice cream.

I was also interested to note that except for the children, there was a distinct segregation between the sexes. The younger women were seated comfortably together in a harmonious huddle, smiling and nodding and appearing, in spite of some very up-to-date outfits, somehow reminiscent of an earlier age. There was nothing unworldly about their husbands however. They loped about, dark eyed and watchful. They eyed me with obvious interest but kept their distance. Chris was nowhere to be seen. And I, who had absolutely no business being here at all, felt very much alone.

Soon I became conscious that it wasn't only some of the predatory husbands that were checking me out; I was now the subject of much interest to the whole room. This was not comfortable. I wandered over to the table and helped myself to an olive. Then I had another. Briefly I considered dipping into some taramasalata, but didn't want to be smiling through a mouthful of pink glob if Chris approached me unawares.

I was just thinking about leaving when there was a shuffling in my direction and I recognised the restaurant owner heading towards me with a glass of white wine in both hands.

"Good evening, you are very welcome here Miss?"

"Pennhaligan. Clarry Pennhaligan." At last, there was somebody to speak to.

He smiled and offered me the glass of wine, which I accepted gratefully.

"I am Thanos Tsoumanis," he said and held out his hand. I shook it and there was then an awkward pause.

"You were here earlier this week I believe," he said eventually. "As you see tonight we are celebrating. We Greeks do not observe our actual birthdays once we have grown out of childhood, rather we honour the Saint after whom we have been named. Each Saint has a name day and so there will be many who share festivities tonight."

I nodded politely and he continued with a hesitant smile as if fearful of losing my interest.

"It is a happy day for me. A man is always relieved to have reached the age of sixty. To have seen his sons and daughters settled and his grandchildren growing strong."

He turned slightly and indicated a beautiful dark-haired boy of about seven who was careering about the room issuing great cowboy whoops whilst cracking a pretend whip.

"It certainly seems a family occasion," I replied.

The clannish atmosphere was beginning to oppress me. Where the hell was Chris I thought? I determined to give him only another five minutes before making my get away. I flashed an appeasing smile at Thanos.

"I only hope that I'm not intruding?"

This time his smile seemed genuinely warm. "Not at

all, a stranger is always welcome. We have a superstition in Greece that a stranger could be a God in disguise and therefore we extend our hospitality to a guest."

I laughed appreciatively and made a mental note to tell Flan who would love that.

He explained, "You see we are a very close-knit community. Perhaps it is because we have left our native land that we cling so to our old traditions and to each other. It is very important to us to maintain our sense of being *Greek*," he emphasised the word with pride and then shook his head. "But it is more difficult for our young people, they become integrated."

"Isn't that a good thing?" I wanted to know.

"In one way yes, it is. To do well in this country, or indeed anywhere, it is necessary to adapt and be accepted, but…" here his voice dropped and for a moment he sounded much older than his sixty years, "It can also mean the loosening of our cultural ties and for old men like me that is sad."

A voice from behind us cut in, "But you are not old Thanos."

It was Chris. He had caught me unawares after all. His eyes scanned my face and then turning he made a sweeping gesture to include the whole room and slapped Thanos lightly on the back.

"For a man of sixty it is the time to enjoy the fruits of a life of labour and to appreciate all that he has achieved."

The older man laughed good-naturedly, nodded at me, and then left us. Chris and I looked at each other. "I'm glad you came," he said smiling into my eyes. Again, he was wearing a dark suit and I found that it was hard to imagine him in anything else. The formal cut became him and lent

124

him an air of authority. I liked the way that his hair showed just a few strands of grey on the sideburns and that his eyes were so dark they were almost black. His olive skin looked healthy and well cared for. He looked expensive, sure of himself. Dangerous, just as Flan had said. He reached for a glass of wine from a nearby table and clinked my glass with his own.

"What are we toasting?" I asked.

"Getting to know one another," he replied.

"Perhaps we should start then," I said. "You know my name is Clarry. I'm twenty-six and I'm in the restaurant business." I thought this sounded better than, 'I wait tables.' I went on, "I don't like carrots. I'd love to go to Egypt. I'm very kind to animals except daddy longlegs which I'm scared of. I've invented my own cocktail… which is really good by the way." I checked the list off my fingers. "And I sometimes wish I was slimmer but I know that I never shall be."

He laughed as I finished my recital. "So now it's my turn?"

I nodded. You bet it was.

"I am forty-four years old," he began. "I have various business interests mostly in property."

This much I knew.

"My family comes from Thessaloniki. I drive my car too fast. I like twelve-year-old malt whisky. I am impatient with fools but rarely lose my temper and… I enjoy beautiful things."

The way his eyes never left mine as he said this made his meaning clear.

Slick, I thought and a little too practised for my taste, but there was something about the way that he didn't fidget or look about the room that was oddly compelling.

"The food looks terrific," I said waving a hand towards a dish of shiny purple aubergines topped with cheese and at a platter of glistening stuffed tomatoes. "What's that?" I asked pointing to a huge earthenware casserole of something richly aromatic that pulsated with herbs.

"Ah, that's Kleftiko or Robbers lamb. You'll like it."

"Interesting name," I said.

"Bands of guerrillas hiding out in the mountains during the Second World War devised a method of cooking meat in a tightly closed oven, so they would not draw attention to their presence by smoke from their fires. This makes the meat tender and moist. Try it. It's perfumed with bay leaves." He picked up two plates and ladled out generous portions, then led the way to a table in the corner where we sat down.

The noise level in the room had upped a decibel. The backgammon boys were clicking their worry beads in earnest now and a couple of kids who had been surreptitiously sneaking down dregs of ouzo from abandoned glasses were being berated by their mother, a woman of about my age in a plain black dress. As she passed our table she gave me a swiftly appraising glance that had a hostile edge to it. Why? I wondered. And I couldn't help but notice that despite the relaxed party atmosphere, the guests appeared to be keeping their distance from Chris. Every now and again he would give a polite nod or word of greeting in Greek and although I didn't understand what was said, the body language was clear enough; in each case the response was formal and slightly wary. I noticed that it was the women in particular who seemed the most guarded, looking from him to me and then exchanging significant looks. He didn't introduce me at all.

As we ate I asked him about his native homeland and he seemed relaxed and content to tell me of its customs and its geography. Framed by high mountain ranges that included Mount Olympus home of the immortal gods, and bordered on its eastern side by the Aegean Sea, the place sounded beautiful and in many ways still unspoilt. I sat back with my wine as he talked of ancient Byzantine monasteries dotted amongst the mountains and of foothills studded with picturesque villages that had been rooted for generations amongst the olive groves. All very interesting but it was time to do what I'd come for and try and worm out a little information.

"Restaurant life is great fun but I'm not sure that I see myself doing it forever and I…"

"Which restaurant is it?" Chris interrupted me.

It was on the tip of my tongue to tell him Abbe's, but instead I said, "Oh, nowhere fancy. You wouldn't know it."

"I might?"

"Just a place in the village," I said, trying my best to sound vague. I then hurriedly asked, "What about you? Do you enjoy what you do?"

He relaxed back in his chair. "I suppose that I never stop to think about it, but yes I do."

"You said property, didn't you?" I asked playing with my fork. "What does that mean exactly?"

"I'm a developer. I buy properties cheap, do them up, and sell them on."

I forced myself to look impressed. "That sounds fascinating. I've seen programmes about it. Are you busy with any particular projects at the moment?"

"One or two." He smoothed a hand across his well-cut hair. Nikko's hadn't done a bad job. I wondered what on earth he'd think if he'd known that I'd been sitting outside the barbers on Tuesday secretly spying on him.

"I have a refurbishment project on in Clapham and there is a big house in Wimbledon that I should exchange on next week. So, there's enough to keep me busy."

That had to be Alwyn Road. And from his manner he seemed totally confident that the deal was in the bag. Don't count on it I thought. Teasing a strand of my hair around my ring finger, I smiled encouragingly and probed some more.

"How impressive. It sounds like you have your own empire. I should imagine that finding the properties in the first place can't be easy, however do you do it?"

As in my dealings with Simon, I wondered if I was laying it on too thick. This man was a whole different ballgame to Simon and it didn't do to underestimate him. But as before, I had misjudged the male capacity for a flagrant display of ego. Chris seemed to find nothing suspect in my breathy admiration. That he should be praised and flattered was something he appeared to take as his due.

"In this business, it's all about contacts."

"Really? I suppose you mean estate agents. But surely there are so many buyers looking for a good deal?"

"Estate agents are a particularly greedy breed but they serve their purpose." He took a sip of wine, his eyes grazing

128

my neckline and I sensed that he was just about to change the subject but I wasn't done yet.

"I seem to remember from those programmes that some developers can be pretty unscrupulous and do all kind of things to bring down the value of the properties they are interested in… things like… um… turning off the water mains… or getting in squatters… that kind of thing."

He smiled. "These programmes. Must they give away all our little secrets? So…" And this time he wouldn't be diverted. "Let's talk about something else. For example, do you like fish?"

And as I couldn't for the life of me see any way of continuing the topic, I decided to let things roll.

"Because there's a restaurant I know that I would like to take you to where the sea bass is excellent. And they serve a goat's cheese from Thessaloniki, "Graviera" that is sweet and fresh and like nothing you have ever tasted. One thing I believe," he said looking directly into my eyes, "is, that anticipation is everything. We Greeks have a saying *slowly slowly wins the day.*

And we have a saying in Wimbledon I thought; *brush up your pulling patter if you want to get laid.* I was conscious, however, of a feeling of relief. This man was undeniably attractive but he should never ever speak. Before I could make any kind of answer however, his mobile rang.

"I must take this. Wait for me please." And he got up and went out of the restaurant.

I exhaled. There really didn't seem much more to be gained from staying any longer. I'd make my goodbye to Chris and then I'd be off. Deciding that I needed the loo first,

I made my way to the back of the restaurant and pushing open the door walked slap bang into the woman in the black dress who had looked at me with such hostility earlier.

"Oh, I'm sorry," I said, making way for her.

She glanced at me as she was about to leave and then her expression sharpened as she recognised me. With remarkable speed she banged the door closed behind us with a decisive slam and placed her back against it thereby barring my exit. Then folding her arms in front of her she stood glaring at me. It was clear she was seriously pissed off. I kept my expression neutral.

"You *do* know that he has a wife?" she hissed, her accent thick and her voice reverberating with anger.

"I'm sorry?"

Her eyes flashed fiercely. With clear olive skin, thick black glossy hair pulled up and away from her face, and with a strong bone structure, she was very striking. "Don't pretend you don't know," she spat.

"I honestly haven't the faintest idea what you're talking about," I replied.

"Well you're screwing him, aren't you?"

Suddenly everything clicked into place – all those meaningful looks between the women. Of course, he was married. I should have guessed that. But, I told myself, I hadn't done anything wrong. It was Chris. Why hadn't he just asked me out rather than to this intimate party where people obviously knew his wife?

The woman continued in a tight angry voice. "I pity Maria for having a husband who parades his whore in public!"

130

Was that what he was doing, parading me in front of people? Why would he do that? But I'd have to think through this later because right now I had something to say. And no one likes being called a whore.

"I am not sleeping with Chris. And… I have absolutely no intention of doing so. Actually, I didn't even know he was married. I'm sorry if that's what you all think but it simply isn't true. Look, let's start again. I'm Clarry." I smiled and stuck out my hand and after a brief hesitation she took it.

"I'm Nuala."

"I take it you are a friend of Chris's wife?"

"Maria doesn't deserve to be married to a man like that. The Zakiats are an important family."

Zakiat. My brain did a quick backflip. That was the name of the other director of Cornett Developments which had bought the house in South Park Road that Simon had previously sold.

"So, if you are not with him in that way then why are you here?"

I considered lying, considered claiming that we had some kind of business dealings together, but this woman wasn't stupid and besides there was something about the way that she had championed her friend Maria that I liked. "I'll tell you the truth," I said. Well at least part of it I thought. "I was in for a meal earlier this week with a friend and Chris got talking to us and he invited me here today. That's it."

Her gaze was steady and unblinking. "Why did you come?"

I held up my hands. "Well I didn't know he was married or I wouldn't have. A good-looking man put a move on me and I responded."

Her face had darkened and I asked quietly. "You really dislike him, don't you?"

"I despise him," she shot back. "He's a hypocrite. He demands respect from our community yet he pursues only his own interests."

"And those interests are?"

"Money. I don't know exactly what his business dealings are and I don't want to know. But that club he is involved with…" she broke off shaking her head.

"Club?" I pressed. This was interesting.

"It's only what I have heard. It's not a place I would ever go to. *Knights* it's called – somewhere around Waterloo."

"But why is Chris respected if he is such a shit?" I asked curiously.

"Because of his family," she answered flatly. "The Lianthos are one of the old families, as are Maria's family. Stavros Zakiat, Maria's father, is so generous with his time and with his money. Even though he lives here, he still organises aid for all those poor refugees that wash up on our shores. He comes from Samos where many thousands have come to escape their country. But Chris is a very different man. I heard that Stavros was so happy when his daughter married into the Lianthos family, but now who knows? Chris is powerful. No one wishes to speak against him and yet so many have been humiliated by him." The bitterness in her tone was unmistakable. "I've said too much I must go."

She had. And whilst I didn't doubt that she believed what she had told me, it seemed clear that her information was limited. Was she aware for example that Maria's father was working with Chris on his property scams? I was guessing not.

"And his wife?" I couldn't resist asking. "She knows all this?"

Nuala's shrug was eloquent. "I don't know for sure but I suspect she does."

"Have you seen Chris with women before?" I asked.

She nodded.

"And you've told Maria that? Told her directly I mean?"

"No."

"Why not?"

She looked away and then said, "I am not a close friend of hers even though we see each other most days. She has her hairdressers and my husband and I have our delicatessen next door but we are not close. She is a proud woman and would not want to know that other people knew of or discussed her affairs, so, no I have not…"

I nodded and then asked, "Where is your delicatessen?"

"Just around the corner on the Green," she said hesitating. "I have to go now. You will not tell Chris what I said?"

I shook my head. "No, absolutely not. I will go back and talk to him a while longer as if nothing has happened and then I'm off."

"And will you see him again?"

I raised my eyebrow. "What do *you* think?"

I sat back at the table and moments later Chris returned.

"I am sorry for keeping you waiting."

"That's fine," I said. "I have just been soaking up this warm family atmosphere."

From then on I kept the conversation light but I sensed that he discerned a change in my demeanour and I was relieved when I spotted Nuala, her two children, and a man that I presumed to be her husband making signs of preparation to leave. For form's sake, I gave it another ten minutes and then with an air of a woman who was packed and ready to depart, I glanced at my watch. "It's late. I must be going."

"Must you?"

I got up and held out my hand to him. "I'm afraid so. Please say goodbye to Thanos for me and goodbye, it's been fun."

He kept hold of my hand. "Let me take you home."

"No don't worry, I've got my car."

"I will walk you to it."

There was no way I could graciously refuse this offer and so without a word to Thanos or any of the other guests, he took my arm and together we made our way out of the restaurant. Once in the street he dropped my arm and silence descended upon us. At last we reached my car and I turned to him.

"This is me. Thanks again."

He didn't speak and for a moment I felt a shiver of apprehension. I didn't know this man and yet here I was alone in the dark with him. Instinctively I took a step back, the handle of the driver's door pressing into the small of my back.

"Well," I said brightly. "So I'll say goodnight then and…"

Still he didn't speak but as he looked at me I could see that an assessment was being made and that he'd come to a decision. What that decision might be I could only guess. I waited. After a beat, he turned and with slow deliberation walked back along the street in the direction of the restaurant. It was only when he had rounded the corner and was lost from sight that I let myself into the car.

CHAPTER SIXTEEN

Sometime during the night, I had been dimly aware of the sound of rain drumming against the windowpane, and when I awoke just after eight, it was still beating a steady tattoo on the casement. I drew back the curtains to gaze out on to a glowering grey sky where sulky little rags of cloud did their best to block out the light from a watery sun.

Whilst I was in the shower I missed a call from Laura.

"Hey babes." She sounded happy and excited. "Sooooo much to tell you."

I winced. So she'd slept with him. Well of course she had.

"I wondered if you're about today for a coffee. I don't have to work because of the Norwich trip. How about I come around to yours at about noon? Right, if I don't hear from you then I'll assume that's OK. See you later."

Ordinarily I would have loved the idea of a lazy Monday morning gossiping on the sofa with my best friend but not this time.

I needed milk and so walked into the village. Although rain still fell in steely rods from a gunmetal sky, I felt the fresh air was doing me good. I'd shoved my newly washed hair up into a beanie to keep the dreaded frizz at bay. Little did I know that before this day was out, hat-hair would be the least of my worries?

I opened the door to Laura who was standing on the mat under a dripping umbrella and proffering a packet of chocolate digestives.

Taking in my appearance with a swift glance, she asked, "What's with the hair? New look?"

She strode into the hall, laughing and pulling off her wet jacket. Her long brown hair, I noted, fell about her face in damp strands, without even the slightest suggestion of frizz.

"Hi. Come on in." Luckily she didn't seem to notice the stiffness in my voice and I made a concerted effort to pull it together. There's no point in carrying on like Lady Macbeth and wringing my hands, I told myself. Laura would be OK. I would just give her the facts, she'd get upset, we'd talk it through, she'd start to feel better, and then that would be that.

"You look well," I offered putting the kettle on.

"Oh I am love, I am. It's true what they say about sex being good for the skin? See." She pulled her hair back from her face. "Apparently, all the blood rushes to the surface which then…"

She was animated and just a bit hyper and as she described the boost that exercise gives to the epidermis, my thoughts instinctively turned to Karen and her skincare advice. Perhaps they had more in common than just Simon after all?

Coffee made, we went into the sitting room and sat down together on the sofa. I took a deep breath as Laura kicked her shoes off and curled her feet up under her, balancing the plate of biscuits on her thighs.

"Laura, I need to…" I began, but she cut across me.

"Right, I'll start at the beginning, shall I? Or at least from when I last spoke to you. When *was* that… oh yeah, the day after we'd gone to the Lighthouse, before I had to go to Norwich?" She took a sip of her coffee "OK. So he called me every day when I was away. Every day, now you have to admit that's a good sign?"

"It is," I reluctantly agreed.

"And, you'll be really proud of me, I didn't call him, not even once – just like it says in 'The Rules.'"

In spite of myself I couldn't help but laugh. She and I had had many a heated discussion over glasses of wine about this bible of Dating Rules. We'd always had mixed feelings on the *treat them mean to keep them keen* approach.

"Good on you," I said.

She nibbled at a biscuit. "Don't let me have more than two. There's nothing like having your clothes slowly peeled off item by item to make chocolate public enemy number one." She stretched across and put the plate down on top of the old pine trunk I use as a coffee table. "So… I get back from Norwich…"

"On Saturday night," I encouraged. "And?"

"We arranged to meet at San Lorenzo."

This is a classy Italian restaurant in the town that has been there for years and is popular with the more affluent of the locals. During the Wimbledon Fortnight, it's impossible to get a table unless you are in the company of one of the players or have slept with an umpire (I know this for a fact as my friend Althea did actually do this and not only got to sit at a secluded corner table in the conservatory with full view of any incoming celebrities, but also added some new and highly imaginative skills involving two balls and a whistle to her already considerable sexual repertoire).

Laura continued, "Lovely food and you know how nice the place is and then…"

I interrupted her suddenly curious about something. "It's an expensive restaurant and so I hope he paid?" I softened the question with a playful shrug.

"No, we went Dutch."

"And when you went to the Lighthouse?"

This time she must have registered the slight edge to my voice as she looked up in surprise. "What? No we split the bill then as well."

No surprises there then. I'd already known he was a tightwad. Laura looked at me, but then her face lightened. "Oh right," she laughed sounding relieved. "You're back to 'The Rules' aren't you? But seriously Clarry." A slight frown appeared. "I don't want you thinking the worst of him for that."

I winced, wishing, for her sake, that meanness was the only character flaw I knew about.

She continued earnestly, "Why should a guy nowadays be expected to pay for dinner? We're both working. It's only right that I pay my share."

"OK OK." I lifted a hand in surrender. "So maybe I'm old fashioned and just appreciate a man playing the gentleman from time to time."

She shot me a look. "How many gentlemen have you been out with recently?"

She might have a point there. I moved swiftly on. "So nice place, good food and then?"

"And then," she replied. "We had a fucking great shag."

We both laughed and for a moment I forgot all about the news I was yet to deliver.

"He's got a grrrrreat body." She gave a contented sigh and nestled back more comfortably into the sofa. "Really fit and he's got one of those nice straight penises that hang properly and don't kink off at some weird angle."

"Always my favourite," I nodded sagely.

"And not a bad size either."

"Even better."

"I think it's time I was in a relationship again. I feel ready for it. I've done casual."

"And some," I remarked dryly.

"And you haven't?"

I let that one go right past me, because it was her we had to focus upon. She was falling for Simon and I knew the drill because we'd been down this road before. In her mind, she had already picked out a dress and reserved the caterers.

"I can't think why I was so mistrustful of him to begin with," she said. "What the hell was I worrying about? Just because a guy takes a genuine interest in my work, I have to go and get all paranoid."

And here something in my face must have betrayed my feelings as her eyes suddenly clouded with uncertainty. She made a stab at pretending to ignore what she thought she'd seen and continued blithely. "Because obviously you couldn't have found anything bad out, could you? Clarry did you?" she swallowed hard. "Find out anything that is?"

I cleared my throat. "Well actually I did."

Instantly she bridled and was on the defensive. "Well I don't suppose for a minute that it was anything important but you may as well tell me." There was an edge to her voice and she'd gone very still.

I felt a moment of misgiving as something about *don't shoot the messenger* flashed across my mind. "Well," I said again. "The thing is…"

But just at that moment the landline rang. "Don't worry I'll let the machine pick up," I said and then heard Flan's disembodied voice.

"Darling. I've been worrying about Laura. Have you told her yet? That poor girl really needs to know… "

That was as far as she got. With a swift glance at Laura's stricken face, I leapt to my feet and ended the call.

CHAPTER SEVENTEEN

I sat back down upon the couch and turned to Laura. She'd gone very pale. It was as if all the vitality and joy had been drained out of her and what was left was a limp rag doll sitting back against my cushions.

As I looked at her she made an effort to collect herself and with studied carefulness put down her half-eaten biscuit on the table before asking, "What does the *poor girl* need to know?"

"Laura!" I made to move towards her but she stopped me with a bat of the hand.

"Just tell me Clarry. Tell me whatever it is because it's obvious that… in fact now I come to think about it you've been acting a bit weird ever since I got here but I was just so caught up with telling you that I…" She broke off and then added in a low voice, "So, it isn't me he's really interested in after all?"

"He's not what you think love. He's not a good guy."

"He's been using me?"

I nodded. "I think so yes."

She immediately straightened and her eyes flashed with a flicker of hope.

"You think? You mean you're not sure?"

This was worse than I'd thought. "I am sure. Look wait while I tell you."

And so I did. Incoherently at first and in no particular order but with growing assurance, I laid out what facts I'd discovered and what interpretation of them I'd made. Two things I left out though. The break-in to Simon's house and the night he'd spent with Karen. The first I had resolved never to impart and the second I was holding in reserve in case the evidence I presented of his crimes weren't enough to convince her.

As she grasped the extent and ramifications of Simon's actions she grew angry. "The fucking bastard." She was on her feet now and pacing moodily about the room. "I knew that the prices he got for the houses were low but I thought that it was just the state of the market. I should have checked, done some proper research but it never crossed my mind that he'd been making money out of them on the side."

She stomped over to the window and stared out at the rain that still fell in unrelenting silver arrows against the streaming glass. Turning back to me she said, "This means that he... no wait a minute... my firm... has cheated the beneficiaries of those wills out of money..." She'd come to an abrupt halt in front of me. "And I'm responsible. I'll have to tell the senior partner."

She covered her face with her hands and then blurted out through her fingers. "I'll never get promoted now. In fact I'll be lucky not to get fired and that'll be the end of my career. Oh my God I'm about to lose my job. How could I have been so stupid? What a fucking mess."

She crumpled back down on the sofa besides me. I put my arms around her and hugged her close for a moment and then pulling myself away said, "You are not stupid and it is not your fault. Come on. Look, if we can stop what's happening with Alwyn Road…"

Something in my tone must have got through to her as she straightened and offered in a thoughtful voice, "Which actually we can stop…"

"Which we definitely can and will," I agreed.

I then went on to fill her in on my encounter with Gary and his rental arrangements.

"But you don't think that Simon knew anything about it?" she asked.

"No, I'm certain he didn't. You should have seen his face. I'd swear his surprise was real but equally I feel sure that it has to be connected to this guy Chris."

I told her of my discussions with Chris at The Vine.

"In the meantime, the way Simon and I left it on Friday was that I'd get back to him to confirm the offer and organise his little down payment. And also, to give the OK that my phoney consortium would get rid of Gary and crew."

"And, he's bound to be on tenterhooks. He can only be offering the house to you rather than to Chris because he's expecting to get a higher backhander from your side," said Laura.

"Exactly. What other reason can there be?"

"Well," cried Laura "What are you waiting for?"

I hesitated. I'd thought that my dealings with Simon were over. I didn't want to have to talk to the creep ever again.

"All you've got to do is stall him. Play for time until I've talked to Mr. Garstein, the senior partner and then it will be out of my hands, and yours. If Simon doesn't hear from you then he might agree a deal with the Greek and that just makes matters more complicated."

I dialled Simon's number. "Hi it's Gemma."

Laura grinned at this.

"I haven't a lot of time and so I'll make this quick. We're on. Yes, we've got ourselves a deal. We get the house and you get your fee, £25,000 upfront, and £25,000 on completion."

My eyes met Laura's. She wasn't smiling now.

"Good so we're agreed. I'll phone you again in the next couple of days and we'll do the handover. What? Ah yes the little question of our friend the Skinhead. Now don't you worry about him… that will all be dealt with."

We moved into the kitchen and I made more coffee.

"I haven't thanked you yet I know," said Laura.

"You don't have to."

"I do but I think I'm still trying to get my head around it. He seemed so plausible. You are quite certain, aren't you?"

I stared at her. "You've just heard my conversation with him."

She dropped her gaze.

"Oh, come on." I felt a mounting impatience "He's committing fraud and he may very well have got you fired, what more do you need to convince you? A handwritten confession signed in his blood? Any minute now you'll start making excuses for him."

"I'm not trying to defend him. It's just that despite it all and no matter what his motives may have been at the beginning, I can't help wondering if he really does like me. For myself I mean. Nothing to do with the houses and the money."

I hesitated. This was of course the question I had asked myself in the early stages of my investigations. I had worried at it and discussed it with Flan but that was before I knew about Karen.

"Couldn't he have grown to have feelings for me?" she whispered.

No he couldn't I thought. I kept my tone light. "Well sure he could Laura but what difference does it make? You can't possibly forget and forgive the other stuff."

"But perhaps he could change?" she said. "I'm wondering now if we should perhaps give him a chance to explain. Talk to him, find out his side of the story."

I suppose I should have been prepared for it, but that she could let her feelings of disappointment and betrayal so affect her judgement gave me a real jolt. And I felt cross with her. Who hasn't tasted the sourness of disenchantment and felt the sting of rejection? She was too old to be reacting like this.

"That's the last thing we should do." I knew I sounded sharp but I couldn't help myself. "He could turn nasty for all we know."

"Of course, he won't! He might be a crook but he's not violent."

Standing with my back against the fridge and gazing at my best friend's truculent expression I felt the first stirrings of misgiving. I knew that expression of old and it had never boded any good.

"You don't know that Laura. You don't know *what* he's really like. That's just the point." Her expression darkened as I continued, "What matters now is that he is stopped."

"I know that. Of course, I do," she retorted. "But I'm just wondering if it wouldn't be better to tackle him about it ourselves."

"It won't do any good!" I shouted, finally at the end of my store of rapidly dwindling patience. "He's a liar in more ways than one Laura. In more ways than I've told you."

It was out now. Too late to take it back. I stood there looking at her and the oppressive silence between us remained unbroken for several minutes.

"What do you mean? What aren't you telling me?"

It didn't take long. As briefly and with as little emotion as I could, I described exactly what I'd seen outside Simon's house yesterday morning and recorded faithfully the conversation that Karen and I'd had. I explained that whilst she hadn't actually mentioned any names, I believed that Simon was the casual fuck buddy she'd referred to.

Laura listened intently and at no point did she interrupt me. With her eyes levelled over my head and fixed on the old painted dresser that displayed some of the most decorative of Grandma P.'s vintage crockery, she heard me through to the end. The question she then asked was a predictable one. "What's she like?"

"Ordinary."

"Clarry tell me exactly what she looks like."

"OK. She's pretty but a bit… well cheap looking."

"More…"

"All right, all right," I gave in reluctantly "She's not particularly tall; slim, big boobs. They looked fake to me. Blonde, green eyes, heavy on the spray tan…"

"Enough. I think I got it." She nodded and I winced at the expression of defeat on her face as she said miserably, "Totally different from me then."

"Yeah totally different in that you're a brunette," I protested. "And your boobs are real."

"But that's what men like isn't it? The obvious. A woman who looks like a blow-up doll. And why is that? I'll tell you why," she said flatly. "It's because that's what men really are into, it's what they want. Even when they say they don't; even if they're happy in their relationships and love their wives. It's what they all secretly respond to."

I shrugged. "Look this is a whole other conversation for a whole other time. Forget about Karen. She doesn't matter. You do. And what we need to do now is put our heads together and work out how you're going to break the news to the senior partner. What did you say his name was?"

"Mr. Garstein."

"Right. Mr. Garstein. So, how do you think you should…"

Tears were forming in Laura's eyes and immediately I changed tact. "I'm sorry love. I'm sorry that I had to tell you about Karen."

She sniffed hard and wiped a hand across her eyes and then, without missing a beat, lobbed what would turn out to be an unexploded bomb straight at me. "What I don't understand is why didn't you tell me about this straightaway?" The note of challenge in her voice was undisguised. "Why were you keeping it from me?"

I blinked in surprise. "I wasn't *keeping* it from you. I didn't want to upset you."

"Well I'm certainly upset now, aren't I?"

"Yes, but that's not my fault. I was just trying to protect you."

"I'm not *saying* it's your fault but…"

This was getting us nowhere. "Now come on. You know what I meant. Let's just try and…"

But she wasn't finished. "And I suppose Flan knows all about it and that was what she meant in her message. So you've both been feeling sorry for me?"

"No. Of course not. You are getting this way out of proportion."

"Oh, so now I'm overreacting, am I?" Her tone was blistering. "And the thing is Clarry, I'm just wondering if you're not getting a bit of a kick out of this. I think maybe you've enjoyed all the prying and spying and snooping. It could be the start of a whole new career for you."

Suddenly I was furious. "Why the hell can't you have the guts to admit that you misjudged the situation with Simon?" I was shouting now. She was the one who had asked me to investigate and now I was being punished. I'd been right about the messenger. I glared at her. "Stop blaming me for your own mistakes. You *asked* me to find out about him Laura. Remember? Or has that conveniently slipped your mind? Well I did exactly that. I found out what his real motives were and OK so you don't like what

I've had to tell you but that is no reason to take it out on me."

Tears were streaming down Laura's face now and I felt my own eyes filling up.

"What's going on? Why are you being like this?" I asked more gently. "He's not worth getting so upset about and certainly not worth us falling out over. There's always another man out there. You know that. That's what we've always said isn't it?"

"Ah! But will you approve of him if I do meet one?"

"What?" I jerked my head back in surprise "What do you mean?"

The look she gave me was cold. "No matter who I meet they're never good enough are they?"

"What?"

"I think it's because you're jealous. You're on your own and you're jealous that I had a chance to be happy with a guy. You're jealous that I'd found someone."

"No!" It came out in an angry squeak. "Of course I'm not. That's insane. How could you possibly think that?" I looked down at my hands resting on the table. They were shaking. The bomb had exploded and I didn't know how we would get back from here. "That's a fucking awful thing to say."

"Well that's that, isn't it?" she said. "I'm obviously a *fucking awful* person. I'm useless with men and now I've screwed up my career. Great, Just great."

And before I could say another word she walked out of the room, crossed the hall and slammed the front door behind her.

CHAPTER EIGHTEEN

Mechanically I washed the coffee mugs and put the biscuits in a tin. Then I straightened the sofa cushions and gathered up some old newspapers and magazines, but all the time my conversation with Laura kept running through my head in a continuous loop. How could Laura have said those things? We'd known each other for most of our lives and she thought me capable of the meanest kind of jealousy? Then I remembered that I hadn't phoned Flan back. She would want to hear about what had happened last night at The Vine and I needed to offload about Laura.

The minute I heard her voice I felt instantly better. She does that. There's something in her manner of giving you her full concentration, combined with the admirable restraint she displays in not butting in and telling you where you went wrong, that makes her the perfect sounding board. I poured out the whole story and she listened sympathetically making the occasional tutting noise as I filled her in on what Nuala had told me about Chris and then moved on to the episode with Laura.

"Oh dear, she really is confused isn't she? Poor girl. She's hurt and her feelings are in turmoil. No wonder she snapped."

"But what about me?" I protested. "What about my feelings?"

"They may be a bit bruised but I think you'll live."

That's the thing I always forget about when talking to Flan. Whilst it's true that she always cheers me up, she doesn't automatically take my side.

"And what about what she said at the end?" I exclaimed. "The bit about me being jealous. Do you think she meant it?"

"Do *you*?"

"Well she said it and I suppose she must. But no… honestly I can't really believe that she did."

"Exactly. You can't and that probably means that she didn't. It's most likely that it just leaked out as part of the great gush of emotion she was feeling during the heat of the moment. You two are so close Clarry. Don't let it get in the way."

I thought about it for a moment. "But this has to have affected our friendship. In fact I think it may well have ended it."

"Is that what you want?" asked Flan gently.

"No! Of course it isn't, but it's not just about me. I mean if she's been thinking all those awful things."

"*One* awful thing," put in Flan.

"Well OK," I acknowledged. "Just one, but that one was pretty loaded wasn't it? And you know something? I've been going over it and over it in my mind and she's wrong about it. Dead wrong."

"Well you need to tell her so."

"Oh no. It's up to her to make the first move."

"Well darling. If that's the way you feel," said Flan dubiously. "But I wouldn't wait too long to make up if I were you or Laura may have lost her job, her romantic illusions, and her best friend all on the same day. Now that's a lot of heartache."

I looked at my watch. Nearly three o'clock. I chewed my lip. I needed something other than my row with Laura to think about and an idea that had been gradually taking shape somewhere in the back of my brain had skittered its way to the forefront. And for it to have any chance of success I'd need some help. Looking up *Knights* I found that it was on Bayliss Road and that it was listed as a bar/club. It didn't appear to have a website. Then I picked up the phone, dialled the restaurant, and spoke to Ian who listened and said he'd call me back. Half an hour later he did so.

"Right, we'll be with you at eight. A bit early I know but Steph has an audition tomorrow morning and so can't have too late a night."

For several hours, I tried to distract myself from thoughts of the evening ahead but couldn't seem to settle to anything. So, I did a few chores, put out the rubbish bin, and threw away the dead forget-me-nots from the old blue vase. I nipped out into the garden, where the rain was still falling with dreary persistence and picked some more. Looking down at my muddy footprints on the kitchen floor reminded me that I'd been meaning to clean it for over a week now and this seemed as good a time as any and besides it would keep me occupied.

I keep my Hoover, broom, and cleaning odds and ends in a walk-in cupboard by the back door. It would originally have been used as a larder and there were still the slatted shelves for the storing of pots of home-made chutneys and preserves. As I'm not known for my pickling and bottling, the only provisions in this cupboard today were of the alcoholic kind. I got out the mop and bucket and created a nice soapy lather and made a start. I was only half way through when glancing at my watch I realised that it was after seven and Ian and Stephanie would be here in less than an hour. Propping the mop up behind the larder's open door and abandoning the kitchen floor, I pelted upstairs to get changed.

Ian scrutinised my black halter-neck dress and then nodded approvingly. "That'll work." He rummaged in the carrier bag he was holding and with a flourish produced a tangled assortment of wigs. "You said brunette or black? Well there's *Jessie J*, *Katie Perry* in her early years or my personal favourite *Kim Kardashian*."

"Let me try the *Jessie J*."

Steph looking sensational in a short red dress, high at the neck and plunging to a deep V at the back, laughed as I began cramming my hair into a jet-black, mid length bob. "Can't I have one as well?"

"It's not you that mustn't be recognised," Ian, admonished.

"Some of my best performances have been as a blonde," mused Steph. "I was Rapunzel in Panto at Brighton two years ago. I had these lovely long plaits for the prince to climb up and in the Madonna tribute band I had this one wig for Like A Virgin and..."

"Oh, go on then if you want to," interrupted Ian. "I've got a *Dolly*, a *Brittany,* and a *Christina* in the car." Then turning back to me he said, "You want to scrape every bit of your own hair up first. I've got some clips... Ah *no.*" His gaze was critical as we both studied my reflection "Not your look love. A little too Vicar of Dibley. All you need is a dog collar and a crucifix."

"Right," I said. "Pass me the *Kim Kardashian.*"

I opted for the independence of my own car and stop-started through the evening traffic around the backstreets of Waterloo, in the wake of Ian's MINI Coupe. It had started to rain again as I pulled up behind him in front of a launderette on Bayliss Road and it occurred to me that another advantage of this whole wig thing is that synthetic hair doesn't frizz. No worries about hat-hair now. As we picked our way down the street, Steph who had insisted on the *Brittney* agreed with me.

"Some actors when they are getting into character start with a mannerism or a habit of speech, but I always think accessories are much more fun." Tugging on her wig she asked Ian (who under the name *Fancy Nancy* performed a drag act at a Burlesque club called Jezebels a couple of nights a week), "Why do you need so many?"

"It's all about variety now love. It's what the punters want," he said gloomily. "And the competition's fierce. I have to hold my own against a new boy *Lady Frou-Frou* who works with a live snake." He brooded for a moment. "And that tired old has-been *Maid of the Mist* is still twirling his tassels."

My eyes met Stephanie's – *Fancy Nancy* and *Maid of the Mist* were not friends.

"Right just run this by me again Clarry because I'm not used to working without a script. Our cover story, if we need one, is that you and I are here possibly looking for a job and you can't use your own name in case this Chris guy recognises you." She broke off thoughtfully. "Is Mallory the best you could come up with?" and then to Ian, "What's your role again?"

"Manager or agent. Whichever..."

"More like pimp in that outfit," she shot back.

Ian looked down at his skinny leather jeans, silver lurex tuxedo jacket, and white low-necked T-shirt. "Too much?" he asked innocently.

I snorted. "When is silver lurex ever too much?"

We almost walked straight past the club, as there wasn't a sign above the door.

"Is this it do you think?" I asked.

Sandwiched between a betting shop and a Korean food store, its windows were obscured glass and reinforced with security grills.

"Doesn't look much," said Steph. "But come on let's ring the bell."

She pushed at the buzzer and we waited looking at each other expectantly.

As the door slowly opened Ian started singing, "*I'm coming out, and so you'd better get this party started.*"

"Oh, you're definitely out alright," said Steph and then joined in, "*Let's get this party staaaaarted!*"

"Will you shut up," I hissed warningly. "Remember. The most important thing is not to draw attention to ourselves."

156

"That's not always easy for me darling," drawled Ian. "Being so good-looking can be really rather a curse."

"I know exactly what you mean," agreed Steph patting her *Britney*.

I don't know what I had expected, but the Gate Keeper should have provided a clue. He was a tall heavily built man somewhere in his late twenties, dressed in a pair of jeans that were seriously in need of a wash and a tan leather blazer that looked like something a 1970's cop would have worn in an American TV show. He had slicked back dark hair and a pale unsmiling fleshy face that was pitted with acne scars. The smell of his aftershave was astringent as he ushered us into the confined space of a narrow lobby.

"That will be £20 for you," he said to Ian in an Eastern European accent. "The girls go in for free."

"Couldn't you consider me an honorary girl?" Ian appealed smiling broadly up at him and showing a lot of white teeth. "I take just as long as them to get ready for an evening out and besides I…"

"£20!" the man repeated in a monotone.

I nudged him, "So much for the lurex."

"Never mind," he said fishing out his wallet. "The night is still young."

And it was. Nine o'clock on a Monday evening is never going to be a club's busiest time, but this place was dead. We had entered a large room where a bar dominated most of one wall. Tables set with chairs of twos and fours took up most of the floor space and built-in banquettes edged the remainder of the walls. In the far corner there was a tiny raised stage with a solitary pole upon it, where, ignored by the half dozen or so customers sitting talking, smoking or playing cards, a stringy girl wearing nothing but a thong, disconsolately grinded her pelvis to the slow ponderous beat of canned music. She was the only other woman in the room.

"Uh oh," said Steph taking a step back.

Everyone had looked up at our arrival.

"Very low rent," said Ian in a voice that carried. "Not what I'm used to at all. I think drinks are what we need don't you?"

I scanned the room. Chris was not here. I breathed a little easier and followed Ian and Steph to the bar.

"Situations like this demand cocktails I always think," said Ian and turning to the barman raised an eyebrow, "Oh 'Ello. There are two of them."

The man perfunctorily swiping a cloth over the counter was the mirror image of the Gate Keeper. Same build. Same slicked back hair. Same pale watchful face and unsmiling expression, but this version, was minus the acne scars.

"The Brothers Grim," Steph muttered. "Blimey this place is a bit rough. I needn't have worn my Pulling Dress. Not that that was…" She broke off on catching my expression and then in an effort to distract me, pointed disapprovingly at a dirty plastic ashtray. "Smoking in bars isn't allowed anymore. And look everyone's puffing away."

Ian appeared to be having trouble placing our orders. "Two cosmopolitans and a mojito," he enunciated loudly as Brother Bar Keeper looked blank. "You must know how to make them? It's simple. Three sprigs of mint, some lime juice…" he broke off impatiently. "Never mind, I'll come around and show you."

"Looks like Ian's the one who's job touting now," laughed Steph, but stopped as the barman held up a restraining hand.

"Not come behind the bar." His accent was even thicker than his brother's.

"I'm just going to get you started," persisted Ian bustling his way behind the counter. "Now I take it you have cranberry juice for the cosmopolitans? It's one measure of vodka to two of…" He began hunting through a selection of beer mugs and wine tumblers. "Where are the martini glasses? They're just not the same in an ordinary…"

"No," said Brother Bar Keeper laying a thick hand on Ian's arm. "Not come." And forcibly pushing him back out to the customer side said flatly, "No cocktails."

"You are strong," said Ian. "Usually I go for a 'Roughty Toughty'… but, I don't think we're bonding."

"They do a pole dancing class at my gym," remarked Steph some five minutes later when we were propping up the bar and sipping at glasses of acidic white wine. "It's good for flexibility."

The three of us studied the girl on the stage.

"She's certainly that," said Ian and then turned away with a grimace. "Oh, must she bend over like that?"

"I think that's rather the point," I said.

Steph grinned. "There are always ads in The Stage for exotic dancers. In fact there are more of those than for regular gigs."

"Ever thought of giving it a try?" Ian asked with a smirk. "Not that I'm any judge but you seem to have the right equipment. And especially now you're a blonde."

Steph made a face and yanked on her wig. "Actually I love this look. I could really get into it. Like get into character. In fact I'm asking myself what Brittney would do in this situation for example. Right now?"

"Burst into a song and dance routine most likely," I said and then as I saw her strike a pose put in hurriedly, "but don't."

"If she's as white-trash as they say she is," pondered Ian, "then I think she'd order some fried chicken."

My mouth watered. And I realised that I hadn't eaten anything since this morning.

"Not here," said Steph wrinkling up her nose. "She'd catch something. I mean look around you."

Ian observed our fellow customers. "Yes they certainly drained the swamp for this crowd."

I had to agree with him. At a nearby table three middle-aged men in crumpled office garb with their ties askew and their suit jackets flung over the back of their chairs, were drinking beer from a pitcher and scrutinising Steph and I like we were their next meal. Conducting a furtive conversation in a language I didn't recognise, their eyes skittered over my bust and Steph's legs as they dragged on their cigarettes. Oh for heaven's sake I thought in irritation, why do you have to *mentally undress us*? There's a naked woman at the other end of the room slithering up and down a pole. Isn't that enough tits and ass for you?

At another table a man in his sixties with a flushed face and a comb-over, gave great jarring grunts as he yelled, "Raise" and slammed down his card deck.

160

His companion, an older black man, with a huge stomach and frizzy grey hair muttered, "Fold!" with obvious bad grace.

Because of Chris's involvement with the club I had assumed that most of the clientele would be Greek, but there were only a couple of guys talking intensely to each other on one of the banquettes who looked even vaguely Mediterranean. The average age range was probably fifty and in their various groups I received an overall impression that these men were not what would be considered successful, by anyone's standards.

"So?" asked Steph breaking my reverie. "What's the plan?"

I must have hesitated a moment too long because it was Ian who answered for me. "Looks like she doesn't have one, do you?"

"Well… not exactly no."

They looked at one another.

"But that's fine," I protested. "That's just how these things go. One has to work off the cuff."

"One does? Does one?" smiled Steph. "Off you go then… do your stuff."

She had a point. It was time to get serious. I had spotted a door in the far corner by the stage that I hoped might lead to the back rooms or offices and that seemed a good a place as any to give my ill-thought-out plan a try.

Hey *Mallory…*" called Steph in an undertone as I started away from the bar. I looked back at her.

"I hope you know what you're doing?"

I squared my shoulders. So the bloody hell did I.

As I neared the stage, the girl in the thong now grimly welded on to the pole with only her thighs, met my gaze. I smiled trying to fight down my sense of distaste. Sure I knew places like this could only ever, under the sequins and cheap costumes, be seedy, but there was something so curiously sexless in the girl's mechanical gyrations that the effect was utterly dehumanising. Perhaps that ultimately is the attraction for men? The girl didn't smile back.

I half expected someone to stop me as I turned the handle of the door. One of the Brothers Grim perhaps – coming after me with a guttural "Not Go."

But I passed through into a dank corridor unmolested. Although the building was two storeys, I had no idea if the club occupied the upper level as well as the ground floor. I made my way past stacks of spare chairs, crates of beer, and an old slot machine and came to a staircase where I hovered doubtfully for a moment. Nobody was about. All was quiet but for the dim thudding of music from the other side of the wall. I felt hot suddenly. Sweat was breaking out along my hairline under the heavy tresses of the wig.

What if Chris was up there... or indeed what if anyone was up there? And someone was bound to be. What could I say? That I thought the loos were up here? That I was looking for a job and wanted to speak to the manager? I swallowed and then started slowly up the frayed carpet of the stairs. As I neared the top I could hear a faint muttering sound coming from a half-open door on the left of a gloomy passageway. I stopped and listened intently. A sound of heavy breathing and then a woman's voice drawn out in muffled exasperation, "Come on!"

Oh God I begged, my thoughts turning instantly to the idea of a private lap dance with extras, please don't let it be someone having sex. I waited. Nothing. The top stair creaked as it took my weight and I inched my way towards the door. More murmuring and then a thump as if someone had fallen over something followed by a cry of "Fuck!"

I was outside the room now and as stealthily as I could, I edged my head around the door and peered in. Mercifully there was only one person in there. A woman wearing thigh-high black boots was bent over with her back to me and struggling to get out of a tight pink latex dress. I coughed politely to announce my presence and then asked, "Would you like a hand?"

She shot around. "Who the fuck are you?" There was a trace of the Midlands in her accent. Her body still askew and her face partly concealed by the dress, she looked me up and down but didn't give me a chance to reply. "Well now you're here. Don't just stand there. Pull."

I approached her warily. The room was narrow in dimension, brightly lit, and very untidy. Clothes on plastic hangers were draped across the window. They dangled from hooks upon the wall and fanned out over the back of two of the chairs from the bar. More spilled out from a zip-up sports bag on the floor. A table where a red suspender belt drooped over the corner of a super-sized plastic mirror, doubled as a make-up station and a food counter. Bottles of foundation, lipsticks with their lids off, and mascara wands were scattered amongst empty coke cans, crumpled fast-food wrappers, and cigarette packets. Discarded shoes littered the floor. Huge white platforms, six-inch strappy black sandals, and a pair of gold lace up boots that I thought looked interesting. In the corner, a bin overflowed with wadded up tissues and beside it was a half-full bottle of vodka.

The girl raised a pair of skinny arms and bent her head as I took a tentative hold of the dress's pink striped collar and then yanked hard. With a squelching noise the rubber made one last show of resistance and then came slithering off with a snap. Once freed from its constraints it was obvious that not only the girl's improbable breasts but the small hard protruding swell of her stomach were the cause of the obstruction. She reached for a grubby white towelling bathrobe which she wrapped around herself and glared at me.

"You're two days early," she said sullenly and picking up a cigarette packet from amongst the debris on the table, pulled out a fag, drew it to her mouth unlit, and took a long deep pretend drag. She was in her early twenties and small framed. Her long dark hair which had magenta streaks at the front was sticking up in a frizz from the static of the latex. Under thick pancake make-up her skin looked spotty around the mouth and under the nose.

"I'm giving up," she explained returning the cigarette to the pack. "It helps." And then shoving a pile of clothes onto the floor, she sat down, crossed her legs, and examined me. "That real?" she asked.

For a moment, I didn't know what she meant. I'd forgotten all about The *Kim Kardashian.* "Doesn't it look it?"

"No. But I'll say this for you. You're not the usual type. Posh accent. And you're too big."

I couldn't resist a glance at her stomach.

"Sod you!" she snarled and rose in one angry movement from her chair to the collection of outfits hanging from the wall. I could see that her hand was trembling as she raked through the clothes, selecting and then rejecting first a black lace corset with a frilly apron and then a sheer bodysuit in dayglo yellow. I didn't know what to say and had just decided to retreat when she spun back to face me.

"They're my shifts until Sunday. That bastard said I could finish the week and I need the money. After that it's all yours." She lifted her hand in an ironic gesture that took in the whole of the shabby meagre room. Daylight dawned. For some reason this girl seemed to think that I was going to be replacing her in the club, on the stage, on the pole! I held up a placating hand.

"I'm not here to take your job. Honestly I simply couldn't do what you do."

Her look was serious and assessing. "No. I don't think you could. You'd never get up the pole."

That wasn't what I'd meant at all. And although it wasn't exactly flattering, I laughed. Suddenly the girl turned very pale and sat back down heavily on the chair. Dipping her head between her knees she gasped, her breath coming in short pants. I crouched besides her and pushed some of the magenta strands of hair back from her face.

"Can I get you some water?"

She nodded and pointed in the direction of the table where I found a plastic litre bottle. I held it to her lips and she took a few small sips.

"Shall I open a window?" I asked.

The air was stale and tainted with a greasy whiff from the empty takeout bags. I scooped them up from the table and

165

jammed them into the wastepaper basket. The girl hadn't answered and was still concentrating on her breathing and so I lifted down hangers bearing a nurse's outfit, something floaty in a leopard-skin print, and a collection of nylon teddies from the top of the window frame, and looked vainly for somewhere else to put them.

"Not much room in here is there?" I remarked as finally I laid them on top of the sports bag.

The window casement was old with flaking paint and rotting timbers. I don't think it could have been opened for a very long time, because it took a certain amount of shoving before I managed to get the bottom sash to open a few inches. I stood inhaling a moment. Even the polluted air of central London was sweeter than the stale odour of that room.

"Better?" I asked taking the bottle from her.

"Yeah. Thanks for that." Her breathing was more even now and the colour was coming back into her face.

"How far along are you?" I asked gently.

"Three months, and been throwing up for most of it," she said and the Midlands twang was more pronounced now.

"Is that why you're leaving? Because you're feeling so sick?"

"Na. I could dance for another few months yet, with the right outfit obviously. But that fucker Chris wouldn't have it. He came in here last night and caught me just about to barf. Put two and two together and told me that tomorrow would be my last night. As he said who wants to pay to see a pregnant pole dancer?"

"I'm not sure that's legal," I said. "Employers aren't allowed to just terminate a…"

166

The girl gave a hollow laugh. "What? You think we're given a fucking contract? You're pretty green, aren't you? It's cash. All cash."

"I see. No tax, no records of employment I suppose?"

"No records of any kind," she said. "Just like all these places."

"Have you worked in many?" I asked.

"Enough."

"So Chris owns the club?" I asked. "Is he here now?"

"No he's not here and yes he does, him and another much older man that I've only ever seen a couple of times."

She must have seen my look of relief and instantly she was suspicious of me again. "Know him do you?"

"I've met him," I offered cautiously, and then said in a rush, "And like you I think he's a complete fucker. Look... I'm..." I was just about to say Clarry but recovered myself.

"I'm Mallory. Who are you?"

She took her time before answering as if giving her name committed her to something that could come back to bite her. "It's Paula. So if you're not a dancer what are you doing here then?"

This girl could help me I thought but I wasn't going to explain myself. I ignored her question and shot out one of my own. "Does he have an office here?"

She nodded. "Down the hall. Why?"

I improvised. "He's hurt a friend of mine and I wanted to leave him something that will let him know that I know... that *she* knows... that..."

I trailed off deliberately keeping it vague, but it must have stirred something as Paula smiled for the first time.

"Like a personal Fuck-You message?"

I laughed, "Just like that!"

"Whatever it is you're up to I hope it really screws him over."

I shrugged and was this time at least able to give her an honest response. "Probably be no more than a mild irritation but it makes me feel better… and my friend… of course," I corrected myself.

She looked at me. She knew perfectly well there was no friend.

"What will you do when you leave?" I asked after a moment.

"Go back to Dudley." She took a glance in the mirror. "Once she knows about the baby my mum will have me back."

"And the baby's father?"

"He wanted me to get rid of it. And I nearly did. I thought that that was what I wanted. I didn't want to be saddled with a baby but now… I dunno… I figured it would be good to have something of my own, to look after. To love."

I thought back to the two young mums I'd seen with their babies at the swimming pool and asked, "And to love you back?"

She ignored that and looked at her watch. "I'm on in five minutes and so if you want to get into the office you'll have to be quick."

Going to the door and taking a hasty look along the passage she whispered to me, "He keeps it locked but I know where the key is. Sometimes, the Karmanskies – that's the twins – go in there to make private calls. The key is behind a loose bit of wood. Come on."

And with that she whisked out of the room moving pretty fast despite her thigh-high boots. I followed at a sprint and watched as she crouched down, wriggled free a section of skirting board, and retrieved a key. She handed it to me and pointed to a door at the far end of the hallway. "That one. Put the key back when you're done. And you better hurry. One of the twins could come up at any time. I've got to get dressed."

I took it and watched as she disappeared back into her room and shut the door. Forcing myself to stay calm, I ran swiftly down the hall to Chris's office and put the key in the lock. It turned easily. I was in. Not daring to turn on a light my eyes took a moment to adjust to the darkness. I couldn't make out much but that didn't matter. I wasn't here for a look around. I pulled off my shoulder bag and removed a folded-up piece of paper upon which I had typed in bold capitals: *If you think you'll be getting the Alwyn Road House... think again. Ask Simon.*

Even if Chris hadn't already paid Simon upfront to secure the property, then I didn't think he would take Simon's reneging on the arrangement at all well. It was a small and ultimately impotent gesture, but at least it was payback of a sort. Payback for his arrogance and his complacency; payback for the trouble he had, indirectly, got Laura into and payback for the pain that he caused his wife. Also, it was a way of punishing Simon. And that felt really good.

I crossed to a desk. There was a pile of Greek newspapers and a stack of files. It was frustrating that I would not have the opportunity to search through the folders. Perhaps there would be something here that connected Chris to Gary? Or to other estate agents and maybe even to solicitors? There could be all kinds of deals detailed here, criminal or otherwise. For a moment I toyed with selecting some at random and shoving them in my bag, but rejected the idea. I would do what I came here to do. It was enough. I placed the paper in the centre of the desk where anyone sitting down would be sure to see it and within seconds I was locking the door behind me.

A minute later, having returned the key to its hiding place, I was making my way back along the landing to Paula's room when from behind a closed door I heard a muffled sob. I stopped and listened. There it was again, but louder this time. Quite distinctly now, I could hear the sound of a woman crying. Now there are many different reasons for tears. Not all of them profound or even intensely felt but this... this was something different. In these tears, there was loss and there was hopelessness and almost like a tangible presence, I could feel it. Behind the door, a woman was weeping in despair.

"Hello," I said quietly.

The crying abruptly stopped.

"Hello," I said again. "Are you OK in there?"

No answer.

I glanced up and down the hallway. No one was about. I hesitated and then knocked lightly on the closed door. No response. Oh well I thought, it's none of my business but, there'd been something so utterly bleak in her cries that I couldn't just walk on by.

"Are you alright?" I said again more urgently this time.

I was just putting my ear to the door when Paula, poking her head out from her room, called, "All done?" She had changed in to a short denim blue dress that had chevron cuffs and a silver badge on the breast pocket and was something of a cross between a Meter Maid and a Prison Guard.

I nodded. "Yes. Thank you so much. Um Paula… I…" I looked again at the door. "I heard someone crying in there. A woman."

Paula disappeared back into the room and I followed her.

"Who is she?" I asked as she peered into the grubby mirror and picked up a lipstick.

"No one."

"It definitely sounded like someone to me."

She turned and looked at me then. "What you don't know can't hurt you. That's what my mum always said and it was one of the few things that she ever got right so I remember it. I don't know anything about that girl or any of the others and I sure as hell don't want to know."

"Others? What others?" I said. "What do you mean?"

A look I couldn't decipher flickered across her face.

"Something weird is going on here isn't it?" I pressed. "Just tell me if whoever it is in there is all right. That she's not in any… oh I don't know what I mean really… that she is not hurt… or in any danger I suppose?"

This time I could read her expression. It was one of mistrust mixed with uneasiness and, I thought fear. "Paula. You know something don't you?"

She didn't reply but carefully placed an American style police cap on her head and then walked out of the room.

It was when we were nearly halfway down the stairs that she caught the heel of her boot in some strands of the frayed carpet. She lurched forward losing her footing and would have fallen if I hadn't shot out an arm to save her.

"Fuck!" she exclaimed as she steadied herself against the banisters and I could see shock in her face as her hand went instinctively to her stomach. "I'd have gone then if you hadn't caught me." She looked up at me still clutching hold of her arm. "Mallory's not your real name is it?"

I shook my head feeling a little shamefaced and pulled my hand away.

"It doesn't suit you and neither does the wig by the way. Blonde are you?"

I nodded again.

"I thought so." She turned and picked her way carefully down the remaining steps. "Like my mum said it's probably best if I don't know your real name anyway. Once they've found out that someone's been in the office they'll be asking questions."

We were in the passageway now and sidestepping around the slot machine. I hesitated and then blurted out, "Who's in that room Paula? What's going on?"

"I told you," she said. "Not my business."

I stared at her "Why do you do this awful job Paula? Don't you hate it?"

Her eyes were quite expressionless as she regarded me steadily. "For a posh bird you're fucking thick aren't you?" She made to open the door to the club but I put a hand on her arm.

"Wait. Take my number." I fumbled in my bag, snagged a pen and a scrap of paper, and scribbled it down. I held it out to her.

"Why would I want that?"

"I don't know really," I said and I really didn't. It just felt the right thing to do. "But, I think you do know more than you're saying about the woman in the room. And I think perhaps you're frightened? Look, if you ever want to talk to someone or you need help…" I shrugged.

"You need to watch out for yourself never mind about anyone else," she said, but she took the paper, folded it, and stuck it down her cleavage. "And I'm nearly out of here, just one more night."

"So, this is practically your last dance?" I smiled at her. "You should be wearing a corsage."

She looked blank. "You what?"

"Nothing. Oh and good luck with the baby," I called as she turned to leave, but she didn't look back just opened the door and went out into the music and the cigarette smoke.

The place had filled up a little since I'd been gone. At first I couldn't see Ian and Steph and then I spotted them, still standing at the bar, but now encircled by the three men that had been staring at us. They were evidently making themselves very much at home. Steph with her arms extended in front of her and with a mildly beseeching look upon her face was delivering a speech.

"You once said that you liked me… Just as I am."

Ian clapped. "Go on love it's marvellous." He turned to me. "This is the bit where Bridget lets Mark Darcy know she's mad about him. You know… from Bridget Jones's diary. It's her audition piece for tomorrow."

"Steph," I said. "Come on now. We really had better be going."

But there was no stopping her. *"And I feel the same. Even if you do wear jumpers that your mum's made for you and…"*

To approving whistles from the three men who I don't think fully understood what she was saying, but were just smoking and enjoying the show, she continued addressing an imaginary Colin Firth. *"I mean that tie's a classic… and I seriously believe you should reconsider the length of your sideburns but…"*

Ian whispered, "She's going to walk it!"

"Ian honey," I said. "Which bit of… Don't Draw Attention to Yourselves, didn't you understand?"

Unfortunately for me at that moment there was a break between songs, so my voice came out loud and distinct. People were turning around and staring. But at least Steph had stopped declaiming which was something. I took hold of her arm. "We're out of here. Let's go."

But the movement had taken her by surprise, knocking her against Ian who in turn cannoned into one of the three guys who dropped his cigarette. He wasn't happy. Even in a foreign language one always knows when one is being sworn at. But I was too het up now to care and began frogmarching Steph towards the door. After a couple of steps I became aware of a commotion behind us. I turned and looked. The men were talking in highly excited voices and pointing at Ian who was hopping up and down on the spot frenziedly flapping his hands at a glowing circle the size of a penny upon the lapel of his jacket. Within a second it had spread. The lurex glimmering gold where it should have been silver. Ian was on fire.

I dashed towards him shouting, "For Christ sake Ian, just take it off."

"It's designer!" he yelled frantically. "Ted Baker."

But Steph beat me to it. Making a lunge at the bar, she yelled, "I know exactly what Britney would do in this situation." And grabbing at a soda siphon from the counter she aimed at Ian's chest and pressed down hard upon the nozzle. She missed. The spray hit me full in the face. "Ah!" she said with an apologetic giggle and then recovering, started to sing *"Hit me baby one more time!"*

She aimed again and this time she was on the money. The sparks that were just flickering into flame were thoroughly doused. The fire was out. All that remained was the acrid metallic odour of burnt lurex.

A desultory round of applause broke out from the customers that were close enough to have seen what was going on, but they soon settled back to watching Paula on the stage simultaneously unzipping her dress and twirling her cap.

"Now you have to admit," said Steph. "That was classic Britney."

Ian and I standing dripping side by side made no comment.

Steph regarded me evenly. "Clarry forget The *Kim Kardashian*. Now with those waves you're more Russell Brand."

Ian was busy examining the scorched remains of his jacket. "You owe me for the lurex," he muttered darkly.

I did, but this was not the time or place to discuss it for out of the corner of my eye I could see Brother Bar Keeper bearing down on us and if he was unsmiling before, now he was positively glowering. In silent accord we headed swiftly for the door.

CHAPTER NINETEEN

B ack in the car I was surprised to find that it was only ten thirty. I felt bedraggled. The top of my dress was damp and heavy tendrils of The *Kim Kardashian* were dripping down my neck. I pulled it off and ran my fingers through my hair. I was hungry, I was drained but I was feeling pretty pleased with myself. After the morning I'd had with Laura I would never have thought that the day could have ended on a high. Laura. The memory of Flan's words slipped uninvited into my mind and took up a holding position… "*She may have lost her job, her romantic illusions, and her best friend all on the same day. Now that's a lot of heartache.*"

Switching on the engine I came to a decision. There was well over an hour until midnight so there was still time. One thing Laura definitely wouldn't be losing today was her best friend.

Last year on the back of a generous salary, Laura had wisely invested in a lovely Victorian conversion flat in a side street off Battersea's Northcote Road, which is an area that is always buzzing. It may have been late on a Monday evening and the start of the working week, but it seemed to me as

I backed the car into a parking space that all the bars and restaurants in the street, and there are dozens of them, were still doing a roaring trade.

Although the rain had stopped the sky still looked threatening, but there were plenty of determined drinkers and diners occupying outside tables. Their hum of conversation and good-natured laughter competed with a medley of musical styles belting out from the various restaurants: Italian opera issuing from the pizzeria, the irresistible beat of a Latin American rumba from the Argentinean and the plaintive strains of Edith Piaf from a bistro whose white tablecloths gleamed with candles and silverware. It was like stepping into an irrepressibly lively continental street party and never wanting to leave. I could fully understand why Laura loved living here.

Laura's flat occupied the whole of the first floor of a dignified stucco house set on three levels. As I opened the gate, I noted that there were signs of someone having been busy recently giving the communal front garden a seasonal facelift. Two polystyrene trays of scarlet geraniums sat ready to be planted alongside four empty terracotta pots, a bag of compost, and a trowel. I knew that the green-fingered enthusiast couldn't possibly be Laura. She doesn't do gardening.

As I trotted up a short flight of stone steps, I knew that I should have phoned in advance but I hadn't wanted to give her the opportunity of putting me off. I buzzed on the intercom. No response. Maybe she was out or had gone to bed. I buzzed again and this time her voice crackled through to me.

"Simon it's no good… just go home."

Simon? I blinked in surprise. I yelled into the speaker, "Laura it's *me*… Clarry."

"Clarry?" Even through the static I could hear the catch in her voice. "Oh thank God… Come up."

The door latch clicked and I charged through the lobby and sprang up the stairs. I'd just made it to the top as Laura opened the door.

"You thought it was *Simon*?" I demanded going straight to the point.

She glanced nervously around as if expecting to see him lurking in the stairwell. "He just left. Am I glad to see you."

We glanced at one another for an instant as if each were measuring the degree of the other's absolution, then Laura grinned shamefacedly. "All right?" she whispered.

"All right," I nodded and we immediately closed in for a hug.

After a moment she released me and I could hear in her laughter a mixture of contrition, relief, and emotional exhaustion. She led me into the sitting room. This was an airy, high-ceilinged room with its original picture rail still intact and with three casement windows that looked out upon the busy street below. The entire flat had been painted white when the developers had converted it and Laura hadn't seen any reason to change that. What saved the room from being characterless was a trail of the flotsam and jetsam of Laura's life. Her briefcase spewed its contents out on to the floor; a teetering pile of paperbacks were stacked against one wall and a pair of shoes which judging by their position, the left one tucked behind the sofa and the right one lying discarded under the window, suggested that they might have been kicked off in rather a hurry.

She yanked me down on to the sofa where I looked meaningfully down at two half-empty mugs sitting on the glass-topped coffee table.

"So, what happened? What was he doing here?"

She shrugged apologetically. "He just turned up. I spoke to him earlier and…"

"What?" I interrupted. "You called him?"

"No," she was firm. "*He* phoned me at about six and asked me out for tomorrow night and so I…"

For an awful moment, I thought she was going to tell me that she was going to carry on seeing him but I needn't have worried.

"I said that I didn't want to see him anymore."

I realised then that we should have guessed he might well get in touch before she'd spoken to her senior partner. We should have come up with a stalling tactic.

"I started off by saying that I was really busy this week but I suppose he must have guessed something was off by my voice. He asked me if there was anything wrong."

I looked keenly at her.

"That threw me a bit," she admitted. "But I just said no. He said I sounded weird and asked what was going on. Well what could I say? I tried but I couldn't think of anything there and then and so stupidly I just said that I'd heard something about him that had worried me and that I thought it would be a good idea if we didn't see one another for a while. And he was really pissed off Clarry. You should have heard him."

"I'm very glad I didn't," I said heavily. "I've seen him in a flap before. He's not at his best under pressure."

"He was obviously really annoyed even though he was trying hard to suppress it. His voice was icy and he asked what the hell I was talking about. When I tried to brush it off he said that if it concerned him then he had a right to know. Which I suppose in a way he did."

"So what did you say?"

"Well he kept pushing and pushing and I tried my hardest to stonewall him but he wouldn't let up, kept demanding that I tell him what I'd heard. I wished then that I'd never said anything at all and had just made a date with him. I could have cancelled it." She shook her head. "And so in the end I just put the phone down. I didn't know what else to do."

I'd have probably done exactly the same I thought and told her so. "I think you handled it pretty well," I reassured her.

"But then about half an hour later the buzzer went and it was him. Well you can imagine how I felt."

I could. I'm sure I would have just pretended not to be home. "But why did you let him in?" I wanted to know.

She brooded on that a bit. "I know I shouldn't have but it just seemed so mean to leave him standing on the doorstep. After all we had spent a night together and now he was being dumped without an explanation. I would hate that if it was the other way around."

I was forced to acknowledge the justice of this. "And? What happened when he came up?"

"Well it was fucking awkward."

"I bet it was."

"When I opened the door he tried to kiss me but I pulled away and he looked all hurt and sulky."

Now that I could quite picture. He'd be the very image of the spoilt little boy who couldn't get his own way.

"I offered him a coffee."

I looked at her in surprise "Why not lay out the welcome mat and give him a blow job whilst you were at it?"

"It was more because I didn't know what to say, so I needed something to do. Anyway, he followed me into the kitchen. By the way do *you* want a coffee? Or a drink?"

"In a minute," I said. "Finish telling me what happened first. Oh and I'm starving. Got anything to eat?"

She flashed an apologetic grin. "Not a bloody thing." But, on seeing my disappointed expression got swiftly to her feet and disappeared into the kitchen. When she returned a few minutes later she was carrying a bottle of white wine, two glasses, and a large packet of crisps, this last she threw into my lap. I snatched them up gratefully and noisily chomped down on a great handful as she went on with her story.

"I made our coffee and we came in and sat down, but all the time I was thinking about how much I didn't want him here… in the flat. And so I started babbling on about work to cover up the silence because he didn't say a word at first but just kept giving me these meaningful looks. Eventually when I'd run out of breath, he started on me. He absolutely insisted that I told him what I'd heard. *I demand to know* he kept saying. I felt I had to tell him something just to get rid of him. What other choice did I have?"

"Why didn't you simply tell him to leave?" I asked reaching for my wine glass. "You didn't have to explain yourself, you could have just told him to sod off."

"But that's just it," she said. "Somehow I found that I couldn't. It was as if… and this is going to sound pathetic… as if it would be impolite. I mean we had slept together."

Good manners shouldn't have to come with such a price I thought. "Well so what did you tell him?"

"I said that a rumour had reached me that he was selling off properties cheap to a developer. And as a result I felt no longer comfortable dealing with him professionally or seeing him socially."

I took another swig of my wine. "That sounds really controlled."

"I wasn't feeling in control I can tell you!" she shot back. "He got really shirty on hearing that and started blustering on about defamation of character and libel laws and…"

"To a solicitor?" I gave her a wide-eyed look and was rewarded with a genuine laugh.

"I know! Anyway then he really started to press me for details."

"What did you say?"

There was a pause and she shifted uncomfortably against the sofa. "Probably a little more than I should have I'm afraid." She wouldn't quite meet my eye and I suddenly didn't like the way this was going.

"What exactly did you say Laura?"

"Well I'd had no intention of getting into the details but I had to say something."

I put down my glass. "Please don't tell me that you mentioned my investigations?"

She cut in hastily, "No. Your name never got mentioned!"

"I should hope not!"

"Of course, I didn't say that I'd asked my best friend to spy on him… that's if we are still best friends?"

I nodded impatiently. "Of course we are. Don't be so bloody silly. It would take more than one little…" That was as far as I got.

"I'm so sorry Clarry. I don't know why I reacted that way. I just felt such a fool and I took the whole thing out on you."

"Do you really believe that I'm jealous of you or of any relationships you might make?"

She flushed and blurted out, "I don't know what made me say it. It was crazy. I was crazy!"

I wasn't going to argue with that.

"I'm grateful to you Clarry. Honestly I am. I mean without you I would have got myself in deeper and deeper with Simon."

"Right OK then." I was brisk. Real friends aren't that easy to find and shouldn't be discarded lightly. I was ready to move on. "Back to Simon."

"Well he kept on trying to get me to tell him who had said what. But I refused to give him any names and would only say that I'd had it on good authority from someone I know and trust. And that I suspected him of acting fraudulently and against all the codes of… blah blah blah. And ethics, blah blah blah. Which he denied flatly."

"But of course," I remarked dryly.

"He was seriously pissed off. He said that whatever I'd heard was a complete fabrication, that it was ridiculous and that whoever it was that had said it was a liar and out to make trouble for him, and finally that I must be stupid to pay attention to any of it," she said, pursing her lips.

"Nice. But you seem to have taken it in your stride," I remarked. "I mean I know it has upset you but you seem OK."

She shrugged. "I guess it's because now there's no doubt in my mind about him."

"That's not what you said earlier this morning," I reminded her.

"I know I know. But when he was in front of me and was working so desperately to convince me, it was like he protested too much. And as a matter of fact he's a pretty lousy liar. It was obvious he wasn't telling the truth."

"How so?"

"He kept fidgeting with his car key, taking it in and out of his pocket and twisting it around and around his finger. I just knew somehow. And then I told him that I would be withdrawing the Alwyn Road house and that I'd already told my senior partner all about it and that he would be contacting Dunstan Stead."

"No!" I gasped. "What did he say?"

"God it was awful. His face went white and he looked furious."

"I bet he was. Think of the money he'll be losing."

She gave a bitter laugh. "Good. Well then I told him that he'd have to go and that's when it all got a bit out of hand." She took a sip of wine before continuing. "He started shouting and saying that I was being totally unreasonable and why wouldn't I believe him and what proof did I have and oh I don't know. I couldn't really take it in. I just wanted him out of the flat. He started pleading with me not to take it any further. He was practically crying, Clarry, saying that he'd lose his job and that his whole career would be over."

"Precisely what your own worries have been. I hope you didn't start feeling sorry for him?"

"Not for a second. His self-pity was… well not just sickening but embarrassing."

I could well imagine. "And so how did you get rid of him?"

She was proud of herself now. "I went to the front door, opened it, and said that I'd had quite enough and insisted that he leave. And after a few moments when it was obvious that I meant what I said, he did. And that's why when the buzzer went literally five minutes later I thought he'd come back for another round. And tomorrow morning I've got to tell Mr. Garstein all about it."

I nodded. "The senior partner? And you told Simon that you'd already done that. Clever."

She stretched and yawned. "Yeah I thought that would be wiser. God I feel knackered. All this drama really is exhausting. But tell me what's been going on. Why are you dressed up? Where have you been?"

I kept it short and to the point. I too was feeling drained.

As I got up to leave I asked the one question that still puzzled me. "What I don't get Laura is what you ever saw in him."

"It's weird but I don't really know. I think I just wanted him to be the right guy because this felt for me to be the right time."

"And now?"

"Oh no," Laura called as she waved me goodbye. "I'm well and truly off men for the time being."

CHAPTER TWENTY

As I let myself into the car an insistent and fretful wind tugged at my hair. There was about to be another downpour. I drove with care, conscious of the two glasses of wine I'd had on an empty stomach. As I passed along Parkside I could see how the wind had whipped itself up into a fit of temper and was lashing out at the chestnut trees that lined the common on its eastern side. And even with the car windows tightly shut I could hear great rolls of thunder in the distance, growling a deep percussive bass as the rain came down in torrents. There wasn't a parking space immediately outside the house and so by the time I'd legged the fifty metres or so from the car, I was wet through. I could see from afar a first rapier gleam of lightning flicker into quivering life and illuminating the inky blackness of a starless sky.

As I fumbled for my keys I felt glad to be safely home and out of the rapidly gathering storm. Peeling off my sodden jacket and draping it over the stair banister I headed for the kitchen. The mop and bucket were still where I'd left them propped up against the open door of the walk-in larder, but that I decided could certainly wait until the morning.

What I needed now was food. I reached for cheese and

tomatoes out of the fridge, switched on the grill which is old and part of the ancient oven that takes ages to heat up, and took a pitta bread out of the freezer. Rubbing at my wet hair with a tea towel, I sniffed at a bottle of Merlot that had been open for a couple of days and poured myself a glass.

I was just taking my first sip when there was a knock at the front door. I put down the glass in surprise and looked at my watch. It was after midnight. Who could be calling so late? Perhaps it was Flan making her way back along the Ridgeway from one of the local History Society's Dos that she attends at the Wimbledon Museum? Maybe she'd seen my light on and thought she'd take shelter from the storm. Well I was always glad to see her. I'd order her a taxi and whilst she waited we could have a drink and I would fill her in on the day's events. I went out into the hall and opened the door.

"It's a ghastly night to be…" The words died on my lips. Not Flan but Simon Napier. A rain sodden Simon Napier. There he stood, all six foot of him, solid and immense on my doorstep and scowling at me with a look of intense malevolence. I gulped. "What are you doing here?"

"I just thought that we could have a little chat." His tone was light, even social, but the way his steely grey eyes bored into mine was chilling.

My mind somersaulted through the possibilities of how on earth he could have found out where I lived. "Um," I stuttered. "Now is not a good time."

He laughed derisively and took a heavy step across the threshold pushing me back into the house with his body.

"Now Gemma that's not very nice, is it? Not very friendly, and after all, we've got so much to talk about."

My initial reaction of shock turned swiftly to one of anger. Who the fuck did he think he was forcing his way into my home? "Look I've just told you Simon…" I began.

"You and I are going to have a talk whether you like it or not."

We *were*? I didn't think so. I made a move to usher him out, but he suddenly thrust past me and kicked the door behind us with a slam.

"No! My boyfriend is here and he won't…"

Simon tut-tutted at the transparency of the lie. "Now now Gemma! There weren't any lights on when you came in. We both know that there's no one here. And there's no need to look so worried. As I said I just want to talk to you."

Why when I first opened the door and saw it was him hadn't I just slammed it in his face? I didn't want him in my house, especially at this time of the night but something in me had baulked at making a scene. I now understood exactly what Laura had meant about an innate sense of social convention having crippled her ability to follow through on her instinct. Well I wasn't Laura. I could live with a breach of good manners. I hadn't invited him in and he wasn't a guest. I wanted him the fuck out of my house.

"Simon," I concentrated on keeping my voice level. "It's late. I'm quite happy to talk about anything you want, but not here and not now."

I might as well have saved my breath. He took a purposeful stride and went on into the kitchen. I followed him uncertainly and watched as he look a long look around.

189

"Very nice. Quaint these old cottages. Located in the heart of Wimbledon Village and offering spacious accommodation with all the charm of a bygone era." His voice had taken on a sneering parody of Estate Agency Speak. "Equidistant from the station and…" He looked at the bottle of Merlot on the table. "Aren't you even going to offer me a drink?"

"No, I'm not."

"Well I'll just have to help myself, then won't I?" Reaching for the bottle, he lifted it to his lips and drank down greedily. He stood in front of the dresser and I took a position opposite him with my back to the fridge. We looked at one another across the width of the old pine table. He was wearing one of his pin-stripe suits, a white shirt with the top two buttons undone, and a pale-yellow silk tie at half-mast. His wet hair was plastered to his dripping face.

"I expect you're wondering why I'm here Gemma? That's if Gemma *is* your real name." His tone was bitter, "Which I very much doubt."

I didn't answer. I was trying to steady my breathing and think my way out of the situation. It's important to keep calm I told myself. Don't let him see that you're rattled. There's no threat here, nothing to be afraid of because he says he just wants to talk to me. But how had he found me? It had to be that Laura, when they'd had their confrontation, had given away more of the truth than she'd thought. Or more than she'd told me. I batted away the treacherous notion. And as a result, somehow or another Simon had found out where I lived.

"Don't want to tell me huh?" I was brought sharply back to the moment. "I *saw* you going into that bitch Laura's flat

190

and…" He registered the flash of surprise in my eyes and he laughed mirthlessly. "Oh yes. I'd just been thrown out on my ear by that patronising cow spouting bollocks about ethics and professionalism and so there I was sitting in my car and thinking about how I could get back at the stupid whore when who do I see but you."

When I didn't answer he said, "You were in there a fucking long time."

He took another deep swig from the wine bottle and wiped his lips with the back of his hand. Something animalistic about the gesture made me shudder. My heart was thudding wildly. Steady I told myself. You can handle him.

"Having a nice gossip about me, were you?" he asked. "Told her a load more lies about me did you?" His voice dropped to an insinuating note. "Or were you two getting cosy? Perhaps that's what you're both into?" The look he swept over my body made my skin crawl. "Invite me round next time. I like a bit of girl on girl."

"Get out!" I yelled.

He smirked and lounged back against the dresser with his weight on his heels and his crotch pushed forward. "Oh I'm not going anywhere and I must say that I'm very surprised that a well-brought-up girl like you hasn't asked me to sit down by now. Where are your manners?"

"Fuck off Simon," I flashed back.

"So where were we? Ah yes I'm waiting outside. I watch you come out and get into that crappy old car of yours and then I follow you back here. It wasn't difficult," he sneered derisively. "You drive like an old woman."

I winced. I'd been so proud of my new-found tracking and surveillance skills and yet I was the one who'd been tailed.

He began again. "So let's start with who you really are."

I said nothing.

"Not going to tell me are you? Well it shouldn't be too difficult to find out." He scanned the room and then swinging behind him gave a grunt of satisfaction as he caught sight of a sheaf of papers on a corner of the dresser. Topmost was my credit card bill. He pounced upon it and scrutinised the figures. "Dear oh dear. Someone's been treating herself. Right let's see the name…" He turned his attention to the top of the page. "Ms C. Pennhaligan," he read aloud. "Now what does the C stand for I wonder? Claire? Cathy?" He raised an ironic eyebrow but the menace in his voice was unmistakable. "Oh I've got it. Cunt. That fits."

"If you don't get out right now," I croaked, "I'll call the police."

"Oh I don't think so," Simon said and then turning casually to examine the contents of the dresser shelves behind him, he picked up a white china teacup ringed with violets that was part of a set that Grandma P. had owned. He examined it dispassionately and remarked, "Don't like this. Not my style at all."

Idly he played with the cup juggling it from hand to hand catching it like a ball and pretending to drop it. I made an abortive movement forward, but he waved me back. Then slowly and deliberately he allowed the cup to slip through his fingers and crash to the floor where it shattered into a dozen little pieces. I couldn't suppress a cry of outrage.

"Oh sorry," he said but there wasn't an ounce of apology in his tone. "Careless of me. Oh and by the way there'll be no police. I can't see a phone in here which means that it has to be in the next room or upstairs. And I'm not at all convinced you'll be able to get to it. Not till we're through."

I felt the hairs prickle on the back of my neck and a trickle of sweat run down between my breasts, but I made a concerted effort to subdue my mounting panic. I needed to get control of this situation. And fast.

"Look Simon." My attempt at being calm and reasonable sounded hollow even to my own ears. "There's nothing to be gained by this, by you being here. So I want you to leave. Now."

His gaze was frigid. "What you want doesn't concern me in the slightest. It's what I want that matters. And I want answers." He banged his fist down heavily on the table and the violence of the movement made me jump. "Who set you up to this?" he hurled the question. "Who are you working for?"

"No one," I faltered.

"I'm beginning to lose my patience Miss C. Pennhaligan." He snarled and reaching again for the bottle drained it in three long swallows. As he drank I could see a dribble of red wine make its way down on to his crumpled white shirt. It looked like a droplet of blood.

"Honestly Simon I…"

"Don't fuck with me," he shouted and there was real fury in his eyes.

I tried again but it was clear that the impulse that had driven him here in the first place was now intensifying. I was starting to feel really afraid of this man.

"I'm telling you the truth," I returned shrilly. "I don't work for anybody. I…"

"Lying bitch," he yelled and a dab of spittle appeared at the corner of his mouth as he pressed on. "That offer you made on the Alwyn Road place wasn't genuine was it?"

"No it wasn't," I admitted resignedly and raised my eyes reluctantly to meet his. What else could I have said? Desperately I tried to come up with some story that would placate him, at least for now and as my mind groped for ideas I became gradually conscious of a channel of heat coming from behind me, somewhere off to the right. I didn't have time to compute it. Simon was back on the offensive.

"I bet you were feeling pretty pleased with yourself. Thought that you'd made a real fool out of me didn't you? Well," he spat. "I had my doubts about you from the word go. Turning up out of nowhere and interested in the house when there was no legitimate way you could have known about it."

"Legitimate!" I shouted forgetting my fear now in blind indignation. "That's rich coming from a crook like you. That house wasn't ever on the open market. It was just a moneymaking scam for…"

I broke off as he stepped away from the dresser and lurched menacingly across at me. Panic threatened. My perspective of him had dramatically altered. I had known him to be vain and greedy but had believed his display of pride masked some deep-rooted male insecurity that could be dispelled only in the most ostentatious form of arrogance. I had dismissed Simon as essentially harmless. I realised now that I had got that very wrong indeed.

"And so what if it was?" he demanded. "It was all going very nicely until you and that interfering bitch Laura starting poking your noses in. Why couldn't she mind her own fucking business? I was *selling* the houses wasn't I? What difference did it make to her or that fucking firm she works for who I was selling them *to*?"

I should have kept quiet then. I shouldn't have said another word. I knew that I was only antagonising him further but I just couldn't stop myself. "But you weren't getting the right money for the vendor, were you? You were lining your own pockets, getting enormous kickbacks from…" It was on the tip of my tongue to mention Chris, but I reined myself in at the last minute. "Whoever you were selling them to."

"Ah," he pounced on this. "So it must be Laura's firm you're working for! You've really set me up haven't you? And now I'm about to lose my job all because of a fucking woman."

The impetus of his anger moved him forwards around the table bringing him closer to where I stood. Measuring him with my eyes I saw a man as taut with tension as a tightly curled spring. A spring that was about to unravel. Something of my understanding must have transmitted itself to Simon as a consciousness flickered across his features. I witnessed a brief internal struggle where he weighed up whatever his own version of morality amounted to against the primitive need to strike out at what he believed was the perpetrator of his downfall. Opaqueness descended over his eyes and I knew then that a line had been crossed. This man was dangerous.

I knew that I'd never make it past him. He was blocking my exit to the hall. Leaning back as far as I could, I edged a step away from the fridge in the direction of the door to the garden. My brain worked feverishly. Had I unlocked the door when I first came in? I couldn't remember. I didn't think I had. But I couldn't be sure. I felt derailed. I was losing my footing. I'd only ever before observed violence from afar. It was on a distant horizon. Something glimpsed but never experienced. In the comfortable security of my own world I had never yet looked it in the face. Now the landscape that I knew was shifting and I found myself ill-prepared to confront the new territory before me.

Both of us were watchful, both wanting to deduce from look or manner what the other would do next. Simon took another step towards me. I flinched and he laughed. He feigned another step. The opaqueness had dispelled and there was now something even more unsettling in his eyes, a gleam of triumph as he scented my fear. Like a cat playing with a mouse he was enjoying the thrill of the hunt before lashing out.

He advanced again, took a step, a check back, and then another step. I inched away. I was pressed against the cooker now and suddenly I could feel a lick of heat upon my skin. I'd forgotten I'd turned the grill on. Simon appeared to have noticed nothing. Perhaps the effects of nearly a full bottle of red wine downed so quickly had deadened his senses. That and the magnitude of his anger. His focus was fully upon me. He was the hunter and I was the prey.

How had this got so out of hand? Why hadn't I even considered the possibility that what I'd been doing had an inherent risk factor? I recognised now that until this point, my investigations into his affairs, into his life, had seemed like a game. I'd congratulated myself on my daring and nerve. I'd boldly and without scruple broken into his house and unlocked his secrets, persued the clues I'd discovered, and made what sense I could of the evidence. Now the game had come to an abrupt and terrifying finale. It was all too real. It was as if the energy I'd expended had been steadily escalating, gathering momentum to then turn traitor and work against me and ultimately to reach this climax.

Abruptly Simon made a stabbing movement towards me with his arm and laughed as he did so. He was alcohol and adrenalin fuelled. He'd discovered a new extreme sport, he had all the time in the world, and it felt good.

"Come on don't be shy…"

His manner was coaxing and his arm snaked out to me again and this time close enough to make me recoil and cry out. Irrepressible tears started in my eyes, tears which he mistook for weakness. A look of derision lit up his face, his smile was both dismissive and salacious. But dimly I registered the fact that with this scorn came a relaxing of the threatening stance, a loosening of his body. His mouth was slack and his eyes were glazed. Oh Christ. He was getting turned on.

I took a furtive glance to my left. The mop and bucket were still leaning against the open larder and next to that was the door to the garden. Could I fight him off sufficiently to give me time to get to it and to make my escape? The garden was walled and fenced, but I could at least scream and make one hell of a noise. Surely someone would hear me? My eyes fixed upon the key in the latch, but I now felt sure that I hadn't unlocked it. With a sinking heart I knew that he'd be on me before I could even make a move. And for the first time in my life I fully understood what it was to be truly afraid.

Through the upper glazed section of the door I could see that the rain had become torrential. The trailing creepers of a clematis plant that clambered up and over the lintel were agitated by an angry squall of wind, so that they beat like phantom fingers against the glass. The stabs of lightening were much closer now. But it was in the sudden explosive retort of a great crash of thunder sounding so close that it must have been almost overhead, that a suggestion whispered and I felt the first mutinous stirrings of defiance. A renewal of hope presented itself. I was a woman wasn't I? So, why not use what I had.

I rallied and retrenched. I had one chance. In his contempt for what he had believed to be my powerlessness, Simon had committed the cardinal error that the combatant so often makes in the face of impending victory. He'd underestimated the enemy. The quarry was in his sights and was to his mind too defeated in spirit to put up any more of a fight and so I'd been written off.

Well the bastard wasn't as in control as he thought. He might be bigger and stronger than me, but brute force doesn't always overmaster the driving instinct of survival. I am your match Simon Napier, I thought. You may well see yourself as the cat toying with the mouse before tearing it to shreds, but you'd better look out you fucker because this mouse bites back.

And so instead of twisting away, I forced myself to remain where I stood allowing him to come closer, the sham of a hesitant smile preying invitingly across my lips.

For a moment this change of tack threw him and he halted in surprise, then the overmastering egoism that was his chief characteristic regained its hold and he asked with a self-satisfied smirk, "Hmm, changed your mind have you?" There was a kind of smugness to the set of his mouth and he could afford now to be gracious. "I thought you'd come around in the end – knew you'd see sense."

He was only a foot away. I looked up at him but all the time I was conscious of the blaze of heat on my back from the grill. Simon still didn't seem to be aware of it. And I was determined that he shouldn't. It was vital that I kept his attention fully on me.

"Well Simon," I said softly and looking squarely into his eyes added, "It's just that you took me by surprise."

It was enough. With another step he was directly in front of me, his body pressing against mine. I could smell the tang of his sweat as he leaned in and put his hands on my shoulders jamming me up hard against the oven. With a butting motion of his head he then brought his face in close and his mouth down on to mine. I could taste the wine on his breath and feel his hard-on as he rammed his pelvis against my hips.

The intimacy was obscene to me, but in simulated passion I curved my body into his and brought my left arm up to caress his back. But slowly I inched my right arm up behind me feeling my way for the grill pan. His hands were at my neck and starting to move down to my breasts. I felt a sob of fear and disgust rise in my throat, but I forced it down as my hand continued to grope up and over the controls of the oven. He was pulling at the halter-neck tie of my dress, his tongue pressing hard against my teeth, as at last I got a tight grip on the handle.

I needed air. I felt I was suffocating and drowning in panic. I had never struck a blow in my life and I prayed for courage. It was now or never. Drawing my mouth away from his, I murmured, "Hang on. Wait a bit. Let me get more comfortable."

He grunted and relaxed his hold on me giving me the chance I needed and allowing me enough space to bring up my right arm and grab the handle of the now red-hot grill pan behind me.

"What the fuck?" Simon spluttered.

"Take *that* you bastard!" I screamed and then harnessing all of my strength I batted him full in the chest with the pan. The blow pushed him back against the kitchen table, which shifted against his weight causing the empty Merlot bottle to teeter ominously for a moment and then crash noisily to the floor.

Instinctively Simon had put up his hands to fend off the attack and then yelled out as his fingers clasped around the scorching hot pan. Instantly, he released it and it started to fall between our two bodies.

Prepared for this I hastily jumped back, but he, dazed and stupid with surprise, wasn't quick enough. As it descended, the scalding cast iron pan hit him full on the crotch.

"I couldn't have hit you in a better place Simon!" I shrieked.

His knees buckled and howling in pain he clasped at his genitals, but I wasn't going to be offering a cold compress and a sterile bandage. I struck out, side stepping the mop and bucket and made for the back door. I reached it and found that it was locked. My hands fumbled clumsily with the key but they were sweaty and I couldn't get it to turn.

In panic I risked a look over my shoulder and saw that Simon, still bellowing, was now lurching towards me. Frantically I worked at the lock but he was nearly upon me and I'd run out of time. I whirled around to face him looking desperately this way and that for something to defend myself with. But there was nothing to hand, nothing I could use as a weapon.

My eyes lit upon the mop. I grabbed hold of it just as Simon reached me and like some free-styling matador, I struck out at him with as much force as I could muster, jabbing him hard in the stomach. It barely checked him. He gasped, still in obvious pain, and then recovered himself almost immediately and charged forward to get at me. But he hadn't reckoned with the bucket. He hadn't seen it, hadn't known it was there, so he tripped, lost his footing, and pitched violently forward. The momentum of his descent brought him cannoning into me with a glancing blow to my shoulder but nothing could break his fall.

The bucket knocked over by the impact had shed its contents of scummy water and now rolled futilely against Simon's feet as he lay sprawled face down upon the floor. Winded, I scrambled to right myself, vaulted over him, and hurtled towards the hallway.

It was going to be all right, I was going to get away. I would run out into the night, would bang on my neighbour's door, and call the police and… But instead I did none of these things. Something prevented me.

Whether it was a feeling of culpability in that if I hadn't interfered with Simon's affairs I would never have found myself in this position, or an element of wounded pride that I couldn't handle this myself, I had no idea. Whatever it was it halted me in my tracks. All I knew was that I wasn't done here yet.

I walked back towards Simon who was now in the process of easing himself up to his knees. His breath came in ragged grunts and gasps.

"You bitch," he spat and started to pull himself upright just as an almighty clap of thunder booming directly overhead startled us both.

And it was then, acting purely on the instinct of the moment that I picked up a heavy bottomed saucepan from the top of the stove and without hesitation, stepped forward, and brought it down hard upon his head. With a whimper he slowly slumped back down to the floor. And in the crackle and fizz of the lightening streak that then flashed and flared through the kitchen in an unearthly radiance, I looked down at his prostrate body. The enemy had been vanquished. The cat had got his comeuppance. He'd thought himself the hunter, but what he hadn't bargained for was contending with a woman who hadn't eaten a square meal in twenty-four hours. I get mean when I'm hungry.

Without further thought I grasped hold of his ankles and alternately pushing and dragging him, succeeded at last in heaving the unconscious Mr. Simon Napier, manager of Dunstan Stead estate agents, into my walk-in larder. Wincing a little from the wrench to my shoulder I shut and bolted the door. And then leaning back against it and dusting off my hands I heaved a great sigh of satisfaction. *Now* I was done.

CHAPTER TWENTY-ONE

There was only one person I could think of turning to. Flan. She answered the phone on the third ring. "Flan it's me. Bit of an emergency here. Can you come over? I mean now."

If she was surprised at the request and by the fact that I was phoning so late, she didn't express it or shower me with questions. She merely answered smoothly, "Certainly darling. And I've got company. We're on our way."

"Thanks. I can't really explain over the phone but…"

Suddenly there was a sound of banging from the kitchen. Somebody was coming to.

"Please hurry. It's important."

With a click Flan rang off.

I couldn't face the kitchen. The door to the larder was solid wood and although I thought it unlikely that Simon would be able to kick through it, nevertheless the muffled thumps, thuds, and curses were unnerving. I paced about in the hallway and then as a precaution, opened the front door wide ready to make a quick getaway if it should prove necessary.

The rain had stopped and the wind had eased. The storm

had either passed on to inflict its tantrums on someplace else or had blown itself out in a fit of pique.

A car drew up and a minute later Flan came hurrying up the path with Mr. H. two paces behind her. She was looking fully alert and dressed in navy trousers and a cream sweater, and although the rest of her face was bare of make-up she had applied lipstick.

"Darling what is it? What's happened?"

"Well," I explained breathlessly still on the doormat. "I've caught a cat and it's in the kitchen. Because you see mice sometimes *do* turn. Or is that a worm? Anyway doesn't matter." My previous calm had abated and I was jangling with a manic energy.

Flan and Mr. H. exchanged a look before she said tranquilly, "Clarry you don't have a cat."

I laughed in what I hoped was a reassuring way but it came out more as a cackle. "No it's alright. I haven't completely lost my mind. It's Simon. He turned up here and well he attacked me." I felt the sudden sting of tears. Angrily I dashed them away explaining, "I managed to fight him off. And then I smashed him over the head with a saucepan and locked him in the larder. But now he's waking up. So at least I haven't killed him. Which is a good thing I suppose," I trailed off.

Flan put a comforting arm through mine and turning to Mr. H. who had been hovering anxiously during my outburst, said, "George perhaps we should investigate?"

"Righto my dear." Mr. H. may be seventy-two years old, a little barrel-chested and with dodgy knees, but there was something in the resolute set of his shoulders and the look of quiet determination in his faded blue eyes that was instantly cheering. "In we go then," he said. "In we go."

The crashes from the larder were louder now. Flan took in the wrecked kitchen: The table pushed off-centre, broken glass underfoot, and dirty water pooled over the lino. The grill was still on and the room was hot. Carefully picking her way across the debris she turned off the grill and then she unlocked and opened the back door, allowing in a draught of clematis-scented air. Turning to Mr. H. she asked, "Shall we?"

He nodded and made his way to the larder. The volley of abuse had reached a crescendo as Simon picked up on the sound of voices. He was yelling and kicking in such a paroxysm of indignation and rage that for the first time I was struck by how ludicrous this all was. I fought to suppress a spurt of nervous laughter and I could see by the look of droll enquiry on Flan's face that she had also picked up on the absurdity of the situation.

She and I maintained a position at the entrance to the kitchen, whilst Mr. H. took his stance to the left of the larder door. Stretching out his arm he placed his hand on the bolt.

"Ready?" he looked from Flan to me.

"Ready," said Flan.

"Ready," I agreed swallowing convulsively, my throat feeling suddenly dry.

He silently slid back the bolt and Simon who had been mid charge as the door swung open, came catapulting out into the light. Swearing horribly he skidded on the wet floor nearly losing his balance. Righting himself he took in the sight of Flan and Mr. H.

"Who the hell are you?" he demanded angrily and then not waiting for an answer yelled, "That bitch…" pointing an accusing finger at me. "Almost killed me and then she locked me in the…"

Flan held up a restraining hand and said firmly, "That'll be quite enough from you young man."

Simon gulped in surprise and said nothing. His hair was sticking up on end and there was a trickle of blood on his forehead, the sight of which made me feel slightly queasy. I'd done that. I'd drawn blood. Swaying slightly but resisting the desire to sit down, I noticed and was heartened to see that he was limping from the impact of the heavy grill pan upon his testicles. The fingers of his right hand were swollen and red from the heat of the pan. The front of his shirt and trousers were soaked from the dirty water. He was not at all his usual sleek groomed self. And one thing was for sure his yellow silk tie would never be the same again. Serves him right I thought with a jolt of satisfaction. He should have bought drip-dry.

Simon taken aback by Flan's tone of scornful disapproval broke off in mid rant, looking from one to the other of us to add querulously, "But I've been in that fucking cupboard for…"

But it was now Mr. H.'s turn to remonstrate. "And there'll be no more of that language. There's no call for it. Especially when there are ladies present."

Simon opened his mouth to object but seemed unable to find the right words and so stood gaping fish-like at the pair of censorious septuagenarians before him.

"Now," said Mr. H. assuming command. "I think we had all better sit down." He moved to the table and made to lift one corner to reinstate it in the centre of the room, when turning to Simon he exclaimed, "Well come on then. What are you waiting for? Give me a hand with this."

Simon still dazed, and for the moment seemingly docile, obeyed. He glowered at me as I took the seat furthest away from him. It was strange though. I was no longer in the least afraid of him. He was reduced. His moment of dominance had expired. He was just a bewildered and contemptible man. And I despised him.

"Now," said Flan turning her eyes upon him with haughty distain. "I believe your name is Simon Napier and that you are an estate agent. And I understand from what Clarry has told me that you are guilty of…" and here she enunciated very distinctly, "of some highly questionable practices."

Simon made to interrupt but she ignored him.

"However, what I don't in the least understand is what you are doing here, in this house, and in the middle of the night."

"And neither do I!" declared Mr. H. stoutly.

Simon shifted uneasily in his seat as Flan fixed him with her gimlet gaze.

"I came to talk to her. That's all," he protested.

"Funny kind of conversation you've been having by the look of this kitchen," observed Mr. H.

"That may well have been your intention," continued Flan. "But the fact remains that you committed an act of violence upon a woman. Nothing excuses your behaviour. It is the grossest form of outrage and also the action of a coward." She gave him a withering look.

Simon blanched.

"Hear hear!" chimed in Mr. H. "You deserve to be horsewhipped and if I had my way you..."

Flan cut across him. "Well?" she demanded imperiously. "What have you got to say for yourself?"

Simon squirmed but had the grace to look ashamed. "I'm sorry about that." Then looking across at me, "Honestly I am. I don't know what came over me. I just felt so angry that I flipped. I'm about to lose my job." A note of self-pity crept into his voice as he looked back at Flan. "I've worked really hard. I've turned that agency around. They weren't even shifting ten properties a month until I took over and now that's all gone to waste. All because of her," he pointed at me, his self-pity swiftly turning to accusation. "She was the one who blew the whole thing."

"I have to say that you are making yourself intensely disagreeable," interjected Flan. "After all from what I gather it's nobody else's fault but your own. There's no earthly point in blaming Clarry, or anybody else. You have been found out. Your dishonourable conduct has thankfully come to light. As it inevitably would have done at some time or another with or without Clarry's... er... endeavours... and so now you must take the consequences."

"Exactly!" I shouted no longer able to contain my smouldering anger with his blatant self-justification. "You have cheated God knows how many people out of their rightful inheritance and yet you expect us to feel sorry for you? You make me sick!" I slumped back in my chair feeling spent and exhausted.

"I think that what we all need now is some tea," suggested Mr. H. getting to his feet.

"No don't you get up Clarry dear," he said as I started to rise. "Just point me in the right direction. I'll see to it. I'm quite domesticated you know. I have had to be, as I've been on my own for a good few years now." He shot a look laden with meaning at Flan who pretended not to notice.

I sank back down suddenly aware that a cup of tea was what I wanted more than anything else in the world at that moment. Whilst Mr. H. bustled about with the kettle I noticed that Simon was now staring at Flan with a look of deep mistrust.

"Haven't we met before?" he asked.

I froze. I'd completely forgotten about Flan's rash but brilliant venture into his house to retrieve my car keys.

"I don't think so," replied Flan with perfect equanimity. "I have a good memory for faces and I don't believe that I have ever seen yours before."

"Well it's funny," he pursued with suspicion, "But you look just like a woman who knocked on my door late one night last week feeling faint."

"I have never felt faint in my life," Flan returned crisply. "It's an indulgent weakness I wouldn't dream of allowing myself."

Apparently satisfied with this, Simon dropped his gaze.

Mr. H. who didn't do things by halves had actually unearthed a teapot and after laying out the milk and mugs he resumed his seat to ask, "Shall I be mother?"

I laughed. The incongruity of us all sitting down to a midnight tea party in the exact same spot where less than an hour before I'd been threatened and attacked, where I'd been desperate, was farcical. And yet I asked myself why not?

What was the point in being melodramatic about it? I was a little bruised and undeniably shaken, but I was all right. I'd survived and here we were sitting down and discussing it over a nice cup of tea. It was all so terribly British.

I felt another spasm of laughter. And then another. And then they kept on coming. Really I couldn't seem to get them under control. This was just too ridiculous for words. Perhaps it was the after-effects of shock combined with a lack of food that was making me feel so light-headed, but one way or another I was suddenly feeling a whole lot better. Flan stood up and crossed over to me.

"Drink your tea darling. It'll do you good."

Dutifully I did as I was told, took a few sips, gradually regained my composure, and after a few moments Flan once again took charge of the proceedings.

"So what happens from here? Clarry you have, my dear, a perfect right to call in the police."

I sobered instantly, conscious that I now had a very important decision to make.

Flan's expression was very grave. "This young man has forced his way into your home and has attempted an assault upon your person." She sounded just like a lawyer and I remembered what she'd said about the cop shows. "You are fully entitled to redress and should you choose to go down that route then informing the police is the natural course of action."

"Quite right," agreed Mr. H. staunchly. "I was just about to suggest it myself."

Simon had sat up very straight, his body rigid, and his eyes fixed upon mine.

I closed my eyes uncertain of what to do. Part of me wanted him to endure the indignity of being questioned by the police. That would knock some of the arrogance out of him. It would be his turn to feel cowed and afraid. But then again did *I* want to face all the questions?

They would be bound to ask me what his motive in coming here had been. How much should I tell them? Wouldn't then the whole story inevitably come out? What about the implications for Laura and her company? And in the end what would be the point? The whole process would probably take forever what with statements and things, only for Simon to get a ticking off. And maybe not even that. After all it was my word against his. Wouldn't it be better for everyone to leave the police out of it? Wouldn't my best revenge be to outmanoeuvre him and get him off the scene for good?

"Well," I let out a reluctant sigh. "I am very inclined to involve the police. This has been a very frightening experience for me and I do feel traumatised by what has happened."

Simon's expression of despair was a tonic to my jaded spirits. There were sheens of sweat on his face and his eyes were pinpricks. "Look, please Gemma... or what is it? Clarry. I really can't be arrested. It would be on my record. Please can't you just..." He was begging now.

I screwed up my face in a show of deep contemplation and from the corner of my eye I could see the merest suggestion of a smile hovering at the corners of Flan's mouth. She knew me too well.

"So, OK," I said when I felt that a sufficient amount of time had passed and that I'd put Simon through the maximum level of anguish. "Here's what's going to happen."

"Anything," he said and I could almost see the tension physically drain out of him. "Anything you like."

This could be fun I thought. Think of the mileage I could get out of it. I was pretty broke at the moment and I could really do with... No. I veered away from the thought. I was not like that. I was one of the good guys.

"I will not go to the police but only on the following condition: First thing tomorrow morning, before your office even opens, you are going to deliver back your car and leave your boss a note of resignation from immediate effect. Say it's for personal reasons or whatever you like. And you are not to work again as an estate agent in this area, or in fact anywhere again. Take up a new career. You're young enough to start again and besides I feel sure you've got some money stashed away from some of the other deals that you've made."

Of course I knew that he had plenty of money. I was thinking of his £200,000 investment with Lehman Black. Simon's face fell and I fought down a laugh.

Well what did he think I was going to say? That he had been a bad boy but it was OK now, we'd just forget all about it and he could go on as before as if nothing had happened? I think he'd got off pretty lightly. On consideration I thought I'd actually been rather magnanimous, although realistically how would I ever know if he did work as an agent in another area? I knew that that part of my conditions was just hot air. But I was enjoying the feeling of empowerment that the dictating of terms was giving me and so why should I deprive myself of a good feeling by getting bogged down with the details?

"And listen Simon," I pressed it home. "Of course I can't promise that your boss whomever he or she may be won't get to know the truth. That much is out of my hands. Laura's firm may have already contacted Dunstan Stead. But I will do what I can to see if I can swing it so that they don't prosecute you. But I don't know if they will even give me the opportunity to voice my opinion."

He was trembling now but I went on without compromise.

"Because trust me they might very well pursue this. They might investigate every sale you've ever made and maybe not just at Dunstan Stead, but wherever you were before, because I'm betting that this is not a new thing for you. And then you'll be well and truly screwed."

He looked truly afraid as I said this and I wondered fleetingly just how dirty his hands were. Not my problem thankfully. I'd done my bit for the greater good.

"Oh and just one more thing," I added casually.

His eyes met mine in the full expectation of another body blow.

"You will never get in contact with Laura or me ever again. Understood?"

He nodded in undisguised relief but I didn't take it personally.

I sat back crossing my legs in a show of elaborate unconcern. "So take it or leave it Simon. The choice is yours. You can try and brazen it out with the police, with your firm, with the solicitors at Laura's company if you want to, if you've the stomach for it, but if I was in your place I know what I'd do."

It took him all of ten seconds to decide. "OK OK." He made a gesture of surrender. "I agree. I'll do it. I'll resign. But I think that you are being very unfair about this – unnecessarily harsh."

"Unfair?" bellowed Mr. H. who over the last few minutes had become increasingly agitated and who now rounded on Simon. "Harsh? Why you cheeky little sod. You should by rights be prosecuted. And not only that, I for one would like to give you a damn good thrashing." His blood was well and truly up. "And don't you think I couldn't. Even at my age. I keep myself fit and I could still beat the living daylights out of you. You just see if I bloody well couldn't."

He broke off and turned with an apology to Flan and me. "Sorry about the language but it makes my blood boil to hear him when he's been given the chance to…"

Flan leant across the table and patted his hand with the kind of smile that explains why even in her seventies she could still inspire devotion in a man.

"Nobody doubts that for a moment George. You're twice the man he could ever be."

Simon dropped his head in mortification. Even someone as self-satisfied as he couldn't fail to feel some semblance of shame.

"Well I think that's all don't you?" said Flan slicing through the tension and rising to her feet with the air of one who was just bringing a neighbourhood watch meeting to a close. "Although just wait one moment whilst I take a look at that cut."

Simon seemed inclined to object but glancing at her expression decided to think better of it.

"Clarry do you have a first aid box?"

"No. But I do have some plasters."

"Good but the cut needs to be cleaned up first."

She turned and went over to the dresser for a bowl and registered for the first time the broken teacup on the floor. "One of your grandmother's favourites. You did it I suppose?" She glared at Simon who coloured.

"I'll of course make good any damage. Just let me know how much," he offered hastily.

I waived the offer away. I was feeling exhausted now and just wanted him to go.

"Right," said Flan after she had filled a soup bowl with water and taken a clean tea towel from a drawer. "Let's see what we have here."

Like a chastened schoolboy, Simon submitted to her ministrations and I was suddenly reminded of Maggie tending to Dan in the pools parts place. Perhaps as a revenge for the attack he'd made upon me or possibly as payback for the broken teacup, Flan was not quite as gentle as she might have been. Simon flinched under her touch but wisely kept his mouth shut.

"There's no harm done." She stood back to examine it. "It's very slight but head wounds do bleed a lot."

Once the plaster had been applied, Mr. H., still rather red about the face, asked, "Are you alright to drive?" He may have lost his temper and all but challenged Simon to a duel, but he was a very kind man and would not have allowed someone in a weakened state to get behind a wheel.

"I'm fine," Simon mumbled and for an instant I saw a look of respect for the older man flash across his eyes. "Well goodbye then. And well… thank you…" He trailed off miserably and was quite unable to look at me.

Flan looked at him sternly. "I don't expect to be meeting you again but I just hope and pray that you have learnt your lesson from what's happened here tonight."

And remembering the look he gave Mr. H., I wondered if perhaps he had. Simon nodded mutely and then gathering what shreds of dignity he had left, walked out of the kitchen. A moment later we heard the front door close behind him.

"Thank you. Thank you both for everything." I bit my lip. "I don't know what I would have done without you." My voice wobbled and I felt close to tears again.

"What you need is a good night's sleep," replied Flan tenderly and hugged me close. "You've had a nasty shock. Get straight into bed and you'll feel more like yourself in the morning."

Flan is rarely motherly but in her simple response I could feel a wave of love and concern. I bit back more tears and turned to Mr. H. "And Mr. H., you were magnificent."

He drew himself upright. "Glad to be of help young Clarry and take it from me, if there's ever a bit of a flap on, I'm your man. It's National Service that does that. It's the training. They want to bring that back you know." And then seeing that he was losing the attention of his audience said, "I'll just go and start the car. Bye then now."

He trundled off and once out of earshot Flan remarked, "He *was* wasn't he? Rather magnificent I mean?"

I nodded. "He's a lovely man. A real sweetie and actually I think he must have been rather good-looking when he was younger. And he's still got a good head of hair. Not sure about his teeth though. Are they his original set?"

Flan flashed me one of her rakish smiles. "Listen darling," she drawled. "At this age I count myself lucky if they've got a penis and a pulse. Anything else is a bonus!"

CHAPTER TWENTY-TWO

Sunlight streaming in through a gap between my bedroom curtains brought me around to consciousness at about eight o'clock. It was a beautiful morning. I would have expected to feel a little woozy and punch-drunk after last night but I was clear-headed, light-hearted, and absolutely starving.

In T-shirt and knickers I headed downstairs to find a kitchen that looked like a battlefield. Ignoring the chaos and shoving my feet into a pair of trainers, I made tea, three rounds of toast, and boiled an egg. I felt the need for protein. Taking my breakfast out into the garden I sat down at the old stone table and took in the aftermath of not only the natural storm and its affects upon the garden, but also the man-made tempest and its impact upon me.

Both of us had recovered pretty well I thought. The budding roses clambering up the back fence had taken a bit of a battering; the bird feeder had been shaken off its branch on the lilac tree and as for me I may have become acquainted with the threat of violence, had got up much closer to it than I would have wished to, but my perspective on life hadn't in fact shifted as dramatically as I'd believed.

Most people I reminded myself were just normal and decent and I saw no reason for a prat like Simon to jaundice my view of the rest of humanity. And although my shoulder felt a little stiff and my eyes were slightly swollen, I was alright and still the girl I'd been yesterday. There would be no need to send flowers. But it could, I reflected as I sipped my tea, have been a whole different story.

Shaking my head I banished the thought. Whilst I wasn't going to minimise the fear I'd experienced last night, neither did I regret taking on this investigation. I had been given a brief and for once I'd fulfilled it. I hadn't lost interest, hadn't backed off or simply quit. I'd seen it through.

I decided to tackle the mess before having a shower and by nearly ten the kitchen was looking more like itself again. In fact it was looking rather better. Moving some of the china to fill in the space where the teacup had been and seeing how dusty it all was, I'd decided to clean the shelves of the dresser and give each and every piece of crockery and glass a wash. I'd stopped after finishing only three of the shelves, as my hands were getting pruny with the soapy water and because I saw no need to get carried away.

Gazing in satisfaction at the sparkling glassware, I was interrupted in my labours by the phone. It was Laura and she was sounding remarkably pleased with herself.

"How did it go with Mr. Garstein?" I asked.

"Brilliantly."

"Really?" I asked doubtfully. "But you were so worried."

She cut across me. "Yes but that was before I'd really thought it through and realised that it's all just a question of angles."

"Angles?" I questioned.

"Yes, because if there's one thing I've seen time and time again as a solicitor it's that if a person *feels* guilty then they *look* guilty. Do you see?"

"Well no not really," I admitted. "I mean how does that relate to you and your boss?"

"I changed my approach," she explained. "Instead of going to Mr. Garstein and saying, I may have really fucked up here and please don't sack me, my strategy was to turn it on its head and present the case in a totally different light."

"And that would be in a light that reflected well on you?" I asked now beginning to get it.

"Of course!" she laughed. "I said that I had become suspicious when the sale prices on the two other houses were lower than expected and had decided to look into the matter before the good name of the firm was jeopardised."

"That's pretty slick babes!" I offered and was genuinely impressed.

"I know!" she gave a short laugh. "And Mr. Garstein said I'd done the right thing in coming to him and praised my professional judgement."

I gave a low whistle. "God you're good. And I don't suppose you mentioned that you were sleeping with Simon?"

"Well no, it kind of slipped my mind."

"Very wise," I said gravely.

I then went on to fill her in on last night's drama.

"Oh my God!" she exclaimed. "I can't believe it. Are you OK? Did he hurt you?"

"It was more the other way around. He definitely got the worst of it."

"Bloody hell. I can't wait to hear the full story. So you say he's agreed to resign from his job?"

"Yep. Should have done so by now and…"

"Oh Christ I nearly forgot," Laura interrupted me. "The main reason for calling you. You and I are meeting with the owner of Dunstan Stead at twelve o'clock. James Dunstan. Can you make it? Right got to go. See you outside their office."

And before I could protest, she rang off. I glanced at my watch. Nearly half ten and I was hot and sweaty from my housework. That is so Laura. She delivers a fait accompli and just expects me to comply. Well one of these days I might not automatically fall in with her plans, I thought crossly, and then where would she be? Dismissing this line of thought as a waste of valuable time and energy, I charged upstairs for a shower.

At five minutes to twelve, I was standing outside Dunstan Stead wearing my cornflower flippy skirt with a pale pink wrap top and leaning in to give Laura a hug.

"Fab. You're on time," she said.

She was in her usual business uniform of charcoal suit and white shirt but she'd jazzed it up with a black lace choker and was looking cool and confident.

I grimaced, "Well I nearly wasn't but…"

She gave me a shove and ushered me into the building.

The full strength of the midday sun was shining through the plate glass shopfront, giving the room a hothouse atmosphere. Hanging on the white walls were framed black and white prints of architectural plans, which looked I thought, very similar to the ones Simon had in his sitting

222

room. Perhaps he'd helped himself? Talk about taking your work home with you. On a giant easel to the left of the door were photographs and details of "This Week's Featured Properties" some of which already had sold stickers across them.

My attention was caught by a sketch of a block of New York Style Loft Apartments that was under construction on the south side of the Common. I tried to imagine myself living in it serving pastrami on rye and lox bagels to Flan and Mr. H. but couldn't really picture it.

There were four beech wood desks in the room, in front of which were pairs of upholstered chairs positioned at an intimate and conversational angle. Two of the desks were empty but the occupants of the other two immediately rose to greet us with the forced bonhomie and determined glint in the eyes of those who work mostly on commission.

I recognised the woman I'd seen bringing in the open/closed board when I'd first staked out Simon and she was wearing another shirt waisted dress. The other, a young guy with tufty blonde hair and a suit that looked slightly too big for him was, I could see from the nameplate on his desk, Stephen Oakley. Now I was right in front of him I could see what Flan had meant about his teeth.

"We're not buyers," said Laura with a smile. "Or vendors. Sorry. We've got an appointment with Mr. Dunstan."

The woman, her nameplate pronounced her to be Linda, answered politely, "Good morning. May I take your names please?"

We gave them and she then led us through and out to a private office at the rear of the shop.

"He's expecting you," she said. "Go on in."

Laura nudged me as if expecting me to go in first, but I shook my head and took a step backward.

"Oh no. After you."

She smirked and pushed open the door. A guy in his late thirties with close cut dark hair and a pleasant but plain face rose from behind his desk. He had the build of a habitual sportsman with broad shoulders and a compact well-toned body.

"Hello," he said offering his hand and giving us a warm smile. "I thought I heard voices. I'm James Dunstan."

Laura introduced us both.

"It's very good of you to come," he said and led us to a brown leather sofa. "Now how about some coffee?" he asked when we'd sat down.

He indicated one of those sophisticated coffee machines that look like you'd need to go on a course to learn how to operate and a few minutes later we were sipping at steaming hot and remarkably strong cups of espresso.

"Can't get through the morning without at least three of these," he admitted with a rueful smile. "Terribly bad for me I know, but I can't help myself. Now, I have to tell you that I was shocked to hear from Mr. Garstein this morning. I'm still reeling from it now. At first, I couldn't believe it of Napier. I mean I knew he was ambitious, even a little cold-blooded but I thought he was probably just what the company needed." His large mobile mouth set in a grim line.

And it was then that I became aware of Laura discreetly giving him the once over. Good for her I thought, but I'm sure she'd said only last night that she was off men for the time being.

James was still talking. "I've been blaming myself. I should have kept more of an eye on what was going on." His eyes clouded as he explained, "I haven't spent as much time in the office as I should have in the last few months. You see I've just gone through a messy divorce and…"

I felt Laura beside me stiffen with interest. A disconsolate divorcee needing a shoulder to cry on, this was the perfect breeding ground for her next big crush.

"My wife walked out six months ago leaving me with our two boys. And it's been tough juggling everything."

Laura asked gently, "How old are they?"

"Charlie's seven and Sam's nearly five." His face lit up. "They're great kids. But these last few months have been difficult for them. They miss their mum. Finding childcare for Sam and cover for the school run for Charlie has been a challenge to say the least and so I have to confess that I've rather let things slide here."

He glanced at Laura who nodded sympathetically. Wanting to distract him before he could move on to the subject of bed-wetting or other symptoms of childhood trauma, I was just about to interrupt when she said in a voice full of warmth and understanding, "Being a father is your most important role and it sounds like you are coping really well."

James smiled and I noticed then that there was something particularly open and attractive about that smile. It clearly wasn't wasted upon Laura who was now pulling playfully at a long lock of her hair, which is always a sure sign of interest with her. Here we go I thought. Throw in two motherless children and it was practically a done deal.

"That's kind of you to say," he said and looking directly at her asked. "Do you have children?"

She laughed, "No. I'm not married but I love kids." And then added seamlessly, "I'm single actually."

As she smiled into his eyes a slight blush crept up her throat. Now that was smooth I thought. I could see James digesting the information. But would he take the bait? We would have to wait and see but I hoped so. There was something very likable about this guy.

There was a slight pause. It was time for me to cut in. "And Simon resigned this morning?"

James gave himself a little shake appearing to remember the reason for our meeting.

"Yes when I came in at eight thirty his desk was cleared, the car was outside, and a letter giving little or no explanation for his sudden departure lay on the mat."

Laura said, "My firm, Mr. Dunstan, will not be…"

"Call me James please."

She dimpled. "James, as I said we won't be pursuing the matter. I think Mr. Garstein informed you of that. We believe that there is nothing to be gained by contacting the original owners of the houses in Bathgate and SouthPark Road. It's too late now. The properties have changed hands and all it would do is open up a can of worms, which frankly we don't need. And as for Alwyn Road your company will maintain the instruction and we'll arrange to get rid of the squatters. In fact I think Mr. Garstein has already contacted the police and put the procedures under way."

I heard this with relief, glad that Gary would be sent packing and even more so that Melanie and Ted were safely at Tim's.

"And what about you James?" I asked, remembering my promise. "Are you going to go after Simon? I mean legally that is."

"There's no point in getting bogged down for the next couple of years in mountains of red tape," he grinned and his face seemed no longer in the least plain. "But I do have cause for one area of satisfaction. Napier didn't give me any notice and so he forfeits his salary for notice period and there is also the small matter of his commission cheque for the last three months."

He looked across at me with a significant nod. "So, I'd like you to accept this because I understand from Mr. Garstein that it was down to your efforts that all this has come to light." He pulled an envelope out of his breast pocket and handed it to me. "I've left the name blank as I didn't know who to make it payable to."

I opened the envelope to find a cheque for an amount of money that would take a nice chunk off my credit card bill... but I couldn't accept it. "You can't give me this!" I exclaimed.

"Why not?" James asked mildly.

"Look," I said firmly. "You don't have to worry that I'm going to blab about what's happened. Really you don't have to buy my silence."

"That's not what I'm doing," he protested. "We're an independent company, not one of the big chains. Our reputation could have been seriously damaged by this and thanks to you it hasn't been. So give me one good reason why you shouldn't have it?"

I thought for a moment but strangely enough nothing sprang to mind. I pocketed the cheque and got to my feet. "Well thanks very much. I didn't expect payment but I'll take it."

"You are very welcome." And turning to Laura he put out his hand.

She shook it saying shyly, "Well goodbye then."

James hesitated a moment and then said still holding her hand, "Um. I was wondering if perhaps you'd like to have lunch sometime." He coloured slightly. "To discuss things you know. Napier. Further business that kind of..."

I smiled to myself. The bait had been well and truly taken and I was genuinely pleased for Laura. It looked like James wasn't an inconsolable divorcee after all.

"Yes." Laura's smile was radiant. "That would be lovely."

They both appeared to recognise at the same time that their hands were still interlinked and laughingly relinquished their grip.

Once back outside Laura gave a little skip of sheer happiness. Now normally I don't approve of skipping in anyone over the age of eight and am inclined to make rude remarks to those I catch indulging in the practice, but for once I refrained from comment.

"This is turning out to be a good day," she said beaming at me.

I couldn't find fault with that.

CHAPTER TWENTY-THREE

Laura's right I thought as I made my way home, it has been a good day, but after everything I'd been through yesterday, what I really wanted, what I really needed and deserved... was a bloody good night. I wanted to get steaming drunk and I wanted to get laid. In that order. Luckily for me, both were in my power to achieve. *And* I had options. I could ring around some mates and go clubbing and hook up with someone new or I could take up the invitation left by Not-So-Tiny Tim in a message on my mobile.

"A Tuesday is as good a night as any for Melanie and Ted's house-warming party and so if you can make tonight... and I know you're not working because I checked the rota... that would be great. About nine... See you later I hope."

Melanie greeted me with a hug.

"You're the guest of honour. It's because of you that we met Tim and then we met Barney and then... oh, and did I tell you that I've contacted Kingston College of Art and that I might be able to pick up on one of their courses?" Barely taking a breath she was excited and happy. The pale anxious faced girl that I'd met only a few days before had gone and, as she snuggled under Ted's protective arm I felt glad that not only were things working out for them, but that I had in a small way contributed to their good fortune.

"It'll just be a part-time course because I need to find a job and work at least a couple of days a week to bring some money in and…"

"That's great. Really good news. Good for you," I said.

"And Ted's found some evening work at a tapas bar in Raynes Park. And you're thinking about putting a band together aren't you?" she smiled up at him.

Ted explained, "Barney might even play the odd session himself, him and his sax. He's seriously good and must have been even better in his heyday."

Melanie touched my arm. "I meant what I said about it all starting with you. We really do appreciate your help."

"Absolutely we do," added Ted. "But now I think what you probably need is a drink. Go find Tim in the kitchen. He's making daiquiris."

As I turned to go, Melanie whispered, "Tim's really in to you Clarry."

I made my way down the hall passing a large double sitting room hung with framed posters depicting bands from the seventies and eighties. I spotted Paul Weller's lean frame and distinctive haircut on an album cover suspended above the fireplace, but I only vaguely recognised some of the other faces. Twenty or so people were talking and drinking and listening to something cool and jazzy and syncopated that was playing. Many of them appeared to be contemporaries of Barney the landlord, but there were a handful who were much younger, and were clearly friends of Tim's.

I continued past to the kitchen where even over the noise of half a dozen people talking, I could hear the sound of a blender running.

Tim, surrounded by bottles was alternately squeezing fresh limes and hulking strawberries. "Clarry," he called catching sight of me as he switched off the blender. "Great you're here. Do you fancy one of these? They're heavy on the rum but I think I've got the sweetness to sharpness ratio right."

He grinned and pushed back a strand of hair from his face. I'd been right to describe him to Ian as a puppy, I thought. In his six-foot rugby-playing frame there was something discernibly bouncy and playful, not only in his physique, but in his manner too. And I happen to like puppies. But then who doesn't?

He handed me a drink. "Jerry," he called to a stocky guy in a polo shirt. "Take over from me will you mate?" And he came and stood in front of me. "You look good," he said.

"So do you," I said.

My black dress from last night I'd binned. It wasn't just that the halter-neck ties had been ripped by Simon; I suppose I could have got it repaired, but I just didn't want to wear it again. Even cleaned and re-stitched, something dark and menacing might yet linger in its folds and mar any future occasion on which I wore it, the way a bad dream can sometimes seep out and tarnish a new day. So, I'd gone for an old favourite. Clinging and with that secret support that makes you feel like you're wearing a bandage, it was short and had a zip running down the front.

"I like the zip," Tim said.

"It goes all the way down," I said.

"I see that," he said.

For a moment, the thought crossed my mind that having sex with a co-worker is never really a good idea, but then instantly I dismissed it. We were waiters for god's sake, not running the country or even a company. And besides I was so in the mood. I took a sip of my drink and coughed.

"Too strong?" Tim asked.

"Absolutely not," I said.

The option I'd taken proved to be a highly satisfying one. And the nickname Not-So-Tiny, I discovered, was bang on (Ian, I knew, would be delighted to hear that.) It wasn't going to be anything serious between us; it was just sex. And that was alright with me. Tim was funny and sweet and very eager to please. Eager to please in a whole different way from a puppy.

Around midnight, as Tim lay quietly snoring sprawled upon his back across a bed that wasn't quite wide enough to accommodate us both comfortably for sleep; I took a long breath out. I'd built up a lot of tension in the last week and now, thanks to Tim's energy, stamina, and surprisingly proficient touch, I'd just released it in the best way possible… four times. I ran a finger lightly down his spine. Let's make that five I thought as Tim stirred and looked up at me.

Afterwards, as I padded down a flight of stairs to the bathroom, the realisation came to me that try as I might… and I had tried really really hard, the sound of that unknown woman's sobbing in the club was still with me and that nothing that Tim and I had done and almost certainly would do again in the morning, could drown it out.

CHAPTER TWENTY-FOUR

I couldn't sleep. Tim took up a whole lot of space. Gingerly I slipped out of bed doing my best not to wake him, because after that performance, he certainly deserved his rest. I hesitated and looked down at my discarded clothes. I felt I couldn't just go without leaving a note and so hunted about for something to write on.

His bedroom was a typical young male's room. Clothes and shoes strewn around, a pot of hair gel balanced on a plate of toast crusts, a pile of rugby and gaming magazines, a laptop and a TV on a desk, but no sign of a pen or paper. I picked up a magazine featuring an article about the British Lions and then rooted around in my bag for a pen. As I did so, my phone fell out on to the carpet. I flicked it on and found that I had been left a voicemail message at 12.17pm from a number that I didn't recognise.

"Hi Mallory… or whatever your real name is, it's Paula. I wasn't going to phone but I reckon I owe you. And anyway, I'm out of here in a minute… I'm catching an early train back home to Dudley." There was a slight pause before she continued in a low whisper, "I heard one of the twins talking to someone on the phone. The girls, there's three of them, are being moved tonight. And that's basically all I know. Except I think more are expected because…"

She broke off and in the background there was the sound of a man's voice saying something I couldn't hear. Then the line went dead. I looked at the phone screen. It was nearly one o' clock in the morning. I glanced across to Tim now lying peacefully on his side and then came to a decision. Yanking on my underwear and wrestling myself into the bandage dress, I scribbled a few lines in the margin of the magazine article, grabbed an oversized denim shirt of Tim's from the back of a chair, and slipped out of the room.

Swapping my heels for the pair of trainers that I keep in the boot and cramming my hair into my cap, I started up the Renault and headed towards central London. It was only when I'd been driving for about ten minutes however, that I remembered the daiquiris. I had to be over the limit. Damn. Whatever was going on at *Knights* was happening tonight and even now I might be too late.

Mentally I checked my vital signs. Hands steady on the wheel, vision focused, mind clear – or at least clear-ish. I felt fine and in command of my faculties, but if I was stopped and breathalysed I didn't think the police would see it that way. What to do? I weighed it up and allowed curiosity and the prickling sense of unease I'd been feeling, to battle it out with common sense. Curiosity won and I drove on.

I reached Waterloo and made my way up Bayliss Road slowing down as I passed the club, but I couldn't tell if it was still open as the obscured glass and security grilles made for an impenetrable screen. I took the next left and found myself in a wide and dimly lit street overlooked by a tower block on its eastern side.

I located the rear of the launderette and the Korean food store that sandwiched the club. *Knights'* rear entrance was just a single door. There were no parking spaces directly outside and even if there had been it would have been a bit obvious just to plonk myself there. I continued and then circled back pulling up three spaces down and on the opposite side of the road.

I switched off the engine and waited.

A few cars came and went. Some loud young male and female voices and shrieks of laughter emanated from the direction of the tower block, but the group to which they belonged weren't visible to me. Other than that, nothing happened.

I checked the time. It was now nearly half past one. What the hell was I doing choosing to sit alone in my car in a seedy backstreet in the middle of the fucking night in the hope of catching persons unknown in the act of carrying out operations unknown, over having another hot sweaty bout with Not-So-Tiny Tim? I honestly didn't know, except that Simon and Chris's dodgy dealings made me want to stand up for those who are cheated and exploited. People like the vendors of those houses and Dan and Sheena and Maggie, and Paula... and whoever it was that had sobbed behind that locked door.

At twenty-five minutes to three a van drove slowly past me and then stopped outside the club. I slouched down in my seat and watched as a man got out of the driver's side. All I could make out was that he wasn't very tall and was wearing a dark bomber-style jacket. He walked around the front of the van and disappeared from view.

Five minutes later he reappeared at the rear of the van, the aspect most visible to me, joined by a second man and three women (or girls). The driver unlocked the rear doors and he and the other man ushered the women inside. This manoeuvre, I noted, was carried out swiftly but not furtively and without obvious force or inducement of any other kind. The women appeared to be docile and weren't putting up a struggle, but what did that really indicate I wondered.

Winding down my window a crack, I craned my neck to listen but was too far away to hear anything other than some words pass between the two men in a foreign language. That was it. Both men got into the van and the driver switched on the engine. I had seconds to decide. I followed the van.

Even in the early hours of the morning, London has quite a few vehicles on the road. Delivery lorries, night buses ferrying people home from a late shift or on their way to an early one, taxis with occupants both sober or drunk, voluble or comatose, and a certain dirty white Citroen van that I endeavoured to keep a space of two cars behind.

We travelled through Kensington and Paddington until we hit the Edgeware Road and then up we went through Kilburn, Cricklewood, and Neasdon. On the Hendon Way, we joined the A41 and then hung a left taking the road signposted Watford, Wood Green, and Brent Cross. Where on earth were we heading I wondered, beginning to feel tired and more than a little thirsty.

We passed the giant shopping centre heading north until, eventually, we were on the M1. Usually on a motorway I stick to the middle lane, but for long stretches the van stayed in the right-hand one and so I had to weave in and out of traffic that, although not heavy, came nevertheless in a steady stream.

Now, anxiety about driving over the limit really began to concern me and that coupled with the strain of eyeballing the van and maintaining the appropriate speed restrictions to keep up with it, was making me sweat under Tim's shirt and my too tight dress.

At junction 7, I seriously considered giving up and going home. We could be going anywhere. Nottingham, Manchester or Scotland even and I wasn't sure I was up to the drive. I needed a cup of tea and an aspirin but most of all I needed to get this bloody dress off. At junction 9, I was sorely tempted to take the exit and by the time I spotted the signpost for junction 10, I'd had enough. I indicated a left and switched lanes and as I did so, I realised that the Citroen was also swapping lanes to come off.

As we left the slip road, it was now only one car in front of me and continued to be so as we entered the outskirts of Luton. We drove on. I could feel the adrenalin that my body had manufactured to see me through the demands of the motorway drive begin to dissipate, and that tiredness was taking its place. I'd had no sleep. I was badly in need of a shower, had the parched mouth that results from too much alcohol, and my nerves felt brittle and on edge.

Just stop, I told myself. Turn around and mind your own bloody business, it's nearly daylight. But I can't I argued, I've come this far, it would be crazy to quit now.

We passed a stadium, and signs to Luton airport and to the city centre. Then the van, now two cars ahead, took a left on to a quiet residential road, leaving me no choice but to follow and for the first time without the barrier of another vehicle between us. It was doing about 30 miles per hour and so I slowed to 25 trying to keep as much distance between us as possible. It took a right. Another street and a very rundown one. Several cars had broken windows and there were overflowing dustbins everywhere.

I followed more cautiously now, letting my speed drop to 20 and then to 15, but still I felt highly conspicuous. Would they realise that they were being tailed? How much notice does one take of other vehicles on the road? None if you were just an innocent person going about your business I thought. But what if you weren't?

My arms ached from holding tightly on to the steering wheel and I could feel a fist of tension flare between my shoulder blades. Somewhere nearby had to be the van's ultimate destination. Let's just get this over with I prayed. It can't be long now. Another right and then a left and then we were in a rat run of streets, part of a sprawling estate that appeared to be only semi-occupied.

I could see derelict flats in a low-rise block, with boarded up windows looking, even as the sun was rising, stark and forbidding. Jagged gaping holes had been cut in the chain link fencing that bordered a disused children's play area, where a lone swing hung lopsidedly from just one chain. And then, without indicating, the van suddenly swung a left disappearing around a corner. In pursuit, I picked up speed and swerved after it only to find that it had come to a halt right on the bend. Urgently, I pressed down hard on the brake pedal but it was too late, I was going to ram straight into it. Forcing myself back into my seat as if somehow, magically, the movement of my body could prevent collision with the rear of the other vehicle, I ground my foot down again and pulled desperately at the handbrake. The wheels spun for what seemed a very long minute but in reality could only have been a few seconds. My old Renault rocked violently on its axis but I had missed hitting the van, and with only inches to spare.

I took a long ragged breath. Nausea threatened and briefly I closed my eyes trying to force it down. Instantly, I opened them again at the sound of the van door being opened. The driver was getting out. I could see now that his bomber jacket was of shiny leather and that he was in his thirties with black receding hair. My hand shot out automatically for the door lock and I pushed it to. He was standing on the other side of the glass from me now and was shouting and gesticulating, but with all my windows closed and deafened by the panic that shrieked and numbed my brain, I couldn't hear him.

I pawed at the ignition, switching the engine back on. But I'd forgotten that I was still in gear. The car shot forward and not only hit the van's bumper with a thud, but also crunched down upon the shouting man's foot. As he screamed and fell back, I released the handbrake and tried the engine again. It caught. Frantically I started to reverse as the passenger door to the van flew open and the second man, younger than the first and skinny in a pale grey tracksuit, jumped out.

He looked in disbelief at his companion still screaming and lying in the road clutching his foot and ran towards him. In those precious vital moments that he wasted, I had just enough time to pull the Renault back and execute a clumsy three-point turn. As I shot off in the direction I'd originally come from, I registered, in my rear-view mirror, something small and white that floated out and down from the van's nearside window, to land amongst the scrubby grass that lined the edge of the kerb. Somebody in that van had thrown out a piece of paper.

CHAPTER TWENTY-FiVE

I drove blindly, going I think in circles for a while, until I found that I was clear of the estate and I pulled over. The nausea I'd been fighting resurfaced and, releasing my seat belt and opening the car door, I heaved and threw up into the gutter.

I'd run a man down. I'd driven over his foot. I'd done that. I shivered and switched on the engine. I couldn't drive home in this state. I had to steady myself and I had to get something to drink. A couple of streets down I found a small twenty-four-hour convenience store where I bought two bottles of water and a bar of chocolate.

Back in the car, I wrote down the Citroen's registration number which I had memorised and then forced myself to dismiss everything else from my mind except the piece of paper I'd seen tossed from the window. Was it just a piece of rubbish or could it be some kind of message or cry for help? I didn't want to go back for it. Hell, I didn't even know if I could find my way back to it, but reluctantly I acknowledged that I had to try. Or should I just phone the police and report what I'd seen? But what had I seen that amounted to anything? They'd laugh at me. It was just three women being driven somewhere in a van. That was all. They could be going anywhere for all kinds of reasons, it didn't necessarily mean anything sinister.

However, every instinct told me that it did. Somehow, I just knew that it did. But how, I asked myself, would I even explain to the police my reason for following the van in the first place? Not only that but I probably still smelt of booze and almost certainly of vomit and wouldn't come across as exactly credible. They might even breathalyse me. No. For the moment, I was on my own in this or at least until I had found that bit of paper.

It took me nearly half an hour to locate the right street. Just when I was about to chuck it all in I found the abandoned children's playground, its swing swaying on its one chain, a symbol of a sense of defeat that seemed to permeate this neighbourhood. I slowed down to a crawl and took the left turn where I'd followed the Citroen. I think I half expected to see it still there, because this could have been its ultimate destination for all I knew, but there was no sign of it. I parked and then got out of the car.

This is probably a complete waste of time I told myself. There was a light breeze and the bit of paper could have blown away, or fallen down a grating or been carried off by some huge scary dog. Or, and this was the most likely, retrieved by the man in the grey tracksuit. I thought the bomber-jacket guy would have been too consumed by the pain in his foot to pick up litter. This thought cheered me slightly and I sprinted across to where I thought the van had pulled up.

I found one fast-food burger box, several globs of chewing gum, and a receipt from a supermarket, which I examined in case there was something handwritten on it (there wasn't), a wad of tissues (used), and a page torn from a newspaper and folded into eight pieces. I opened it out but I couldn't read it. It was in Greek.

It was too early to hit the worst of the rush hour, but it still took me over two hours to get home where, being too tired to shower, I fell into bed and crashed out until nearly lunchtime.

Bathed and fortified by scrambled eggs on toast and two mugs of tea, I checked my phone. Tim had left a message asking why I had bailed on him and there were two missed calls from a private number.

I looked again at the newspaper. The date at the bottom of the page was just under a week ago. On one side, there were half a dozen articles with headlines followed by plenty of exclamation marks, but of course I couldn't understand a word of them. The other side was clearly a page of advertisements. Some were in small bordered boxes and others just a couple of lines in the classified section and it was one of these that had a tiny cross printed in blue biro beside it. I squinted at it. There wasn't a phone number, just two lines of text.

I switched on my computer and browsed the translation sites, but after patiently trying to decipher each individual word, the only thing I felt confident of, as an accurate interpretation, was a reference to *flowers*. There are so many nuances to a language, and words have so many different meanings in different contexts, that decoding the ad without help would be impossible.

My mobile rang. It was a private number.

"Hello," I said and then when no one answered repeated, "Hello…"

The line went dead. Irritated, I looked back at the newspaper and then took a mental inventory of everyone I knew. No one spoke Greek. I considered friends of friends, still no one. I phoned Abbe's and spoke to Dave, who then spoke to Laurence and Alec in the kitchen, who spoke to Tara and Ian serving the lunchtime crowd but again I drew a blank. Well I couldn't ask Chris that was for sure and I didn't think consulting Thanos at *The Vine* would be a good idea, but there was one other person I'd met recently who could translate it for me. But would she? And how much would I have to explain to get her to do so?

Nuala's delicatessen on Camberwell Green had a simple rustic charm. There was lots of bare wood, dried herbs hung in baskets from the ceiling, and the walls were lined with racks of wine, vinegars, and olive oils. It didn't go in for gourmet produce, but was more of a family-kitchen affair and was just the kind of place I usually like to browse in, coming out laden with individual portions of interesting delicacies wrapped in greaseproof paper.

And even though today I was here on a mission unconnected with food, I had to admit everything looked delicious. Trays of meatballs in a tomato sauce, plates of stuffed aubergines, and on a chopping board a pile of crusty rolls filled with cheese and Greek sausage. I wouldn't have minded trying them all.

When I entered the delicatessen, Nuala, dressed in jeans, a dark blue blouse, and an apron and with her dark hair pulled back in a ponytail was measuring some stuffed red bell peppers on an old-fashioned weighing scale and didn't immediately recognise me.

I stood to one side as she finished serving her customer who took her time deciding between a portion of dolmades and some butterbeans in a creamy dressing. Eventually the stuffed vine leaves won the day and she left the shop.

"Hi," I said stepping forward. "Remember me? I'm Clarry. We met on Sunday at *The Vine*."

"I remember," she said and the smile she gave me was a bit half-hearted.

"This is a great place," I offered. "Everything looks wonderful. Is that baklava I see over there?"

"Yes. We make it ourselves with honey from Mt. Erymanthos and with nuts from Aegina. How many pieces would you like?"

"Um…well… yes… just one please. That would be great."

Wielding a pair of tongs she lifted a segment of the cake and placed it on a piece of waxed paper. "Is there anything else?"

I hesitated. "Well yes. As a matter of fact, there is."

She looked at the array of food on the counter and I shook my head.

"No Nuala. I'm actually hoping that you might be able to help me with something."

Nuala frowned. "I thought you must want something. What is it? And please be quick. My husband is out at one of the suppliers and I have customers."

I took a quick glance around. "Not at the moment you don't. So please, if you don't mind, I just need you to translate something for me. Just a couple of lines. Here, look." I took the folded newspaper from my bag and handed it to her.

"Do you know this paper?" I asked as she studied it.

"Yes. I think it's from The Kirix."

"Kirix?"

"It means Herald."

"Oh. Right."

"What is it you want translated? There's an article here about how it should have been a record-breaking year for tourism but isn't and another one's about relief for investors and bail-out funds and this one's about…"

"No," I said. "It's on the other side. One of the ads."

She turned the paper over. "So it's just the usual advertisements. There's one for a dress shop, one for a restaurant on the Seven Sisters Road, and one for handmade jewellery. And then there are announcements about a couple of weddings and about upcoming celebrations for the festival of Agios Georgios on the 23rd at both Thyateira church and All Saints church and…"

I interrupted, "No. That one. See. The one with the tiny cross next to it."

"Oh… yes… *louloudia*… that means flowers.

"Yes, that was the one word I managed to work out."

She continued, "It says that there will be an arrival of *freska louloudia*… fresh flowers… on the 17th."

"Two days from now. Hang on," I said. "Let me write this down."

I took a pen and a notebook from my bag. "Right. What else?"

"*Kouti...* that means box. *Sto To Kouti.* At the box... then it just says *pétalo zária*. Horseshoe dice."

"Horseshoe dice? What does that mean?"

"No idea."

She looked thoughtful as she handed me back the paper and said, "It must be from some company that exports flowers to the UK but..."

"But what?" I leant forward eagerly.

"Nothing I'm just surprised that's all. I thought most flowers here came from Holland not Greece."

"And the Scilly Isles," I said.

"Hmm. Well there you are. So now I've done what you asked and so you'd better..."

"Wait a moment please." I looked down at the notes I made. "You said the box. Is that a place do you think – The Box? Have you ever heard of it?"

"No I haven't." She looked at me keenly. "This is something to do with Chris Lianthos isn't it?"

I paused a moment too long before answering. "Why would you think that?"

She stared at me.

"Alright," I said reluctantly. "But it's probably not what you think. In fact, I'm certain it's not. It's something that I came across in... well let's just say... in suspicious circumstances."

"I think you should go now," Nuala said. "I'm not getting involved in..."

She broke off as a tall chunky man in his thirties with a soft jaw but a strong nose entered the shop carrying a crate of lemons. He called out a greeting in Greek and Nuala came around from the counter and kissed him on the cheek. He put the lemons down and hugged her close before turning to me.

"A new customer I think? I hope you are spending lots of money with us." Then he looked more closely at me. "No, I have seen you before… somewhere. I'm Aleksy, this one's husband." He smiled at his wife and then looked back to me. "Well whether you are new to us or not I hope that you have found plenty you like."

"I have," I said. "Some baklava."

"It's fantastic," he said. "Is this it?" He picked up the waxed paper parcel and handed it to me. I put it in my bag. "We make it with honey from Mt. Erymanthos," he continued. "And we use nuts…"

"Yes Nuala said," I said hastily. "And she's just agreed to talk to me about the… about the… the um origins of the recipe… for… an article I'm writing."

Nuala appeared about to protest but her husband interrupted her.

"That's great," said Aleksy. "Make sure you give the shop a good plug."

He turned to Nuala. "There's no one on the bench outside." He indicated a seat on the green directly in front of the shop that I'd noticed when parking my car. "Why don't you talk out there and I'll bring you out something to drink."

My eyes met Nuala's. Nikko's Barbers was on the opposite side of the green and I didn't want to risk Chris seeing me if he popped in for a quick trim. She must have come to the same conclusion because she said, "We'll go out the back."

She led me through to the rear of the shop where cartons of vegetables and sacks of flour sat upon a rack of spotless shelves. She unlocked a door inset with a square mesh panel and I accompanied her outside. We sat, facing inwards, on a low wall that ran the length of the small parade of shops. Nuala took a swift glance around. A delivery was being made a couple of doors down supervised by an old man smoking a cigarette, who raised a hand and waved to her, but for the rest it was quiet.

"He rarely comes to the shop and so we should be OK," she said.

"Who?"

"Chris."

And then I remembered. Chris's wife Maria had the hairdressers next door. I felt a stirring of curiosity about her and wondered if she might come out to get some fresh air and to escape, albeit briefly, from the heat of the dryers. I said as much to Nuala.

"She doesn't work the shop floor anymore but concentrates on the business side. She has just opened another two salons, one in Camden, and one in Bloomsbury. She is very driven, very focused on her businesses."

"That's impressive," I said.

Aleksy then appeared carrying two tall glasses. "Has she told you how her grandmother... *giagia Ragna*... got the recipe from an old lady who lived..."

Nuala laughed over him. "Yes yes *agapi mou* I have, but you'd better get back to the shop."

He grinned. "You can see who's boss around here." And he then left us.

I look a sip of my drink. It was a sparkling orange soda and it was ice cold.

"I don't like lying to my husband," Nuala said.

"Then, why are you?"

"Because I don't want us to have anything to do with Chris Lianthos and so it's better if Aleksy doesn't know."

I considered for a moment. Whilst the translation of the newspaper ad was helpful, it hadn't in anyway enlightened me. So Chris imported flowers from his homeland? Presumably there was nothing illegal about that. And what, if anything, did that have to do with the women?

"That reference to horseshoe dice," I asked Nuala. "Do you know what it means because it sure as hell means nothing to me?"

"No. I told you I don't know."

I could feel that she was beginning to grow impatient and so pressed on

"And if this is just a run-of-the-mill advertisement then surely there should be details of a website or a phone number or something?"

"Well yes," she agreed. "You'd think there would be. Give me the paper again."

I took it out of my bag and handed it to her.

She scanned it. "It's in with the *deltio*... the bulletins, the announcements about forthcoming events..."

"So not an ad," I said. "More of a post or a statement maybe?"

She shrugged, "Again. I have no idea." Then more seriously she asked, "Look, why do you want to know this? What's this about?"

"Maybe nothing." I took a long sip of the orange soda before asking, "I can only assume that The Box is an actual place, right?"

"That's how it reads," she said.

"If there are no contact details and no address then I'm guessing that it's a location that's known… I mean known to whoever this ad or post is aimed at? And you've definitely never heard of it? It's not some Greek community place here in London or…" I broke off thoughtfully. "Or how about in Luton maybe?"

"No. I've already told you." She was getting irritated now. "Why Luton?"

I didn't want to get into specifics and so I batted the question away. "Oh, it's a place that just came up. I thought that there might be a link."

"A link with Chris Lianthos; that's what you mean isn't it?"

"Maybe," I admitted. I rubbed the back of my neck.

"Who are you?" her eyes bored into mine.

"What do you mean?"

"Are you with the police? Is that why you're asking all these questions?"

"No!" I leant across to her. "Nuala really I'm not."

She didn't look convinced.

"Nuala, you have no reason to trust me but… I'm asking you to. Now here's what we have…"

Although she looked askance at the word *we,* she seemed to accept what I'd said.

I ploughed on. "Basically, it's an announcement that flowers… fresh flowers… will be at some place called The

Box on Friday the 17th. Hold on aren't all flowers fresh? I mean that's the point of them, isn't it? That they're fresh."

"Yes," agreed Nuala. "But there are also dried flowers and artificial ones too and some made out of fabric, like on a dress you might wear going to a wedding."

"I suppose so," I conceded. "But this says specifically fresh. Well…. that seems to be that. Thanks again Nuala." There was no point in pursuing it any longer. I'd reached a dead end.

But she wasn't listening. She was looking at a car pulling up outside the back of the hairdressers. A silver Mercedes.

"That's Maria," Nuala mouthed at me.

A slim, attractive woman in her late thirties with long dark hair got out of the car. She was impeccably dressed. The suit of pale pink she wore was clearly a designer one. She had on beautiful coffee coloured stilettos and carried a bag that was cream and boxy and possibly a Birkin. She wore too much jewellery for my taste, a thick nest of gold chains around her neck and a couple of heavy gold bangles, but there was no denying she looked good. She stopped and said something in Greek to Nuala, flicked a casual glance over me and then disappeared into the rear of her shop.

"They're well matched, physically," I remarked.

"Yes," replied Nuala gravely. "But when is that ever an indication of true compatibility."

I thought of the warmth with which she and her husband interacted and knew she was right. Before we parted I gave her my phone number.

"It's a long shot I know, but if you do think of anything else about the ad then please give me a call."

She said she would but I thought it highly unlikely that I would ever hear from her again.

I was just leaving when I realised that I hadn't paid for the baklava. "Oh, I'm sorry I forgot. I owe you for the…" I started to fish out my purse but she waved my offer away. I think she was just glad to be rid of me.

CHAPTER TWENTY-SIX

Tim phoned again around six. "Fancy getting together?" he asked.

"Well… I was planning a quiet night in."

"We can be quiet," he said.

"*Really?*"

He laughed. "It's you that's a bit of a screamer. I'll be round to yours at about eight. Oh, and I'll bring a takeaway."

You've got to love a puppy.

Just after seven thirty my mobile rang again.

"Don't get anything too spicy," I said "A korma's good or…"

But there was no answer.

"Tim?" I said.

No response. I looked at the screen. It was a private number.

"Look," I spoke loudly and clearly. "Whoever you are… I don't want to buy insurance or double-glazing or anything else at all and *no* I haven't had an accident…"

Not strictly true I thought remembering the Citroen van's dented bumper, not to mention Bomber-jacket's foot.

"Hello?" I said again, "Hello?"

The line went dead.

Tim in fact brought Thai food. We ate from plates balanced on our knees in the sitting room and bickered over whom would have the last stick of chicken satay. I won. And in bed, as is so often the case, the second occasion was even better.

At two in the morning I remembered the baklava and we shared it leaning back against the pillows.

"I don't care which Greek mountain range this honey came from," said Tim. "It's lovely and sticky and if I just smear a little over here and a little..." He ran a hand down his chest. "You can lick it off."

I did.

I woke feeling utterly refreshed and clear headed. After coffee and toast, I shoved a reluctant Tim out of the front door.

"I've got stuff to do," I said.

"I can handle stuff," he said.

"You'd only be a distraction. Now Go!"

He went and I switched on my computer and looked up *The Box*. Several storage companies came up, an IT company in California, a cake shop in Edinburgh, cheap accommodation to rent for university students in Lancashire, and a BBC thriller that I'd missed and that looked rather good. There was nothing in or around Luton. But if this ad had anything to do with the women then Luton would make sense I reasoned. The driver and his track-suited friend couldn't have realised that I was tailing them until we'd

255

come off the M1 and were well within the city's boundaries, so that must have been where they were headed to. But to where in Luton and to do what?

I scrolled through page after page, and then gave up. I looked at my notebook. What was this about horseshoe dice? I typed it in and there were loads of references to dice and plenty about horseshoes but nothing that put them together. The nearest thing I could find, on a gift site for racing enthusiasts, was a pair of cufflinks in the shape of dice with a picture of a horse's head on them.

Alright so what about the flowers? *Flowers*, I muttered aloud. *Flowers*. I looked out the window and then, deciding to give myself a break, wandered out into the garden.

The daffodils were nearly over and so I picked a handful. I looked at the rose bush and down at the white tulips growing up through the daffodils and thought how everyone loves flowers. They're so cheering and somehow symbolic of hope and of love and of innocence and even strength. Symbolic. That thought stopped me in my tracks. *The flower of youth*. The expression just occurred to me. Or *in the flower of my youth* meaning when I was young. And how about *The flower of England* used to describe the young men who died on the battlefields of the First World War?

Scraps of poetry learnt at school came to mind, old poems where maidens were described as fresh flowers and a quote on Facebook I'd come across recently – *A woman is like a rose, if you're lucky you watch her bloom*. So, the word flower didn't have to be interpreted literally, it could also allude to something else. And it was most commonly used to represent something young and female.

A truly repellent idea then suggested itself. I stomped around the garden trying to shake it off, but it wouldn't be denied. Oh God, I thought with a sick feeling in my stomach, wasn't there an old-fashioned phrase about... *her flower* – meaning to lose one's virginity – as in the saying *popping one's cherry*? Fresh flowers. I think now I knew exactly what that meant.

I didn't even stop to put the daffodils in water before looking up the number for the delicatessen.

Nuala picked up on the fourth ring. "Hello Demeter's Deli can I help you?"

"It's me Nuala. It's Clarry."

Her sigh came quite distinctly down the line. "I haven't thought of anything else. There's nothing more I can..."

"But I have," I cut in. "Fresh flowers. I think it means young girls."

"Well it could," she acknowledged. "That's sometimes what we call our young girls, our sisters, and our daughters when they are taking the holy sacrament."

"How about young girls to be... pimped out, sold?"

"What?" I could hear the shock and disbelief in her voice.

"I went to *Knights*," I said.

"To that place? Why?"

"It's... It's too complicated to explain. But whilst I was there I heard a woman crying."

"So?"

"From behind a locked door."

"So?" she said again.

"Look I know this sounds crazy. That *I* sound crazy and maybe I am. But believe me when I tell you that I think there are women at that club, and not just there... I think they are being transported to somewhere else, who may be being held against their will."

"Stop," she cried. "I don't want to hear about it. Why are you telling me this?"

"Because you might have heard something." I knew I was pushing her but this was important. "You might have heard rumours, whispers even, within your community and..."

"I have not!" she exclaimed hotly. "Of course I've not. Do you think we'd allow that sort of thing to... how dare you even suggest that."

"Alright alright," I said placatingly. "I didn't mean to offend you but I just wanted to... oh I don't know what I wanted... I'm sorry. I shouldn't have troubled you."

"No you should not!"

That grated with me. "Have you got daughters Nuala?"

Silence and then she finally answered. "No. I have two sons."

"But if you did have daughters?..." I let the question hang.

Another silence before she said, "If you think what you're saying about these girls is true then you need to go to the police, but I don't want you contacting me again. Do you understand? Stay away from me." And she rang off.

I phoned Flan and filled her in on everything that had happened since I'd seen her, early on Tuesday morning with Mr. H. and Simon Napier. That felt like a very long time ago. She listened and then tut-tutted when I told her about the women being put into the van. She laughed and then tried to pretend that she hadn't, when I got to the bit in the story about running over Bomber-jacket's foot, but was truly horror struck when I told her my theory about the ad.

"I think that your Greek friend Nuala may be right," she said.

"She's not my friend. She's made that abundantly clear."

"Nevertheless she has a very good point. This is a very serious matter Clarry."

"I know it is!"

"Well then darling something needs to be done about it. It's time to share your concerns with professionals."

"You think they'll take me seriously?"

"I don't see why not. Would you like me to accompany you? I'm lunching with Harold but I could easily cancel, even though it is his turn to pay."

I laughed. I didn't think she was seeing as much of Mr. H.'s rival, the skinflint undertaker, these days. "No don't do that. There's no need. Where's he taking you by the way?"

"For a ploughman's," she said glumly.

"Do they even serve those anymore?"

"I suppose I'll find out. But one way or another I fully intend to order a decent bottle of Chablis, have a starter and probably a pudding as well, if I can manage it."

Before I said goodbye, I made a brief mention of Tim.

"How lovely for you darling," she observed. "Such a good idea to take up a hobby for the summer."

Next, I tried Laura at her office but she was out at a client's and so I left her a message on her mobile asking her to call. As a solicitor she'd no doubt be in a position to give me advice, and might even suggest coming with me to the police, although that would probably look like overkill and imply I was guilty of something – which of course I was. I had never, to my knowledge, committed a criminal act until ten days ago. Since then I'd broken into Simon's house and Chris's office and run over a man. Not exactly the career path my mother had hoped for me.

I waited an hour but still Laura didn't come back to me. I felt restless and edgy and nervous about the thought of talking to the police but, on the other hand, I just wanted to get it over with. I was also conscious that today was Thursday the 16th and that the ad referred to the 17th. There was little time to lose.

CHAPTER TWENTY-SEVEN

I'd never been in a police station before, not even to report a lost cat or produce my driving licence and so I had no idea what to expect. From watching TV, I imagined being interviewed by some world-weary seen it all before character with a gritty northern accent and that grey complexion that bears testament to a poor digestion. Instead I talked to a bright faced police constable who looked to be about twelve years old with Surrey vowels and the clear skin that only comes from eating up all your greens and getting plenty of exercise.

I sat with him for a long time, he wrote several things down and he even got me a cup of tea, but we didn't really get anywhere.

"We do take reports from the general public very seriously," he told me for the third time.

"That's good to know," I said. "It's why I've come."

"So, let me see if I've got this right," he said, chewing the end of his pencil.

But he hadn't. He'd muddled the few facts I'd given him, which was probably my fault because I'd made a total shambles of explaining myself. I tried again, this time starting at the beginning of the story and not at the end. This made matters worse.

"My job," he said, "is to identify whether or not what you are reporting warrants further investigation."

"It does," I said. "And there hasn't been any investigation except mine so far."

Another hour went by as we went through it again.

"I will tell you what I'll do," he said, "I think I'd better get the guv'nor to speak to you."

"Good plan," I said.

He came back with a tall woman in her thirties who introduced herself as Inspector Lawson. Dressed in dark trousers and a square cut cream shirt she was strong and fit looking and attractive in a very natural way. She shook my hand and regarded me with that cool penetrating gaze that immediately makes you think you've got a smut on your cheek or a ladder in your tights. I was wearing jeans but I couldn't answer for my face.

I went through my story again but naturally left out the break in to Simon's house. I also didn't mention his attack on me (well I had promised). Inspector Lawson stopped me at various intervals.

"This Gary, the individual with the shaved head, he told you that he was charging rent to the illegal occupants of the property in Alwyn Road?"

"Yes. You can talk to Melanie and Ted if you want to. I've told you about them and I'll give you their number. But please, they don't deserve to get in any trouble. They didn't know that the house wasn't being legally rented out and when they did discover that it was, they left straightaway."

Police Constable Twelve-Years-Old jotted down Melanie's number. "And their surnames?" he asked.

"I don't know what their second names are I'm afraid."

"Alright. And let's talk about the other properties," continued Inspector Lawson. "What are the addresses?"

"I can't remember exactly, I've got them written down at home. There are two houses in New Malden and two in Worcester Park."

I decided to omit mentioning the pool parts place in Surbiton in a desire to shield Dan, Sheena, and Maggie from police notice. What harm were they doing where they were? With Gary no longer bothering them, and I hoped that the efforts made by Inspector Lawson would ensure that, then, they could stay on there, undisturbed. It was one bright thought in what otherwise was proving to be a very bleak scenario.

"As I said you can contact my friend Laura the solicitor and her boss Mr. Garstein. I've given them the details."

"We'll do that." She regarded me for several minutes and I felt so sure that I must have something on my face that I wiped a hasty hand across my forehead.

"This is quite a picture that you have painted for us but I'm not sure that any of the pieces really fit."

"Nor am I," I confessed. "And maybe they don't, but none of it really matters does it; except those women?"

"Taking illegal possession of a property does matter Ms. Pennhaligan. It is a serious offence."

"I know. I know. I agree. Of course, it's wrong but

what are you going to do about..." I could hear my voice beginning to rise and Inspector Lawson held up a hand.

"What is it that makes you so sure that these three women in the van were being held against their will?"

"I've just told you why! And no, I'm not sure. I just... have a feeling."

"A feeling isn't evidence Ms. Pennhaligan."

"Well I know that!" I retorted. "That's your job, isn't it? To find it?"

But I could see that becoming irritated was only alienating her. I tried again. "I'm sorry," I said. "This is all a foreign world to me and I..."

"That's quite alright Ms. Pennhaligan."

I wish she'd stop repeating my name because it was starting to grate on my nerves but she was addressing me again.

"I need to understand fully the situation thus far if I am to take action. Now you say that you followed the van – not something I would recommend by the way as it can be considered stalking – and after a while the occupants realised that they were being followed. You then lost control of your vehicle and ran into the back of them."

"I didn't exactly lose control," I protested. "They pulled up half way around a bend and so it was more of an unavoidable accident."

"And you should have reported that accident to the police," she said. "What happened when they confronted you?"

"I didn't wait to find out."

"You're saying that you left the scene of an accident?"

Thank God I hadn't included running over Bomber-Jacket's foot in my tale or they'd arrest me for causing bodily harm.

"You're missing the point. And I've given you the van's registration number, so surely you can do something with that?" I felt my patience wearing thin but I checked myself. "Please look again at the newspaper advert. Doesn't it look off to you? I've explained my theory, isn't that enough to at least check it out?"

"Your theory, yes," Inspector Lawson said. "That is interesting." There was focus now in her manner and for the first time I felt I'd really got her attention.

"And this Paula, do you have her full name? Because I'd like to talk to her."

"No, I'm sorry I don't. All I know is that she comes from Dudley originally. And that she was going back there. On an early train yesterday morning or so her message said."

"I'd like to hear that message. Do you have your phone with you?"

I nodded, handed her my mobile and she listened.

"She owes you?" she asked.

I explained about her being pregnant and catching her heel in the carpet.

"That was a piece of luck for her," was all she said.

I didn't know what to make of that.

The constable made a note of Paula's number.

"So, does this mean that you are going to investigate? Because the 17th is tomorrow," I reminded them.

Police Constable Twelve-Years-Old cut in here. "It's up to the Inspector to decide whether or not to deploy a…"

Inspector Lawson frowned at him and he closed his mouth with a blush. She then rose briskly to her feet. "I'd like to thank you once more for coming in. We'll be in touch if we need to talk to you again. Constable, show Ms. Pennhaligan out."

CHAPTER TWENTY-EIGHT

I felt lighter. I'd done my bit and had left matters, as Flan had advised, in the hands of the professionals. And I had my life to get back to. A small and somewhat limited one I'd recently come to realise, but still it was mine.

"He called," said Laura in excitement down the phone on Friday morning.

"So you're having lunch?"

"Drinks after work."

"Even better. When?"

"Tonight."

I was pleased for her. James Dunstan seemed a genuinely nice guy. "What are you wearing?" I asked.

What followed was an intensely interesting conversation about the perfect Day-into-Night outfit, which Laura maintained was just an unrealistic fantasy dreamt up by fashion editors. "I've had it on all day but I'm telling you Clarry this pencil skirt is so tight I can barely sit down."

"Well then get yourself something nice and comfy with an elasticated waist."

She didn't dignify the suggestion with a reply, so I went on to tell her about my visit to the police station.

"Oh my God Clarry, that's major."

"Well it wasn't really. Not as much as I'd thought."

"I wish I'd known as I would have gone with you."

"I know you would have, thanks and I could have waited, but I felt it was important to tell them about the ad and my theory about the women and how I…"

"Yes those poor women," she cut me off. "Really dreadful…"

There was a pause in which I could feel that what she really wanted to talk about was her forthcoming date with James again. I understood she was preoccupied with her own affairs and I was in no position to judge her, because until a few days ago I was equally as guilty of self-absorption, maybe even more so.

"I've been thinking," she said. "You know if I hadn't met Simon and hadn't asked you to…" she hesitated and then continued, "check him out. And if you hadn't found out what you did and then if I hadn't…"

I knew where she was going with this and so I was brisk. "Cut to it," I interrupted.

"Well I wouldn't have met James," she said simply.

"Is that so very significant? I mean it's only drinks."

"I know but yes. It is. And it just goes to prove, what I've always believed, that everything happens for a reason."

I had nothing to say to this because privately I couldn't help but doubt the importance of our insignificant petty doings in the whole grand scheme of things. But then what did I know?

At five o'clock when I'd just got home from a lunchtime shift at the restaurant and was changing out of my uniform into a pair of jeans and a T-shirt, my mobile rang from a number I didn't recognise.

"Hello?"

"It's Nuala." This was said in a low voice.

"Wow!" I answered in surprise. "I didn't think I'd be hearing from you."

Silence down the line.

"What is it?" I prompted. "Is there something you want to tell me?"

"You mentioned Luton."

"Yes? What about Luton? Do you mean that you do know *The Box*?"

"No. No I don't. I've already told you that."

"OK... So... So what *are* you saying?"

Silence again.

"Nuala? Are you still there?"

Her words when they came were slow and reluctant. "You really think that there is something going on with young girls?"

"Yes," I said. "And so do the police." Not necessarily true I thought, but I pressed on. "Nuala if you've got something to say would you please just say it."

"Alright. I'll tell you, but I'm confident that it has nothing to do with... anything. It's just that I've remembered something. Something I heard some time ago, a year ago or maybe two."

I was beginning to feel like I'd played enough question and answer games in the last couple of days. "What Nuala? What did you hear? Just spit it out for God's sake."

"I remember hearing that Stavros has a depot in Luton. It's where he stores the donations he's collected for the refugees I think."

269

I couldn't place the name "Who?"

"I told you about him when I first met you. About how he privately organises aid for those poor people that arrive with nothing in Samos, the island where he was born. Stavros. Maria's father. Stavros Zakiat."

I sat down heavily. This could be the link. I knew that Chris Lianthos and Stavros Zakiat as directors of Cornett Developments Ltd had purchased a house through Simon in South Park Road. What other properties did they own? I searched online and found details of one other property in Hackney. So that was no good. Then I searched Stavros Zakiat and eventually came up with references to three addresses. One in Willesden Green, another in Leeds, and another in Dunstable. I brought up Dunstable on a map. Dunstable bordered Luton and it was less than five miles from Luton city centre.

I tried to get hold of Inspector Lawson, but she'd gone for the day and I couldn't remember the name of the police constable and so had to leave a message asking the inspector to telephone me.

I paced about the house but I couldn't settle. I looked in the fridge. It was empty, because I hadn't shopped for days. I turned on the TV but everything I watched seemed bland and insubstantial. This isn't real life, I thought, these characters shouting at each other across a London square or having a punch up in a pub in Weatherfield. Real life was going on around me. Real life was in empty properties where the homeless were bullied into paying what little money they had. Real life was in a seedy club in Waterloo where girls gyrated around poles without the protection of employment laws. Real life was women being put into a van and driven away. Real life was in Luton.

I came off the M1, as I had previously, at junction 10. I didn't have a satnav and so had to follow the signs to Dunstable and then pull over to use my phone to locate the address. It was after nine o'clock as I drove through the back roads and it was dark except for the occasional street light. I kept hoping for a call from Inspector Lawson. I'd left another message for her before I'd left, but I had heard nothing.

Following a long winding stretch of road on the far outskirts of the town and having left the few straggling houses behind, I now found myself enclosed on both sides by fields and stretches of woodland. Keeping to a speed of under 20 miles an hour and with one eye on my phone map, I almost missed the gated unit sitting back from the road. I slowed to a stop and studied the premises.

In the dark, all I could make out was that it was brick built and comprised of a single storey and that the gates were operated on an entry phone system. There was no signage, which struck me as odd. Surely if this was a depot for donations then that would be clearly indicated? The idea of pressing the button for admittance didn't appeal. What could I possibly say if someone answered it? I decided to continue following the road and hope that there was some way of snaking back that would bring me out to the rear of the building.

After about a mile, I spotted a gap in the trees on my left and I slowed right down. Pulling into an unmarked track I was now on a potted and rutted path barely wide enough to accommodate the car. Flailing tree branches slapped the windscreen as I made my way forward and I was alarmed to see that ahead of me the path narrowed even further. Fearful of becoming wedged in, I stopped and then reversed back to the neck of the track.

I looked at my mobile willing Inspector Lawson to phone, but it remained reproachfully silent. I'd come all this way without any kind of plan and with only a sense that I should do, had to do… something. I tucked the Renault as close into the protection of the trees as I could, placed my phone and my keys in my pocket, and got out of the car.

It was very dark. I hadn't thought to bring a torch for the simple reason that I didn't own one and I didn't want to use the one on my phone in case I ran down the battery. Creeping gingerly forward a step at a time, I worried that I might fall or wrench my ankle but gradually my eyes became accustomed to the dark. A dull moon sulked behind clouds and the path had indeed narrowed and could not now really be considered a path at all. I pushed my way on whilst something prickly snagged at my jacket and the dark trees loomed around and about me. The urge to turn back was very strong. I thought about Laura on her date with James. That's what I should be doing, not sneaking around in the dark on my own. Just a fortnight ago even the idea of this would have seemed not just unlikely, but completely absurd.

I'll only give it two more minutes I promised myself, because this is probably a complete waste of time and this sodding track is clearly leading me nowhere. Any second now I might fall in a ditch, catch my foot in a snare or be gored to death by a runaway bull.

A few paces later, my arms, which I had been holding out before me, encountered something solid – a rusty three-bar gate. I pushed at it and it gave. Oh, Christ now I was no doubt trespassing and an irate farmer might appear with a shotgun.

I hesitated. I was standing on the edge of a field. A field that even in the dark I could see was neglected and overgrown. I tried to get my bearings when it occurred to me that the map on my phone might show the way, even though I was off road.

I checked it and it indicated that I should carry on going forward and bear to the left. Walking over a furrowed and weed-ridden field is not easy with only the pale glimmer of moonlight as a guide. I stumbled and almost fell several times but at last I was across. Another three-bar gate and padlocked this time, but it was easy enough to climb over it. I checked my phone. Go forward it instructed me. How was I to do that when confronted by a wall of trees? This is insane I kept repeating to myself as I edged between the tree trunks, but I pushed on and suddenly I'd arrived. My phone told me I'd arrived, but… I was the wrong side of a high wooden fence.

I followed the fence around to the right. It didn't run straight but kinked and dipped in several places and I could see that some of the panels were newer than others and had been spliced in amongst much older ones. After about a hundred metres, I reached an original corner section where the woods pressed in even closer and brambles and ivy snaked up and through the rotting timber. That's when I encountered the holly bush. My groping hands got the worst of the sharp spiky leaves and I was about to turn back, when I noticed that the middle of the panel had deteriorated so much that it had started to shred. I gave it a tentative push with my shoulder and felt it give way a little. I listened intently. All was quiet, so I gave it another good hard shove, and this time the centre section disintegrated. It took me another few minutes and some more shoving, all the while being attacked by the holly bush, for me to make a gap big enough to crawl through.

Immediately I dropped to the ground and from the shelter of my dark overgrown spot, looked about me. As I'd hoped I was at the rear of the premises but off to one side. I was on my hands and knees upon cracked concrete where about fifteen or sixteen cars were parked fifty metres or so away. I watched and waited for a while but nobody was about. Why were there so many cars here at this time of night? I wondered.

Following the line of the fence I inched my way along until I was directly opposite the building, but screened by the parked cars and then I sprinted across to the closest of the vehicles and ducked down behind it. I was breathing hard now, adrenalin ricocheting about my body as I darted to and fro until at last I was crouching behind the nearest one to the building. It was dark and sleek and vaguely familiar. I couldn't be certain but I thought I recognised it from the pub car park in Tooting, The Falcon. But was it? I wasn't interested in cars and so they all looked pretty much the same to me.

I felt uncertain what to do. Should I go back, phone Inspector Lawson again and if I couldn't get hold of her then dial 999? But what had I proved? A car that may or may not be Chris's was parked outside a building in Luton. I was still trying to decide, when I heard a scraping sound and peeping out along the flank of the car, I saw that a door to the building was opening. I flinched back. I heard the sound of muffled voices from within and then the door shut again and footsteps rang out on the concrete. One pair of footsteps. Please don't be Chris reclaiming his car I prayed. Please don't let him find me here... but then whoever it was stopped and I heard the flare of a match.

Tentatively I peered around once more and could see the outline of a man with his back to me. I watched as he lifted his left arm up in a long stretch and pulled on a cigarette with his right. He's too tall to be Chris I thought and then instantly retreated as he turned around. A few moments later I heard the scrunching of his shoe as he ground out his cigarette butt, the scraping of the door opening again and then there was silence.

I let out my breath which I hadn't realised I'd been holding and came to a decision. I would risk a quick scan of the building and then I'd get back to the car as quickly as I could.

Swiftly I ran forward and bore a left, moving away from the door until I reached the corner of the property. Now I was close up I could see that the structure was a low oblong and that within this nearside wall there were three large windows, windows that had been blackened out and reinforced with security grilles. Nevertheless, I kept my head low and scuttled along until I came to the front of the property. Here I hesitated, anxious in case the security lights, sensing movement, would activate and flood the area in a blue-white glare. It felt like jumping off a cliff as I darted across the wide forecourt, but thankfully there were no searchlights and no one standing guard at the front door.

It was a heavy metal door with a small square viewing panel at the top. Something pale on the panel caught my eye. I scanned the area. No one was about and so keeping my head down I peered up at the panel. A small white card had been tucked under the metal beading and on the card, was a picture of a dice, upon which, instead of the usual spots to indicate numbers, was the image of a horseshoe.

I snatched it up and then hugging the wall and keeping to the shadows, I raced around to the other side of the building. Here was a direct link to the advertisement. Now all I had to do was work my way around to the rear of the premises and get safely back across the car park to the hole I'd made in the fence. But suddenly that felt like a near impossible feat. I was physically and mentally drained and feeling queasy with anxiety. Right come on, I told myself. You can do this. You must do this. There is no other choice.

I expected that this side of the property would be a mirror image of the opposite side and would therefore have its corresponding three windows, but it was unrelieved brickwork until I had nearly reached the end. Close to the corner was a much smaller window, again blackened out but probably not considered large enough to require a grille. And it was open a crack at the bottom. Stooping directly beneath it I listened. At first I could hear nothing, but then pressing in closer I detected a faint whispering. A conversation was being carried out in a foreign language and the voices were female.

Just keep going I said to myself, head as quickly as you can straight back to the car, but I rarely take my own advice. The window was just above shoulder level and so cautiously I rose to a near standing position and craned my neck to peer in.

It appeared to be a small room, not much larger than a cloakroom. All I could see of the furniture was the legs of one chair, but there were two pairs of feet visible. Two pairs of bare, dusty feet that were quite clearly female. The women were still whispering in quiet undertones, which halted instantly when I hissed.

"Hello… hello… we may only have a minute, but I'm going to try and help you."

Silence.

I tried again. "Are you alright? I'm going to do my best to get you out of here."

Then a small, frightened voice said, "Who are you?" Her accent was strong and difficult to understand.

"My name is Clarry," I said. "But there's no time for that now. I…"

A face appeared and then another. I was looking at two girls somewhere in their late teens, both with long thick black hair, pale caramel skin, and terrified dark eyes.

I felt like crying. I could feel the tears forming as I whispered, "It's alright. It's going to be all right," I smiled as reassuringly as I could. "Are there any more of you? Or is it just you two?"

One of the girls spoke. She had a faded bruise upon her forehead and I took her to be the slightly older of the two. "Rima was with us, but she has been taken by the men into another room. We don't know what is happening to her. We fear for her… and for ourselves."

I looked again at the window. Was it big enough to allow them to squeeze through?

"Does this open up any further?" I asked.

"I don't understand," the girl said.

"The window," I hissed. "Can you open it a bit more? Enough to crawl through?"

They both looked blankly at me for a second and then together pushed up hard on the frame but it didn't budge. They tried again and I heaved on it as well, but still it didn't move.

"It must have some sort of locking mechanism," I said. "But don't worry, you'll soon be safe."

The sound of a door being opened brought them both swinging back around to face the room and instantly I dropped to a crouch.

"What are you doing over there?" demanded an angry voice. It was male and had a London accent. "Get over here. It's nearly your turn."

I didn't wait to hear anymore, but melted into the shadows pressing back against the wall. *Their turn.* I didn't want to think about what that meant, but I couldn't stop terrifying and grotesque images from forming in my mind. I didn't have time to reach the car to telephone the police and maybe did not even enough time to reach the gap in the fence. I had to do it now.

Creeping away from the window I stopped at the corner where I had a good view of the rear of the building and took my phone out from my pocket. I pressed redial and got straight through to Wimbledon Police. With my hand cupped around my mouth and in the softest of voices, I asked for Inspector Lawson. Again, I was told that she wasn't available.

"Tell her it's urgent," I whispered. "Tell her it's Clarry Pennhaligan and that I'm at this address." I rattled off the location. "Tell her to please send help immediately. There are women in desperate need of..."

"Slow down madam," came the reply. "I'm having trouble following you. Can you repeat that address please?"

I gave it to her again my hands shaking.

"Luton, you said? That's not our jurisdiction I'm afraid. You need to contact..."

Why the fuck hadn't I just dialled 999? I was wasting desperately needed minutes here. "Just send someone!" I repeated urgently and cut the connection.

I had only just pressed the number 9 button twice when suddenly I became aware of a slight noise from behind me. Whirling around, I saw the silhouette of a male figure making his way steadily in my direction. I froze. I was in shadow but had he spotted me? Had he heard me on the phone? I thought he was too far away to pick up the sound but if he had heard then he'd know that the police would be coming. And that would give him and whoever was with him possibly enough time to clear out and get away taking the girls with them. And I couldn't even be sure that the police would attend. The operator had said that Luton was out of their area.

I pressed the number 9 button for a third and final time, heard it pick up and then I dropped my mobile into some bushes beside me. At least this gave the girls a chance. The police could pick up its signal and respond to the correct location. Or I desperately hoped so. And then I ran.

CHAPTER TWENTY-NINE

I didn't get very far. The man behind me must have seen my movement and instantly gave chase, but he was slow and lumbering and I might just have been able to outrun him and clear the gap in the fence if it hadn't been for a second man who appeared from out of the rear door.

"Get him," yelled my pursuer and the second man came charging after me.

And he was fast. He grabbed my shoulder spinning me around and took me by both arms. I struggled against him but it was no good for although wiry, he was strong and the grip he held me in was fierce. He was in his thirties and wearing jeans and a black sweatshirt with a hood and had narrow eyes set in a thin white face. The first man, fat and sweating in a dark suit, came panting up and then laughed when he caught sight of me.

"It's a girl. Well we can always do with another one of those around here."

I kicked out at that, aiming a blow to his crotch but I missed. Casually he slapped me hard across the face. I fell back against the wiry man and then, dizzy with shock and with pain, felt myself being dragged towards the rear door.

I was pulled through into a corridor which I just had time to note was lined with boxes of wine and spirits, before the fat man unlocked and pushed open a door and I was flung through it.

"I reckon the boss will have plans for you sweetheart," he leered. "Try not to miss me too much when I'm gone." With that, he slammed the door behind him.

I was in the small room that I'd peered into from beyond the other side of the locked window. The two girls were still there, their eyes now wide with surprise. They came towards me and the girl with the bruise took my hand.

"How did you?… What happened?" she whispered. "You said you were going to help us."

I closed my eyes as my mind swirled in panic. The other girl said something in her own language and shook me by the arm.

"I'm alright," I said opening my eyes. "And I'm sorry. I tried to… but they caught me and I…"

I gave it up. There was no point in explaining. I was here in this room with them and we were prisoners together. And together we had to try and break out but to do that I had to get them to trust me.

"I'm Clarry," I told them again. "What are your names?"

The girl with the bruise answered, "I'm Uri and this is my sister Aischa, but she speaks hardly any English."

"Where are you from?" I asked.

"We are Syrian. We came on a boat. Many died. Many were lost."

"Your parents?"

"They were killed in the bombing. Our brother too."

"I'm so sorry." Inadequate words I knew but what else was there to be said?

They were both thin and were wearing ill-assorted garments. Uri had on a dark pink sleeveless dress with a boat neckline and a full skirt cut just above the knee and which looked to be two sizes too big for her. Aischa was in a short denim skirt with a raggedy hem and a nylon green top with shoestring straps.

"These are not our clothes," said Uri. "They made us wear these."

"How many are there?" I asked. "Men I mean."

"Those two that brought you in and I have seen two others. An old man with a beard and a younger one but... I think there are more... out there."

"Out *there*? What do you mean?"

"I heard voices and some men laughing when they took Rima, our friend. And we smelt cigarette smoke."

She translated for her sister who stood very close beside her and nodded. Their vulnerability was desperately apparent, not just in the immediate horror of their situation but in their history. I felt such a flash of rage and a desire to lash out at those unknown men behind the door that my jaw locked and my fists clenched.

I took a long breath out and then examined the window. I'd been right. There were locking bolts on either side of the frame that allowed it to open only a couple of inches. I tried the door but it was shut fast. I considered it. An internal door like the type you might find in an office, it didn't look particularly sturdy. With our concerted efforts, we might be able to kick our way through but not without making one hell of a noise. Suddenly it opened and the fat man entered. He'd taken off his jacket and loops of sweat ringed his shirt beneath the arms.

Uri and Aischa shrank back but it was me he focused upon.

"Come take a look," he called behind him and a man in his late sixties with pepper and salt hair and a close-cropped beard then stepped into the room.

"Search her." His accent was Mediterranean. Was this Maria's father, Stavros Zakiat? I wondered, as the fat man grabbed me. He stripped off my jacket and went through the pockets finding only my car keys. Then he patted me down thoroughly, lingering over my breasts and between my legs. Revulsion surged through me at his touch but I tried not to flinch. From my jeans pocket, he pulled out the small card with the horseshoe dice upon it. He handed it to the older man who looked at it and then regarded me.

"What is your name?"

I didn't answer. He flicked a glance at the fat man who then took hold of my hair pulling it back painfully.

"What is your name?" the older man repeated.

"Clarry. And tell this clown to let me go. He's hurting me."

He looked surprised and then gave a short mirthless laugh "Yes Perry can be a little rough. But then he is a barbarian and so he knows no better."

Perry the fat man didn't like that. I could hear it by the short intake of breath he took and the way his grip tightened on my hair.

"Me? I am a citizen of the world. I know and do much that a man like Perry could only dream of. Now… what am I to do with you?"

"Show me how civilised you are, how much more evolved you are than Perry here and let me go?" I suggested although of course I knew it was useless. "And the girls too."

Uri and Aischa were cowering together, their arms wrapped about each other.

"Nice try but that's not very likely, is it?" he answered, his glance dismissing me. Perry grunted at that but I didn't respond.

"Well Clarry," the older man continued. "You appear to have involved yourself in things that you would have been much wiser to stay away from. We did not invite you here, but now that you *are* here then…Well it is time that you joined the party. Take her through."

It was a command and Perry instantly responded. "Yes Mr. Z."

Mr. Z. This had to be Stavros Zakiat.

CHAPTER THIRTY

As I was pushed into a wide square room the first thing I noticed was the rich aroma of cigar smoke, and the next, the sound of male laughter. A smartly dressed man with fading blonde hair, a smooth complexion, and a slight paunch visible despite his well-cut suit was standing at a lectern directly under a bright beam of light. He was addressing a room full of men and had obviously just cracked a joke.

His audience, sitting around dimly lit tables in groups of twos and threes with glasses and bottles in front of them, were looking from him to the slight, almond-skinned girl on his left who, in a white blouse and short red skirt, was standing upon a low stool. The man was holding a small wooden hammer and he now banged this down on the lectern.

"I think you will all agree gentleman that we have just witnessed a very good deal here this evening. Fifteen thousand for this lovely piece. She may be small, she may be a touch skinny but feed her up and treat her right and…"

Laughter broke out at this.

"And our friend over here…" he winked at a florid man with a double chin and a glistening bald head sitting at a table near the front, "…will have got a very good bargain indeed. Congratulations sir. Come up and claim your property."

The bald man rose and took the girl by the arm so forcibly that she almost fell from the stool. He led her to his table and pulled her down hard on to his lap.

"Now," continued the man at the lectern. "Let's take a look at our next bid." He looked at me. "Come on my dear, don't be shy, and stand up here by me so they can all get a good look at you."

"NO!" My voice thick with fury thundered through the room. "NO, I WILL NOT."

The effect of shock and then disbelief had left me slow to understand what was going on. But now I got it. It wasn't a hammer that the man at the lectern was holding, it was a gavel. This was an auction. The girl in the red skirt, Rima, had just been sold to the man with the bald head and I was to be the next item on the agenda.

Perry who had my arms pined behind my back now thrust me forward. I flailed and kicked out at him but he held me fast.

"GET OFF ME," I screamed.

"Looks like she's got some spirit," said the auctioneer. "We like a bit of that don't we gentleman? And she's a blonde. The only blonde we have for you tonight I believe. And we all know that blondes like to have fun."

He frowned at me. "Up you get now."

I looked at him full in the face then. He appeared so ordinary, jolly even, like someone's dad. He could easily have been the father of one of my friends making a speech at a wedding or at an anniversary party.

He ran his eyes over me. "But what we don't like is not being able to see the merchandise, so let's get that T-shirt off you, shall we? It seems a shame to have you so covered up."

"Get the hell off me," I yelled as Perry released me and started pawing at my body. He managed to get my T-shirt over one arm and up and over my head. With my other arm stuck and my mouth covered by the material I thrashed about wildly but he was too strong for me. Seconds later the T-shirt was off and I was being hoisted awkwardly aloft on to the stool. This could not be happening. The sense of unreality I was experiencing was so strong that I swayed on my feet and felt myself start to zone out.

"Now who wants to kick off the bid?" asked the auctioneer blandly. "Do I hear ten thousand? Ten thousand? Ten thousand. Yes you sir?"

He nodded at a man in his sixties sitting alone at a table near the door. In a navy suit and tie, he had a face that otherwise would have been utterly nondescript if it hadn't been for the little beads of perspiration that ran across his forehead and the look of intense excitement in his pale unblinking eyes.

"Fifteen thousand," called the auctioneer. Do we have fifteen thousand? Yes, yes we do. We have fifteen thousand." He acknowledged a bid from an Asian man with a bottle of whisky in front of him. "Twenty thousand, twenty thousand. Do I hear twenty thousand?" he looked back to the first man who raised his index finger.

"Yes, I have twenty thousand," called the auctioneer. "Oh and now we have twenty-five thousand." An arm was raised by someone I couldn't see at the back of the room. "Looks like your blood is well and truly up tonight, gentlemen."

Perry still stood behind me holding me by the legs as feebly I tried to cover my chest with my arms and the auction went on around me. My mind was in free-fall. I was standing here exposed in my bra, being sold off like a farm animal or a piece of furniture and there was absolutely nothing I could do to stop it. My brain snagged on that thought and held. I might not be able to stop what was happening but I was fucked if I was going to go passively.

The rage that had been searing through me from the moment that I had seen the girls through the window now completely engulfed me. I felt in a state of heightened consciousness. Everything was real now. I was no longer paralysed by shock, I was no longer hypnotised by terror. I was back in the room. An auction room.

"Stop this you sick bastards," I screamed. "You can't do this. I won't let you. I am not for sale."

I fought desperately to get down from the stool as the auctioneer said with a laugh, "You're going to have fun with this one. She just needs a bit of handling. But let's keep that pretty mouth of yours shut, shall we?" he turned to me. "Or we will have to close it for you."

And that's when the lights went out.

The first thing that happened was that Perry let go of me. The stool wobbled, but I managed to steady myself and step down. It was almost pitch black except for the glimmer of cigar butts. The men in the room, initially stunned into silence, were all now shouting and there was the scrapping of chairs being pulled back and the sound of glass breaking as they rose and started to fight their way to the door.

"Now gentlemen let's try and remain calm." The auctioneer who was standing somewhere off to the right of me, tried to take charge of the situation. "There is nothing to alarm you. It's probably just a power failure. I'm sure we will…"

No one took any notice of him. I was violently pushed aside as someone thundered past me and then another. Like stampeding cattle, the men cannoned into one another. Tables and chairs overturned, there was more shattering of glass when suddenly the lights came back on and the door came crashing open.

"POLICE," called a voice through a loudhailer. "Don't anybody move." "POLICE," the voice repeated and half a dozen armed officers burst in.

Within minutes the room was cleared. A black officer put a supportive arm around me and without speaking I pointed to my T-shirt lying on the floor. It had been trampled upon. He picked it up and gently handed it to me. I shrugged it on and smiled my thanks to him and I thought, in that moment, that he might have the kindest eyes that I had ever seen.

Uri, Aischa, and Rima, reunited in the corridor, stood sobbing in each other's arms whilst being comforted by a female officer.

The auctioneer protesting loudly that he was a professional and that he knew his rights was frogmarched past me. As was Perry, the rings of sweat beneath his arms a tide mark now. I watched as the man in the black hooded sweatshirt, his eyes narrowed to slits, put up a futile fight but was overpowered by two of the officers. Two against one, I thought. Just as he and Perry had overpowered me.

And then finally there was the man I took to be Stavros Zakiat. He put up no opposition at all. I didn't hear him say a single word as he calmly and without hurry submitted to instruction but as he passed me our eyes met. The effect was chilling.

And the customers? They were all led out in handcuffs and I, standing by the front door, made sure to look into each and every one of their faces. With the exception of the Asian man, they were all white and middle-aged. And, just like the auctioneer, I noted how very ordinary they looked. You could pass them in the street or work alongside them in an office and would never know what monsters they truly were. They walk amongst us I thought. They are our fathers, our brothers, and our husbands.

It was then that I started to cry.

CHAPTER THIRTY-ONE

An officer was sent to find my phone. I was taken in a squad car to the local police station where I was questioned gently but insistently for two hours. Then I was driven back to London and deposited home.

When I awoke at nearly eleven o'clock and looked out of my bedroom window it was to see life going on as usual. Out there it was just a regular Saturday morning. I remembered what I had told myself the morning after Simon's attack on me, just a mere four days before. How having witnessed violence first hand, I had decided not to let it alter my perspective and my trust in the concept that most people are intrinsically decent.

Now my outlook had altered. I suspected that there would have been something very wrong with me if it hadn't. And I knew then that I had a decision to make. I could let what had happened shadow me for years to come, I could lie on couches and pour it all out to professionals, or I could confront it myself, out loud. I could listen to my own voice; hear my own words as I described the impotence, the fear, and the fury that I had experienced.

And so that's what I did. I purged and in that outpouring, I found my centre again, which was just as well because that afternoon Inspector Lawson had a lot of questions for me. I went over what I had told the officers last night and she listened avidly. She tried to disguise it but I think she regretted that she had not been part of the take down. To have played a central role in the operation would, no doubt, to her, have been both exciting and rewarding. Try being slap bang in the middle of it, I thought. Exciting it was not.

It was whilst we were going through my statement for a second time that I remembered something. "Ah, it couldn't have been his car after all," I exclaimed.

"Whose?"

"I thought one of the cars I had seen; one of the ones I hid behind in fact, had belonged to Chris Lianthos, but it couldn't have been because he wasn't there."

She looked down at her case notes. "No. He's not on the list of arrestees. We will be talking to him though. How sure were you Ms. Pennhaligan that it was his car? Do you know the make and the model?"

"No I don't. And please would you mind calling me Clarry?"

"OK, Clarry then. But it is a good point you have made. I will check if all cars at the scene correspond with the individuals in our custody. I doubt if my colleagues in Luton will have neglected to do so but it is possible."

As I got up to leave, she added, "Good work on deciphering the advertisement and for tracking the perpetrators down. I would not, however, recommend that you persist in your investigative pursuits. It's not a job for amateurs."

I bristled a bit, at that. Without me, Uri, Aischa, and Rima might have been condemned to a life of sexual and domestic servitude, never to have been seen again. But then so might I.

"Oh, there's no need to worry about that," I replied. "I have no intention of ever playing detective again."

Later in the afternoon, the Renault appeared outside my house and the keys were dropped in though the letterbox. I didn't have any plans. I didn't want to make any plans. My part in the investigations of Stavros Zakiat and Chris Lianthos was at an end and so why did I feel so in limbo? As if I was stuck and unable to take up my ordinary life again? I felt listless and lacking in energy and oddly irritable.

I knew I should phone Flan, but put it off. And Laura, I should speak to her, but I wasn't in the mood to hear all the details of her budding romance when what I'd just experienced was still so raw. I had a good feeling about her and James Dunstan, but did register a pang of regret for the way our friendship would inevitably alter. She would be part of a couple with a man with two children and it would be natural for the demands on her time to increase. I didn't think she could ever become one of those women that she and I rather disliked, the Smuggy Mummies we called them, but you never knew.

And with this thought I wondered if she had been partially right when, in the heat of our row, she had accused me of not wanting her to be in a relationship. Was it true? I knew it wasn't jealousy, but perhaps I was reluctant for things to change. She was my best friend and she was single.

I could always call her and she'd mostly be available or could share whatever plans she had with me. It was selfish of me to mind if this would no longer be the case. I'd just have to live with it and be happy for her. I gave myself a little shake and then brightened at the notion that now all my investigations into *her* love life were over I could concentrate on my own once more. But that would be for another day, when I felt up to it.

Later, still wandering disconsolately about the house it came to me that there was something I wanted to do. A gesture that might help me make sense of the world again because that, I saw now, was what was troubling me. I needed to understand how to balance the small highs and lows and petty cares of my own life with the pain, loss, and despair that so much of the world experiences and not feel forever guilty at my good fortune.

I drove to the nearest supermarket where I picked up two bumper size boxes of teabags, some sugar and milk, a few packets of biscuits, and three bottles of wine, then, I headed to Surbiton.

Again, I parked outside the newsagents and I spotted the same Asian men behind the counter. On my previous visit their shop had been the only one open, but now at nearly six o'clock some of its neighbours were still doing business. At the auto repair shop, giant spanners, jacks, and strangely shaped pieces of rusting metal spilled out on the forecourt. A man in dirty overalls and thick crepe soled boots sitting in a weathered disembodied car seat nursed a mug of something hot. He looked too old to be working still. Maybe he preferred being amongst all this junk to going home I wondered, and then shook the thought away.

In the window of the laundrette sat a solitary Somalian woman in a headscarf gazing vacantly out at the street. I could smell soap powder and steam in the blast of heat that gusted through the open door. The bookies wasn't doing a roaring trade either. In the doorway a stick-thin man in an anorak, sweatpants, and trainers stared down at his betting slip. Was he weighing up the odds of his luck turning? He must have decided to take another chance because, jingling the small change in the pocket of his sweatpants, he turned and made his way back into the shop. I hoped he'd back a winner. He looked like he needed it.

This is seriously depressing I thought, as I got out of the car. I looked around hoping to spot a happy family group or a pair of lovers walking hand in hand, but there was no one else about. Right get a grip Clarry I told myself. Do what you came here to do then go home, pour yourself an enormous glass of wine, switch on the TV, and lose yourself in some soppy film. That should do it.

Since I'd last been here somebody with obviously nothing better to do, had defaced the company insignia. It now read Purbright Pool Farts. Toting three bulging carrier bags, I skirted the entrance and picked my way carefully through the brambles until I was at the back of the building. All seemed very quiet. Putting down the bags I knocked once on the glazed panel of the door and waited. Nothing. I knocked again more loudly, still nothing. I hesitated, reluctant to leave without depositing the supplies I'd bought. I looked around for somewhere to stash them, somewhere that Dan, Sheena or Maggie would be sure to find them.

The scrubby ground to the rear of the unit ran back about fifty yards to a high wall. Overgrown and neglected for what must have been years, I didn't fancy negotiating my way through it. Should I just leave them on the doorstep? It would have to do.

As I stooped to group the bags more neatly together my arm grazed the door which shifted a little. I stood upright and gave it a tentative push. It swung open and without making a conscious decision, I scooped up the bags and walked into the large open-plan room where one week before I had accepted the hospitality of strangers who had almost nothing.

"Hello," I called tentatively, my voice sounding small and a little squeaky in the quiet. "Dan? Sheena?"

Very little light found its way through chinks around the boarded-up windows. Dust motes stirred and settled in the gloom as the echo of my voice petered out. I placed the shopping on the bank of office desks but realised almost straight away that Dan & Co would not need the tea and biscuits, or the wine. They'd gone. The builders' palettes were bare of blankets and the piles of clothes had gone. Oh well, I've left it too late I thought. They've cleared out.

Then I spotted the gas heater and tin kettle in the corner. Probably too bulky to take with them I supposed. I was about to leave when I saw that I'd been wrong about the clothes. In the corner, the chair with the casters was overturned and on the back of it was a long, stripy jumper. The jumper Sheena had been wearing, I was sure of it.

I looked about me. I had only received a dim impression of the place the last time. The desks suggested that this had been where the pool parts company's administration had been carried out and I could see now that there were a couple of official looking documents in clear glass clip frames on the wall. Legal requirements detailing health and safety regulations for signage showing changes in water depth from shallow to deep and for the chemicals used in the various water treatment processes, they didn't make for interesting reading.

I stooped down to pick something off the floor. A blue cardigan. I put it down again. And what was that behind the glazed panel door? A pair of women's shoes, a bit worn but still wearable. That was odd. Why would they leave anything at all behind? Maybe they'd left in a hurry.

My trainers making no sound on the concrete, I crossed to a door at the opposite side of the room from the open rear door and found myself in a narrow corridor. At one end was the front door of the unit, boarded up from the outside and with an empty metal post cage fixed below the letterbox. A door to the left of it revealed a loo, which looked clean and still had two rolls of loo paper. A full cake of soap was in the sink, and above it on a shelf was a can of deodorant and a bottle of shampoo. Again, it was odd. Why leave them when they had so little money? Remembering what Sheena had said about some of the places she had stayed in not having water, I turned on the tap and allowed a trickle of cold water to run through my fingers.

I walked to the far end of the corridor where a pair of doors stood slightly ajar and opening them, walked through into what once presumably had been the storage area. A larger space than the office it had a metal shuttered loading bay taking up one wall which, if I'd got my bearings correctly, I thought would lead out to the rear right-hand side of the building where deliveries would be dispatched. And there was a distinct odour in here. Not a chemical smell, but something rotten and sweet. Maybe a dead mouse or a rat I thought.

Above the shutter was a long oblong window which, probably because it was too narrow for anyone to climb through, hadn't been boarded up. Its blurry spider webbed panes allowed in a sliver of light but it was too weak to permeate fully into the shadowy recesses of the room. The other three walls were set with long deep shelves still bearing labels marked Filters, Pumps, Vacuum Release Systems, and Cast Iron Suction Traps. A few miscellaneous shapes lurked at the back of them. Abandoned parts for pools that no one would swim in.

The air felt damp and the sweet fetid odour strong and pungent. The silence was muffling and complete. I could well understand why Dan and the others had opted to use the office area as their living space. Not just because of the smell, but the fact that there was something spooky and unsettling about this ghost of a failed business. It must once have represented someone's dream or even if not their dream, then at least the focus of their energy and hard work.

Standing there in the soulless concrete block in which Dan, Maggie, and Sheena had made their home; I brooded on how difficult it must be to be anchorless. And I wasn't unaware of the irony of my own situation as I thought this. I owned a house that I had not earned, that I had not worked for. I was incredibly lucky, unlike Dan, Maggie, and Sheena. Where had they gone I wondered? Would they stick together? I hoped so.

I found it hard to imagine what life was like for them. To have no place of shelter, retreat or of comfort. And Maggie was much older than the other two. How was it for her? Did it become easier the more you got used to it or harder as each year went by and the sense of your own vulnerability increasing steadily with age was like a shadow looming closer and closer until it blotted out all hope that things could ever get better?

I shivered. It was chilly in here and I had a sudden longing to be home, away from this dismal place with its associations of broken lives and encroaching despair and away from this bloody awful smell.

I was just turning back towards the door when from somewhere behind me I heard a sound that didn't quite belong. The scrape of something metal on concrete. I stiffened, conscious suddenly that I had no business being here. And with that thought I felt an immediate sense of how exposed I was. How very alone.

I held my breath and listened. Was that footsteps? Yes. I heard them quite distinctly now coming from the office. Dan and the others? I was about to call out but something made me hesitate. What if it wasn't them? Who was out there in the semi-darkness of the office? I swallowed, forcing myself to calm down. There was no need to panic I told myself. It's just my nerves, jarred by last night's experience. My imagination was working overtime that was all. I was getting myself in a panic over what was probably someone with a totally justifiable reason for being here... only right now I couldn't think of one.

It was then that I heard voices, men's voices and they were coming nearer. Two men talking, one of them in a hard, grating tone and the other's low and with an accent. I could hear their conversation quite plainly now.

"What the fuck? These weren't here before."

It was Gary. "There are teabags and milk and stuff in 'em."

I heard again the ring of metal on concrete, but I didn't stop to listen any more. My brain raced through the possibilities. If I ran for the passage was there an exit other than the boarded-up front door? Did the loo have a window? I didn't know. I just hadn't noticed. I glanced across at the giant metal shutter. How did it open? Surely there had to be some mechanical device or some mechanism that operated it.

As quietly as I could, every step a conscious effort at control, I stole across the greasy concrete and in the dim light from the glazed panel above I peered along the entire length of the shutter's base. I couldn't see anything remotely resembling a handle or a lever. Breathlessly I scanned both sides of the wall and at last spotted a switch on the left-hand side at shoulder level. It took me just a second to decide. It would make an appalling noise but what choice did I have? I flicked up the switch. Nothing. I flicked it the other way. Still nothing happened. What was wrong with it? Why didn't the fucking thing open? I flicked it on, off, on again before realising that this kind of automatic locking system operated not mechanically, but electronically. And there was no power.

I cursed myself for not remembering that. I circled the space looking for a hiding place. An upturned palette was propped up in the corner of the right-hand wall. Perhaps they wouldn't see me if I crouched behind it? I approached. The smell was far stronger here, but this was not the time to be squeamish about a dead rat. I was about to pull the pallet away from the wall when my shoe stuck something. I looked down and bit back a scream. There was a foot. A foot in a black ankle boot.

Fighting down nausea, I eased the pallet towards me to see the body of a woman doubled up on the floor. Her face was not visible because she had been folded in two, so that her hands grazed her ankles, but I recognised her hair. Even in the dim light, the magenta streaks in her dark hair glowed faintly. It was Paula. I flinched violently back as waves of heat swept over my body. And then instantly I felt ice cold. Cold and very sick.

The men's voices were louder now and again that squeak of metal on concrete. Desperately I looked about me. The shelves. If I could only haul myself up I might, in the poor light, go unnoticed. Within seconds I was across the room and facing the recess furthest away from the shutter, which would be partly screened from view behind the doors if they were opened fully. I made a scrambling jump for it, swinging my arms high and then gripping down hard with my hands onto the gritty surface of the ledge. For a terrible moment

I swung there uselessly, not sure if I would have enough strength to draw myself up. My shoulders heaved with the effort needed to support my weight. Breathing heavily with one mighty push, I propelled myself aloft kicking up with my legs until at last I managed to get a purchase on the shelf with one foot. Thrusting myself forward, my body fishtailing, I slithered into the dark cavity an inch at a time, my neck muscles in spasm with the burrowing movement. But I had to keep on. Dust filled my nose and throat and I fought desperately to control a sneeze. My eyes blinked trying to accustom themselves to the darkness, which was so thick I felt I could taste it. Another inch and then another. I was nearly there. In a few more seconds I would be safely hidden away. But abruptly my progress was checked. Something at my waist was impeding my crawl.

Clutching with one hand, I fumbled and fought to free whatever it was. It was my handbag. I'd looped it over my shoulder and across my chest where it now had me jammed like a rat in a drainpipe. My other hand flailed impotently across the dirt and I felt a nail tear cruelly against something that stuck up razor-like and sharp. I bit my lip to stop the tears that were now forming. Over the thudding of my heart, I could hear that the men were almost at the door.

There was no time to think. I yanked hard on the shoulder strap of my bag, it gave, and I pressed forwards. The space was too narrow to accommodate my length and too low to allow me to sit upright and so I twisted painfully onto my side facing outwards. The men entered the room and I closed my eyes tight, working on some desperate hope, like a child afraid of bogeymen in the dark, that if I couldn't see them they wouldn't be able to see me.

"Nah, there's no one here," said Gary. "Right let's move it over there and get her out of here. Fuck she stinks."

I opened my eyes. They had their backs to me. The second man was pushing something before him, but I couldn't make out what it was. I watched as he pulled back the pallet and grabbed Paula by the ankles. Her body which had collapsed down on itself, shifted with the movement and for a terrible moment as Gary stooped and lifted her by the arms I caught sight of her face. It was discoloured and bloated and I knew that I would never forget the sight of it. As the two men swung her up and into whatever it was they were pushing, I was reminded of those flickering black and white images on film, of the guards at Auschwitz heaping bodies in grotesque piles as if they were dolls or the carcasses of animals, not human beings at all.

I could see now that she had been dumped into a wheelbarrow and watched as they manhandled and forced her limbs to fit within its narrow confines. Gary then tucked a tarpaulin over her and they trundled the wheelbarrow away and out through the door, with its contents suggesting merely an innocent load of bricks or tools. But there was nothing innocent about its load. The wheelbarrow carried away the lifeless body of Paula and her unborn child.

CHAPTER THIRTY-TWO

I heard them leave. First there was the metallic ring on concrete as they pushed the barrow through the corridor and across the open-plan room and then, more faintly, the sounds of banging from beyond the office door. Then silence.

I don't know how long I lay there wedged within the shelf until the stiffness in my back and in my neck brought me down from my hiding space at last. As I dropped clumsily to the floor, a shot of pain shrieked up each calf and this shocked me back into focus. I groped in my bag for my phone. No signal. I stumbled out into the main room. No signal. I walked unsteadily across to the door and pulled on the handle. It opened an inch or two, but no more, its passage impeded by a heavy chain and padlock. I was effectively locked in.

I righted the chair with the casters and sat down hugging Sheena's long striped jersey about me. I was filthy. Blood dripped from the nail quick on the index finger of my right hand where I'd ripped it. I sucked it away tasting salt and dirt. How long ago was it since I'd last had a tetanus shot I wondered? I'd get septicaemia and have to have my finger amputated. And it wouldn't stop there. Blood poisoning would turn to gangrene and my entire hand would have to come off.

I wasn't sure what the symptoms of shock were but I thought I might be experiencing them. I felt sweaty and slightly sick. But I wasn't disorientated. I knew the name of the prime minster and I knew exactly where I was. That was something. It was the small matter of getting *out* of where I was that appeared to be the problem.

I tried my phone again. Nothing. Then I got up and went and inspected the corridor. The loo was useless, no window. The only exit was the boarded up front door. This was a different matter from the internal office style door at The Box. This was a heavy door but, like its counterpart at the rear of the building, it was glazed on its upper half. I raised my right leg, which felt leaden and aimed a kick at the glass. It shook but didn't break. I tried again and then again and this time it cracked. I needed something to bash it with.

There was nothing in the corridor. I thought of the pallet in the yard but was loath to touch it and had an idea that it might be needed by the police. I went back into the office space. The gas heater was too cumbersome as was the chair with the casters. I picked up the tin kettle. It was light, but it was something. I went back for Sheena's jumper and wound it around my face and wrapped one of its sleeves about my hand. Then I hit the glass with the kettle as hard as I could. It splintered, small shards flying everywhere. I put down the kettle and with both arms now protected by the jumper, I painstakingly knocked out and removed as much of the broken glass as I could. This took time, but whilst I worked I never once allowed my thoughts to return to Paula's face.

Every time I felt the ghost of it threatening my line of inner vision I thrust it away. I couldn't think of her. Not now and maybe not ever.

The glass panel was cleared almost completely. Now all I had to do was get through the boarding. *You can't help me with this one.* I addressed the kettle aloud. *But thank you kettle* I said and then I laughed. I laughed again, a little hysterically now, as I realised how in less than one week, two domestic household items had come to my rescue. The mop that had helped me to fend off Simon when he had attacked me in my home, and this kettle which was helping me to get out of here. And get out of here I would. I stopped laughing and kicked with all my might against the boarding.

It was the Somalian woman in the headscarf that heard me. Her gentle face looked at me in alarm as breathlessly I called out, "Please call the police... Please will you do that?"

She came closer, bringing a scent of soap powder with her and a hint of lavender wafting up from the two bulging bags of clean washing she carried. How strange I thought, I feel like I've been in this place for ever, but in fact I've been here less than the time it takes for a cotton wash and a spin cycle. I started to laugh again as the woman dialled 999.

Over the days that followed, I slept a lot. And I cried a lot. Even when I tried not to think about Paula and her baby, the tears came. And I let them, sensing that the release they allowed could only help me process what had happened. Flan was, as to be expected, wonderful. She listened with calm, warm sympathy only ever gently reproving me as I shared with her the sense of responsibility I felt about Paula's death.

From Inspector Lawson, I had learnt that Paula had died somewhere in the early hours of Wednesday morning, perhaps just moments after leaving the voice message for me.

"We think," said Inspector Lawson. "Gary Marshall and the second man, Michael Myrto, were instructed to move her body only after Zakiat was arrested. And you should have told us about the property in Surbiton," she complained after I had explained how I'd kept the existence of the pools parts place from her in the belief that it allowed Dan, Sheena, and Maggie to keep their home. "They may be valuable witnesses."

"Do you think that's why they disappeared, because they saw something? I don't think they would have left any of their stuff if they hadn't had to get out in a hurry."

She sighed, "We will probably never know. With over five thousand people sleeping rough in the UK, it is unlikely that we'll ever trace them."

Privately I was glad of that, but I didn't say as much to the inspector.

She also told me something of the case that she and her fellow officers were building against Stavros Zakiat.

"The image on the dice indicated what particular *product...*"

She uttered the word with distaste. "Was to be auctioned off. The upward curve of a horseshoe to represent young women, a stirrup for young men... the suggestion there is clear enough... and... a picture of a bridle to indicate children."

I gasped. For some minutes neither of us spoke and then she continued.

"And, as has happened in other cases, an advertisement in the press proved to be the conduit between buyer and seller."

"What about Chris Lianthos?" I asked eventually "Did you find his car at The Box?"

"No," she replied. "And he is denying that he had any knowledge of his father-in-law's activities, but we are still working on that and of course we are questioning him and the Karmanski twins about Paula Fisher's murder."

"This could all take months I suppose?"

"Yes," she admitted. "And you will be called when the cases… or case… because it may prove to be a combined one, go to trial."

What had happened to Uri, Aischa, and their friend Rima in the interval between being washed up on the island of Samos to being taken to the club *Knights* and from there to auction, I never did discover, but I learnt enough from Inspector Lawson about the extent and venality of Zakiat's organization to guess at the horrors they had endured. I didn't meet them again but was told that their case was being considered by the Home Office. Britain having been shamefully slow in offering asylum had a lot to make up for. I hoped that one day all three girls would be able to reclaim their lives and find whatever peace those who have been traded, exploited, and abused can ever hope to find. My heart was with them.

CHAPTER THIRTY-THREE

I'd heard of a theory that time spent online at the office watching fluffy kittens playing with a ball of string, or a cute puppy having his first bath, actually increases productivity rather than reduces it. It's all down to the alleviation of stress apparently. Now I can't vouch for the kittens, but the puppy worked for me.

Not-so-Tiny Tim was just what I needed. His big bouncing undemanding presence lent the finishing touch for my re-entry into life. And so, when just four days after I had discovered Paula's body, Steph phoned asking me to cover tonight's shift for her, I felt ready to face the world again.

"I didn't get *Bridget Jones The Musical*," her voice down the phone was resigned. "They said I can't do posh. But I can. Listen." In strained and fluty notes, she uttered something about *being charmed* and *thank you* and *you're so kind*.

"You sound a bit like the Queen, Steph. Maybe it wasn't what they were after?"

"Never mind," she said. "I've got another audition tonight at six thirty. That's why I'm phoning. I need you to cover for me. Can you do it?"

"Sure, no problem."

Dave had shared my last few shifts about but I had to get back to work sometime.

"What's the part?"

"It's an ad. Excitable young woman dancing around the sofa when she wins twenty pounds, on a home bingo site. I wouldn't have thought I'd have to be posh for that, would you?"

"Anything but, I'd say."

"Great to see you back Clarry," said Dave hugging me as at six o'clock that evening I entered the restaurant.

"Thanks. How's tonight looking?"

"Two parties of eight, a table for six, a table of… oh, and someone called for you."

"Did they leave a name?" I asked.

"No, but he said he'd call back later."

I made my way to the kitchen.

"I'm on the 5:2." Tara had confided this fascinating piece of information on the last occasion we'd worked together and so now, at just after ten o'clock when there were only a few tables still talking over their coffees, I couldn't summon up the energy to congratulate her again on the half a stone she'd lost.

"Yes, you said."

"Did I? Oh sorry," she coloured slightly "I'm sorry to bore on about it but calorie counting seems to be taking over my life and I know that's not healthy. Not long term anyway."

"I don't know how you do it," I said feeling a little guilty at my dismissive tone. "It must be really hard."

"It is. I keep trying to come up with strategies to take my mind off food. And it's not easy working in a restaurant where we're surrounded by the stuff. So now when I see other people eating I just tell myself that what's working its way down *their* digestive tract could just as well be working its way down mine. I simply imagine it's me swallowing the slice of cheesecake or the portion of fries and that it's my intestines it's travelling down to and…"

I hope she doesn't imagine it coming out at the other end I thought. That would be taking visualisation a little too far.

"… And it's like living the experience vicariously do you see?"

I shrugged and then unbidden, the thought of Paula holding an unlit cigarette to her lips for the health of her unborn baby flashed across my mind. Hastily I shook it away. "And does it help?" I asked doubtfully.

"No not at all," she acknowledged with a sigh and went off to take an order for a mint tea from table seven.

When she returned, she asked, "And what about you Clarry? I've been gabbing on about myself. Have you done anything interesting lately?"

"No, nothing really," I answered without thinking. But that wasn't even remotely true I thought. I said nothing to Tara but as I cleared away the cups and glasses and wiped down the tables, I recognised that now everything was over I would miss my investigations. In spite of everything that had happened, it *had* been interesting. And let's not forget, dangerous I reminded myself. But still, it did leave rather a void and it was a void that I had absolutely no idea how to fill. I'd really have to think about getting a proper job sometime soon.

At twenty to twelve I left the restaurant and walked up the high street, my mind occupied with thoughts of a bath and bed. Conscious of a low-lying sense of depression, I felt weary and heavy-limbed. And so maybe it was that which caught me off guard.

I had been dimly aware of the sound of a car engine behind me, but it was only when I turned on to the Ridgeway that I realised someone was kerb-crawling me. It's nothing to worry about I thought. Just some jerk who'll call out something predictably disgusting and then be on his way. And so, I carried on walking whilst the car kept pace behind me. I flung a glance over my shoulder at it. It was sleek and black and expensive. I quickened my step. I looked about for passers-by, but Wednesday nights are quiet in the village and there was no one around.

A black cab with its yellow light on, tick-ticked past and as it occurred to me that I should have tried to flag it down, the car tailing me sped up and without warning came to an abrupt stop just in front of me. Two men got out. One stood directly facing me thereby blocking my path and the other was close behind me and before I realised what they were about, in one swift choreographed movement, they pushed me firmly but not roughly into the back of the car.

My heart thudded in shock and an icy-cold sweat of fear swamped my whole body. I tried to scream but no sound came out. One of the men sat beside me and the other slid into the passenger seat. The driver revved the engine and the door and window locks snapped shut. It was then that I found my voice but I couldn't produce a scream, only a thin forlorn whimper. My brain didn't seem to want to work. I felt stunned and stupid and so afraid that I thought I might pass out.

I looked at the man sitting beside me. Tall, lean and in a smart suit he had a goatee and was somewhere in his thirties. He looked steadily back at me but didn't speak. Instead he reached for my handbag. I must have made a slight movement of protest for he held up a restraining hand. Then he went through my bag methodically until he produced my phone. This he placed in his pocket before handing my bag back to me.

Let him have it I told myself. Let him have it and maybe they won't hurt me.

"Where are you taking me?" I could hear the tremor in my voice. It didn't sound like my voice at all.

His eyes flicked dispassionately across my face but he didn't reply.

"What do you want?" I cried, but this time he didn't even look at me.

I took several big gulps of air, trying to regulate my breathing but that only made me choke. Stay calm. It's vital to stay calm I thought through streaming eyes. Don't let them know what you're thinking. But I wasn't thinking. I knew that. I wasn't thinking at all, I was panicking. Recognising this fact helped me slowly, very slowly, to unclench my body and breathe normally.

I thought of my parents and of Flan. I thought of Laura and of Tim and of the dog, a spaniel called Pepe, which I used to have when I was a child. I forced myself to think happy thoughts until gradually I felt my powers of reasoning revive. My brain was back in business. Not fully, but enough to keep my fear clamped down whilst I tried to work out what the hell was going on. Who were these men and what did they want with me?

I looked at the back of the necks of the two men in the front seats but from this angle couldn't tell if I had ever seen them before. And then I looked, for the first time, out of the window. We were on the A3 heading to central London.

As we sped through the darkness, ideas continued to pitch and roll in my mind. That this was connected to recent events I had no doubt, but weren't all the major players either in custody or being monitored by the police? The image of Paula's dead body flashed through my mind.

We were in the West End now and driving along Park Lane. Not once had a word been spoken by either the man with the goatee or his two companions. Five minutes later we pulled into one of the oldest and most elegant of London squares and came to a stop outside a large but discreet looking, double-fronted town house. The man with the goatee took out his mobile and dialled.

"We are here," he said.

He listened for a moment, disconnected, and then got out of the car. Opening my door, he handed me out on to the pavement. This was it, my chance to scream, my chance to run, my chance to get away and I almost took it. I so nearly took it. But I didn't. What would be the point? Someone obviously wanted to talk to me and if I didn't face whoever it was now, I might be snatched again at a later date and

315

that might be worse. A lot worse. Next time they might… I didn't want to think about what they might do. Better to get it over with and so I followed him up the steps to a heavy blue door besides which was a gold plaque bearing the name of one of the most exclusive private clubs in the capital.

Goatee rang the bell and it was opened by a mild faced man in a braided concierge style uniform.

"Good evening," he said but he didn't stand aside to allow us in.

"She is expected," said Goatee and gave me a slight push forward.

The concierge nodded and I crossed the threshold. Goatee didn't enter with me but merely handed me my phone and then turned and made his way back down the steps.

I found myself in a large hallway painted midnight blue and decorated with gold leaf around the ceiling, in friezes and mouldings above the doors. I had an impression of rose marble and of gilt. Scrolled antique mirrors reflected the highly polished surfaces of walnut sideboards and the glimmer from a stately chandelier. A curved staircase led off and away to the upper floors. I had never been here before, but I knew of the club. A casino, a restaurant, a meeting place for the very rich it had been frequented in the past by the aristocracy, by politicians, and by Old Money. Membership was on a strict for-approval basis.

The concierge hesitated. "It has been requested that you join our member at the table but… we do require ladies to wear evening gowns." He looked at my Abbe's uniform of white shirt, black skirt, and low heels.

"And I look like I should be serving the drinks," I said.

"Indeed Miss."

"And that's because it's precisely what I have been doing."

There was a pause.

"And that's a problem," I offered.

"It is. Perhaps you would care to wait in one of the…"

"Or," I suggested. "Instead maybe I could be passed off as a member of staff? I could blend right in. That way you could do what was *requested* without offending the sensibilities of the Great and the Good. Would that work?"

A flicker of what may have been amusement crossed his face. And he had the face of a man who could not, and determinedly would not, be surprised by anything.

"It would. Follow me please Miss."

Feeling oddly calm, I did so. The sheer solidity and history of the place was reassuring. We reached a pair of double doors opened wide to reveal the casino.

It was a magnificent room. A salon I supposed it would once have been. Two chandeliers even more impressive than the one in the hall sparkled overhead and low table lamps dotted about the room glimmered invitingly. Murals depicting French country scenes of nineteenth century ladies and gentlemen disporting themselves in rowboats or picnicking besides a river, lined the walls. Heavy swathes of fabric looped and nodded above intimate alcoves hung with paintings in thick gold frames. One of the paintings was of a statuesque nude reclining upon a red plush chaise longue and gazing out at the assembled company with an expression not unlike that of the concierge.

And what a well-dressed affluent company it was. No,

not merely affluent, rich. These people screamed money from every pore, and from every diamond. I'd never seen so many diamonds close up. They flamed and shone about the throats, around the wrists, and from the ears of women in evening dresses of every cut and colour. Lace, sequins, chiffon, velvet, in spaghetti straps or off the shoulder, sheathe like and body-hugging on the very slim or draped and ruched upon more substantial figures. No wonder the concierge had looked at me askance. The men uniformly clad in immaculately tailored suits were less interesting to look at, but I caught the flash of jewelled cufflinks and heavy linked watches as they sipped at their glasses of champagne or from cut-glass tumblers of whisky or of bourbon.

Through the tables set for blackjack and for poker I followed my guide until he indicated a table with a roulette wheel. I looked at him blankly. There were half a dozen people around it but I didn't know any of them.

The concierge approached a woman sitting with her back to me. Diamond studded clips held her black hair up on top of her head and she was wearing a form-fitting, white sleeveless cocktail dress. When she turned around I could see that the dress was cut high at the neck and that it had hundreds of tiny seed pearls stitched upon silk chiffon. And then I recognised her. It was Maria Lianthos.

"You will wait here for me until I am ready," she said and it wasn't issued as a request.

I laughed at that. I wasn't sure who I had been expecting, but it certainly wasn't her. Relief that the mystery person was a woman, and was therefore in my mind less of a physical threat than a man, had dimmed the worst of my misgivings and I felt a return of confidence.

"And why would I do that?"

"You've come this far," she said.

"Like I had any choice," I cut across her.

"Have you been a guest here before?"

"Oh I'm a guest, am I? I do wish you had extended me the courtesy of an invitation so then I could have dressed for the occasion."

She considered my Abbe's uniform and the judgement she made clearly amused her.

I stiffened. I didn't like being patronised and felt already at a disadvantage, and so said before she could make a comment, "No. I haven't been here before. It seems a world away from your hairdressers in Camberwell."

"And to the restaurant where you are merely an employee," she said.

Touché I thought.

"So why not observe the play," she continued. "I think you may find it entertaining." Her smile was sardonic as she turned back to the table.

As the concierge left me I felt a desire to scamper after him away from this alien environment where, even if I had been dressed like Maria Lianthos or the other women, albeit without the diamonds, I knew I would never really feel comfortable.

I made to take the empty seat beside Maria when the dealer asked, "Is the young lady playing?"

I shook my head.

"I'm sorry but if you are just watching then you have to stand. House rules."

So, I stood and feeling a little self-conscious, I watched.

Maria gambled a great deal of money. Small change it may have been to her and to her fellow players, but thousands of pounds were being bet upon the spin of a wheel and a small white ball ricocheting among its slots. And it seemed daft to me. To my inexperienced eye it appeared to be only a matter of chance, no skill involved, where the ball landed. Perhaps that's the attraction for the very rich?

I studied the other players. A man in his fifties with a fleshy chin and jowls, staring intently at the carousel as it spun and turned. A sleek couple in their twenties who were much less serious about the business and who laughed and clinked their glasses together, despite a run of obvious bad luck. Two Chinese men who spoke in rapid undertones and who appeared to be in direct competition with each other although their only combatant was the House. And most fascinating to me of all, was a woman of Middle Eastern appearance somewhere in her sixties and elegantly dressed and who drew out great wads of cash from a crumpled plastic bag in exchange for chips. Mechanically she placed her bets and seemed totally unmoved whether the play proved to be in her favour or not.

Maria made gains and made losses and whether the figures were in line with each other I could have no idea, but like the Middle Eastern lady she displayed no outward emotion as the wheel rotated and the ball flew this way and that. That her focus and attention was one of concentration I could see, but I didn't think anxiety about the outcome was the main ingredient. It was clear that she enjoyed the play for its own sake. Not once did she as much as glance in my direction and this fact was beginning to piss me off. I'd been grabbed off the street, abducted by her goons, and she expected me just to hang around watching her play this absurd game when I'd been on my feet all evening.

I was no longer scared, just impatient to know what she wanted with me. And I was thirsty. I hadn't been offered a drink by any of the staff circulating the room, probably because they thought I was one of them.

I nudged at Maria's elbow and pointed meaningfully at her glass. She turned and beckoned a passing waiter, issued a command, and moments later I was handed a long-stemmed flute of champagne.

Another twenty minutes passed.

"No more bets," called the dealer.

The wheel did its stuff once more, but this time when the ball landed Maria cleared her chips from the table and stood up. "Come with me," she said and led the way out of the casino with a slow swinging gait, the pearl beads on her dress shimmying with each movement. Her shoes, I was forced to concede, were to die for. Six-inch stilettos with a pointed toe and in soft silver leather, they had that telltale red sole that denotes one of the most celebrated of shoe designers.

We entered an empty sitting room that had the feel of a gentleman's library. There were paintings of hunting scenes on the walls and serious looking leather-bound books on dark mahogany tables. A bust of a man with a pronounced forehead frowned down from a pedestal and the sofas and armchairs were upholstered in green and gold striped damask. Immediately a waiter materialised and, without consulting me, Maria ordered more champagne.

We sat opposite each other, both taking sips from our drinks as the waiter disappeared back to whatever hidden recess he'd come from.

Silence. I was determined not to be the first to speak. I'd been badly frightened in the car, and, since we'd moved into this room, some of that fear had reasserted itself. Maria looked at me and still I didn't speak. She smiled and crossed her legs. I wanted to do the same but felt that my scuffed pumps didn't bear scrutiny and so I simulated an ease that I was far from feeling, by relaxing back against the cushions. This woman was playing with me and I didn't like it. I didn't like it at all and if I had to, I'd sit here all bloody night rather than give her the satisfaction of betraying my anxiety. Eventually after what seemed an age, she spoke.

"You know who I am of course?" Her Greek accent was barely discernible.

"I do."

"And you are Clarry Pennhaligan?" Her tone was mocking. "What kind of a name is Clarry?"

"The shortening of a more formal one."

Her features were almost too regular I decided. There was something bland about her face as if it had been drawn by a child who had forgotten or was not sufficiently skilled enough to include any lines of individuality or element of character.

"And I expect you are wondering how I found you?"

I had been wondering that of course but I wasn't going to admit to it.

She opened her clutch bag, which was fan-shaped and encrusted with sparkling diamonds. Whether the gems were real or not, it was, I was gratified to note, perfectly hideous. And ostentatious. Good I thought; money doesn't necessarily equal taste. From the hideous bag, she drew out her phone and dialled a number. Instantly my own phone rang. I riffled through my tatty old leather messenger bag and looked at the screen. Number withheld. Maria cut the connection on her phone and mine went dead. She smirked and I remembered all those silent calls I had received.

But I hadn't ever given Chris my number I thought and so how had she got it? But I had told her husband that I worked as a waitress in the village. And it wouldn't have taken much to ring around the half dozen or so restaurants and enquire if I worked there. And then I remembered Dave saying that someone had phoned for me that afternoon.

"Ah," I said. "Abbe's. So that's how your thugs found me."

"Thugs? Oh, I wouldn't describe them as that. And didn't you think Denny rather attractive?"

"The one with the goatee?"

"Yes. I find him an adequate if unimaginative lover, but then as I like to be on top he doesn't have a great deal to do."

"How fortunate for you both," I remarked thinking the conversation was going way off topic. Except that I didn't know what the topic was I realised.

"Weren't my men's suits to your liking?" she continued. "Or their manners?"

"Expensive clothes are no guarantee of respectability," I looked pointedly at her. "And neither is an expensive club."

"It helps. As does money. A lot of money because it allows entry into Society, into the world of The Elite and that's where I belong. But you can see that…"

Her gaze dropped to her designer shoes and then travelled over the elegant furnishings of the room and I was reminded of her father and his belief in his infinite superiority over the sweating Perry. This woman was showing off to me. Why? Why did she feel the need to do that?

"Oh right," I said. "Because living off the immoral earnings of human trafficking goes down so well amongst the very best circles."

Her eyes sharpened. "I was completely unaware of my father's business arrangements until a few days ago."

And what about your husband I thought.

"Really?" My scepticism was evident.

"Thankfully, the police recognise the truth when they hear it and so your opinion is a matter of complete indifference to me."

"Then why am I here?" I'd had enough of this. I just wanted to go home.

"Because I wanted to meet you," she replied.

"You went to a lot of trouble to do so."

"Less than you'd think. But I was curious. Curious to meet the person… the *girl* that…"

There was such derision in her tone that I felt a flare of temper.

"The girl that what? That brought down your father's disgusting evil trade? Yes, I did that. Me. This girl right here that you are so enjoying sneering at."

She re-crossed her legs, took a sip of her champagne, and then put her glass down.

"You do get yourself rather worked up, don't you?"

"Yes of course I do! Over things that really matter. But that means nothing to you, does it? Sitting there in your swanky dress and with your designer shoes and... frankly appalling handbag... you don't give a fuck about what happened to those poor people do you?"

"You don't like the bag?" She picked it up and stroked it. "It's one of my favourites."

I stared at her. I couldn't come up with a single word in response.

"Your interference has been untimely," she said at length. "It has caused me some slight inconvenience but," she shrugged, "I'm over it now. I'm moving on."

"Moving on... right. Do you think those girls are *over it*? Do you think they can easily *move on*?"

Her expression was bland and it absolutely infuriated me.

"Well do you?" I demanded.

Again, she didn't respond to my question but finally offered, "I plan to settle in the US but I may travel a while. Italy is lovely at this time of the year. And there's always the South of France. Cannes, Monte Carlo... the best casino in the world is in Monaco."

"Lovely for you," I said, sickened by her.

"Yes, isn't it? A change is always a stimulant."

"What about your hairdressers?" She wasn't the only one allowed to be curious. "I understand that you have opened some new salons?"

"They are easily disposed of."

"And your husband? Will he be enjoying the delights of St Tropez with you?"

"As I say, time for a change. Besides he may be in…"

"Prison?" I suggested.

"Highly unlikely." Her smugness not only repelled me but was beginning to give me the creeps.

"He may be investing in a new line of business I was going to say." She stroked her fan-shaped bag again. Perhaps it's some kind of fetish? I thought, and she takes it to bed with her?

"Something criminal no doubt?"

She didn't reply, but asked instead, "I expect he came on to you?"

"Who?"

"Don't pretend to be stupider than you are. My husband of course," she snapped.

"You could have meant your poor pathetic perverted old dad for all I knew."

She flinched at that but I didn't let up.

"As a matter of fact, he did come on to me." Well the woman had asked the question, so why not answer it? "But that heavy-handed machismo leaves me cold and so I didn't take him up on it."

"He'd have tired of you soon anyway."

"He didn't get the opportunity to," I retorted. "And I would have thought with your preference for being on top,

326

his swaggering attempts to dominate must have meant a pretty lousy time in the bedroom for all concerned. I mean your husband didn't strike me as the kind of man who'd take it lying down."

I was pleased with that. It was time for a little smugness of my own. "I suppose that's why you need Don….Denny or whatever your thug with the goatee is called."

Her eyes flashed and for the first time I thought that her control might falter. But it didn't.

"I was led to believe that you were quite pretty," she said after a beat as she examined me dispassionately. "But with your face all red like that I really can't see it."

I got to my feet. "Your curiosity has been well and truly satisfied then. So, if there's nothing else?"

"Actually, there is." She got up to face me.

Here it comes I thought. "Well?"

She didn't answer for a long moment and the silence between us seemed to vibrate. This scene had to be played out I thought and so I waited.

"I want to give you a piece of advice," she said and her bland doll-like face was devoid of expression.

"I'm listening."

"It doesn't take much for a life to be taken apart. To be…" she searched for the word "… disassembled piece by piece."

"Is that a threat?"

"Take it how you like. I'm just suggesting that you remember that the next time you interfere in matters that don't concern you."

"Noted," I said reaching for my bag. "I assume that this

327

will be the last time we meet? That you won't be sending your… people… after me again?"

She didn't reply but continued to regard me.

"I'll take that as a yes then."

I crossed to the door but turned back to her. "Well goodbye. It's been fun. I won't shake hands though, because I make it a rule never to go skin to skin with a sociopath."

There are times when you simply have to get in the last word.

CHAPTER THIRTY-FOUR

I t was early, barely eight o'clock when I ran along the track leading down towards Beverley Brook, the lazy trickling stream that threads its way along the A3 side of the Common before joining the Thames at Putney Bridge. It had rained in the night and the air smelt sweet and fresh, the ground still spongy underfoot. Leaping over puddles I could feel splatters of mud splashing up the back of my legs. It felt good to sweat. Good to shake off the ugly memories of the night before, and of the days and nights before that.

Last night after leaving Maria I'd walked through the midnight blue and gold leaf hallway of the club and had stood looking up at the chandelier as the concierge had hailed me a cab.

"Had a good evening Miss?" He'd asked.

"Oh just the best," I'd replied as he handed me into the taxi.

Arriving home, I'd stumbled up the stairs, stepped out of my clothes, and crawled straight into bed where I slept heavily and dreamlessly. When I blinked into consciousness somewhere around seven this morning, I'd felt not just refreshed but light-hearted. This was a new day and if I was going to get on with my life then the strain, depression, and sense of guilt I'd been experiencing about Paula and her baby had to be packaged up and put at a distance. The blue-black bruises on my arms and legs from where Perry had gripped me was reminder enough as was the ragged tear on my fingernail.

Striking out, I headed for Fishpond Wood, a small, protected reserve, hoping that the bluebells would now be out. They were… in their thousands. Their stems straight and firm, the delicate bells of a blue so intense that they seemed to shimmer amidst the shade of the oak trees that lined the timber-decked path. The sight of them refreshed my jaded eyes.

I slowed my pace down to a walk as I came to the stagnant pond where colonies of toads, frogs, and dragonflies make their residence. The surface, a vivid green that bubbled and belched like a vast caldron of primordial soup looked, in contrast to the carpet of bluebells that surrounded it, distinctly uninviting.

With a smile, I remembered earlier in the year looking on in amusement as a dog walker bellowed at her retriever, which, studiously ignoring her increasingly frantic commands had bounded straight into the pond's murky depths. Moments later it had reappeared, one boisterous happy heap of drenched and woefully stinking fur with great ribbons of slime trailing from around its neck. Its mistress had not been at all impressed.

I picked up speed feeling increasingly energised with every step. That look on Maria's face at my parting shot last night had been priceless. The memory of it made me laugh out loud. And from a trill and a warbling in the trees that broke out around me it would seem that the birds thought it funny as well. It felt like they were on my side somehow, as if they were rooting for me. Ridiculous I knew, but comforting nevertheless.

My mind felt clearer. I was more myself. The bruises on my arms and legs would fade and my nail would grow back. Just being outside in the clean, cool air had revived my body and my spirits. Who needs designer gear and glamorous casinos to experience happiness? Jogging along by the brook didn't cost a penny and so perhaps, after all, that old adage about the best things in life being free, might actually be true. Blimey I thought as I trotted on, I'll have to watch myself. I'll be sitting crossed-legged on a yoga mat and chanting next.

And tomorrow night I had a date with Tim to look forward to. Melanie's Ted, their landlord Barney, and a couple of other musicians were putting on a short set at the Bulls Head in Barnes and a bunch of us were going. It would be fun, uncomplicated fun. Right now that was all I needed. And Tim and I long term? I wondered picking up speed again as I followed the track uphill through an avenue of Silver Birches. No somehow, I couldn't see it. The man for me was out there somewhere I was pretty sure, and it wasn't Tim. So that meant I'd have to keep on looking... in a casual way. There was no hurry. Maybe men are like the baby bear's porridge in that old nursery story? I thought. You have to taste test a few to find one that is just right. And so that's what I'd do. Meantime Tim was a playful, energetic, and damn sexy stop-gap. Flan had been absolutely right about him. It *is* good to have a hobby.

"I'm so sorry babe for not being in contact sooner," said Laura down the phone some two hours later.

"That's alright. Don't worry about it. And I should have phoned you to see how your date went. It's just as much my fault as yours."

So, she had been avoiding me as I had been avoiding her. It wasn't the row we'd had, of that I was sure, the dust had settled on that. Perhaps just as I hadn't wanted her bright hopeful enthusiasm about the possibility of a new man in her life to distract me from the cruel reality of what I'd witnessed, she hadn't wanted my newly opened eyes and depressed outlook to tarnish her happiness. And who could blame her? No one likes a wet blanket.

"So how did it go? Tell me all about it."

"Fan-fucking-tastic," she sighed. "He is just Bliss in a Bucket. Oh Clarry, it's been so great. We've…"

And she told me everything. I listened, asked a few questions, and then she told me all over again.

"I knew I had a good feeling about him. About the two of you," I said. "I am so pleased for you."

And I really was.

"Oh, by the way," she said some time later. "Mr. Garstein is very impressed with you."

"He is?"

"Absolutely. He wants to meet you and says that he might have further projects for you."

"But I'm just an amateur," I protested.

"I didn't tell him that this was your first time or anything. I just said that you were a friend of mine who carries out private investigations. Obviously I had to improvise, so I told him that whilst you cover all areas of detection, you usually specialise in affairs of the heart."

"That makes me sound like an agony aunt or a therapist," I objected. "And God knows that couldn't be further from the truth."

"That's for sure," she said. "Because let's face it you've got enough issues of your own to work out."

I *had*? But there was no time to go into this now.

"I know you've had all that stuff about the trafficking and those poor girls," continued Laura. "But I didn't really want to go into all that, too morbid, so I described you as someone who probes into romantic matters, entanglements, intrigues, that kind of thing," she was giggling now. "You're like Cupid's secret little snooper. You're a sex spy. No hang on. I know. A Love Detective."

She was enjoying this way too much.

"I think I got it. Thanks very much," I returned dryly.

"Actually," she said. "I think he likes the idea of you being a woman. I know that the firm does use someone on occasion for divorce cases and things but Mr. Garstein seem to think that a woman might be more effective. So you never know this could be the start of something for you. The Love Detective could be in business."

I digested this. I wouldn't have thought the idea appealing but oddly it was.

"And," she added seamlessly. "He said send him an invoice and he'll settle it straightaway."

"An invoice," I squeaked. "Really? You mean he actually wants to pay me?"

"Sure why not? You've done a job of work so why shouldn't you be paid?"

"But I've already had that cheque from James."

"So? And besides if my firm pays you then I feel that I don't have to."

"Laura, you do know that I would never have accepted money from you?"

"And now you don't have to."

"Well when you put it like that," I said.

"Now," Laura said crisply sounding every inch the solicitor. "I'll check out what the usual rate is and get back to you."

Not bad, I thought. I could get to quite like this line of work, if it wasn't for the human trafficking, being assaulted, nearly auctioned off, and finding a dead body.

I picked up the phone again.

"Flan… great you're in. I've just got a couple of stops to make and I'll be with you by twelve."

When Flan opened the door and spotted the huge bunch of pale pink roses I proffered, her face lit up. "Darling!" she said. "How lovely… and roses as you know are my absolute favourite. Thank you dear. Come inside and let's get them in water."

I followed her into the kitchen. "The woman in the shop told me that pink roses apparently signify elegance and gentility."

"Did she now?" Flan laughed as she crossed to the sink

to unwrap the flowers. "How clever of her, and we haven't even met."

"Oh," I added. "And there's something else." I pulled two bottles of champagne out of a carrier bag.

"One is for now. It's cold and you get the lion's share as I'm due at the restaurant later, but the other is for you and Mr. H. It's a thank you present for the other night, and for last week, and well for everything really."

She stopped arranging the roses and came over and kissed me lightly on the cheek. "Thank you, sweetheart. Anytime. You know that champagne is just the thing to get George powered up. So, that's another treat for me!"

For a moment, the thought of Mr. H.'s seventy-two-year-old body getting into full sexual gear flickered across my mind, but I hastily blinked it away. Don't go there I told myself. There are some mental images best left in a box clearly labelled *do not open*.

"Where shall we sit?" Flan asked. "I think it's warm enough to be in the garden, don't you? You open the bottle and I'll get the glasses."

Outside, Flan scattered a heap of faded candy-striped cotton cushions on to her old wicker chairs and once seated comfortably, I proceeded to fill her in on everything that had happened since our last conversation.

"It doesn't sound quite real somehow," she said gravely. "More like something one would watch on the television."

She reached for the bottle and topped us up. "But you're safe and well and that is something to be grateful for."

"And I'll be richer, slightly richer," I corrected myself and told her about Mr. Garstein and the invoice I was to submit. "I'm still not sure if I deserve it. What do you think?"

"I think it's marvellous. You've worked very hard and put a lot of time and effort into this." She broke off and looked over the rim of her glass at me.

"What?" I said. "You've got that look on your face. The one you get when you are just about to say something rather crushing, which often turns out, very irritatingly I may add, to be true."

"I was merely going to observe," she remarked coolly placing her glass down. "That I think this experience has been good for you."

I didn't answer immediately and then offered hesitatingly, "In spite of everything; I have enjoyed it. And I've met some people that I would never have got to know in the normal scheme of things. Melanie and Ted who I feel sure I will stay in contact with. And although I'll never get to meet the three Syrian girls again or even Dan, Sheena, and Maggie, I am glad that I got even just a glimpse into their lives. So I do feel different somehow. Like I've been on a…"

Flan suddenly looked very stern. "If you say that you've been on a *journey*, I may be tempted to waste a few drops of this heavenly champagne and throw it at you."

"OK, OK," I protested. "It's just a figure of speech."

"An appalling one and much overused."

"But it's not all a success you know. There is something I can't do anything about."

She regarded me keenly registering the seriousness of my tone.

"If you mean that you could have stopped Laura getting emotionally wrung out to dry by that wretched young man…"

"No," I smiled ruefully. "That couldn't have been avoided." I shifted my back against the cushions. "It's Maria Lianthos. I swear she was involved or at least knew far more than she claims. And now she gets to swan off to America and…"

"Darling," Flan interrupted gently. "You're not a one-woman cavalry. What more can you possibly do?"

She was right of course. Time to let it go. I took another sip of my drink and we sat in silence for a while in the shade of an aged crab apple tree, its perfume delicate and its pale pink droops of blossom like puffs of fondant icing. Unlike Grandma P., Flan is what she calls a fair-weather gardener. She lets the borders and the beds take care of themselves and so now in spring, against a backdrop of blackthorn and a tangle of evergreens, the result was a glorious wilderness of anemones, violets, and celandines. It was all so peaceful, and somehow a reminder of the constancy of life.

I looked across to a weathered, timber-potting table where balls of twine, a trug, a smooth grey pebble, a handful of wooden pegs, and trays of white daisies ready to be planted out, sat in attractive disarray.

"And I've also realised," I said picking up from the table in front of us a green glass jug in which Flan had arranged a splash of palest yellow primula and bringing it up to my nose. "Just how lucky I am in my friends. Not just you and Mr. H. of course, but Stephanie and Ian coming with me to the club."

I took in the cool, woody scent of the flowers and then set the jug back down.

"And Laura."

"I rather think my dear," remarked Flan. "That it's you that's been a very good friend to her."

I shrugged and said, "I'm just happy that we're OK now. Back to where we were. By the way she's been calling me *The Love Detective*. I wasn't sure at first but I think I quite like it now. What do you think? Oh and she also says I have issues."

She eyed me thoughtfully and then raising her glass to mine, made a toast, "To The Love Detective. Count me in on her next case!"

In mock solemnity, I clinked my glass against hers and said, "To The Love Detective. Not that there'll be a next case." I laughed the idea away. "But a nice thought all the same."

"I wouldn't be too sure about that if I were you," said Flan. "After all who knows what may happen? And as to issues… of course you have them. I'm seventy years old and I still do. You only stop having them the day you're brought out feet first in a box. They come hand in hand with being alive."

I smiled across at her as we sat peaceably together in the warmth of the April sunshine and finished our champagne. Perhaps she's right I thought. Anything can happen to us and around us. And maybe the trick is not to be afraid of whatever it is that's coming our way? Because after all… no one's story is ever really finished, is it?

COMING SOON...

IN 2019

THE LOVE DETECTIVE: NEXT LEVEL

SNEAK PEAK OF
CHAPTER ONE
AND
CHAPTER TWO
AHEAD

CHAPTER ONE

Evidently, I wasn't making a good impression. The woman sitting across the desk from me flicked a dismissive eye over the one neatly typed page of A4 paper that made up my CV.

"I'm afraid that we have nothing for you," she sniffed looking again at my resume. "Because, as I'm sure you'll agree, it is rather thin."

Harsh, I thought, but basically true. So, alright at the age of twenty-six I wasn't exactly what you might call a high flyer, but she must have something for me.

"I believe that your last temping job for us was cut short after only three days. The notes we have on file are rather unclear as to the reason for this." There was an edge of enquiry to her tone.

I winced at the memory. Things had been going pretty well at the marketing company in Victoria until a somewhat unfortunate incident involving a computer server and my takeout cup of Grande Latte. Apparently, there's something in a double shot of caramel syrup that doesn't quite agree with all its delicate little components. The system went down for two days with many thousands of pounds of potential business lost. I was informed this by the managing director, as he personally escorted me from the premises.

I cleared my throat. The woman was awaiting an answer.

"Oh, it was just that I was so efficient, I dispensed with the company's workload in record time."

Hoping that this would be enough to satisfy her, I flashed what I like to think of as a frank and engaging smile. She didn't smile back. In fact, she appeared to be growing testier by the minute. Well, I reflected, I'd probably be out of temper too if I'd got up that morning and actually chosen, of my own free will, to wear a heavily ruched tunic top in a particularly bilious shade of green. It would be enough to ruin anyone's day.

I took a swift glance at the laminate badge bearing the name Marion that was pinned to the offending tunic and then widened my eyes at the accompanying slogan which promised that she was Here To Help. When was she going to begin? By her manner of barely suppressed irritation I was guessing that it wouldn't be any time soon.

"I only need a couple of days a week, Marion. Actually, at a push, with my waitressing shifts, maybe I could just manage with one." I did my best to look bright and responsible and waited expectantly.

Marion sighed and sat back tapping one of her long synthetic nails on a pile of folders. "Part-time work is always much sought after especially here in Wimbledon. And of course, we have plenty of other applicants. And after all what is it about you that makes you different? Something that would incline me to put you forward as a candidate over all the rest? What's your USP?"

My what? What was she talking about? USP –what did that stand for? Unusual Sexual Practices? Well, I think I'm relatively normal in that department but how could I ever be sure? I made a mental note to ask the very next guy I slept with. Come to think of it, it was actually a very interesting question and one that deserved further consideration, but it did seem a bit odd somehow to have it asked by a recruitment agent.

"Hmm," I faltered.

"Never mind," she said and the nail tapping upped a level. "Let's look at it from the other way around. Let's consider your weak points."

I opened my mouth, ready to admit that I wasn't a big fan of routine, that I didn't like taking orders and wasn't a particularly organised person, when it occurred to me that this might be a trick question. "Well," I floundered. "I'm very flexible and I'm … Um … good with people." I attempted another winning smile. "People like me."

She didn't look convinced. "They do?"

"Yes," I added firmly because that was just plain rude. "Usually they do." There was a pause as we eyed one another, and I decided to give it one last shot. "Actually, I have recently developed some new skills."

The nail tapping stopped for an instant as she again looked at my CV.

"No," I explained, "it's not on there. It's not really the sort of thing that …" I hesitated. I was on the verge of telling her just how much I'd learnt in the last couple of weeks from my first stab at private investigating (or what the narrower minded may refer to as poking my nose into other people's business), when I broke off. What was the point? Somehow, she just didn't seem to be the kind of person likely to be stirred by tales of stake-outs and surveillance. I got to my feet. "Forget it. I doubt you'd consider the experience relevant. Anyway, you have my number."

From the look of relief in her eyes it was clear that we were neck and neck in our desire to bring the interview to a close. As I headed for the door Marion called out, "I don't hold out much hope.'

I turned back. Was she still speaking to me? No, I decided. She was merely expressing her own particular view of the world. Must be the influence of the tunic.

I stepped out into the warmth of a beautiful May morning and strolled up the hill towards home resolving to put all thoughts of my pitiful lack of office experience out of my mind, because here I was on a Friday morning feeling the sun on my face and the sense of freedom that comes from knowing that I didn't have to answer to some ego inflated arse of a boss. I liked my ad hoc lifestyle. I had my waitressing shifts and still some slack on my credit cards and so all in all, life was pretty good. And as for getting another part-time job or landing my next assignment, well something would no doubt turn up.

Something did. And much sooner than I could ever have expected.

CHAPTER TWO

As I let myself into the house I could hear the phone ringing. Dashing into the sitting room and flinging aside my bag I made a grab for it, whilst simultaneously trying to shrug myself out of my jacket.

"Clarry? It's Tara."

"Oh, hi Tara. How are you?" I asked distractedly into the receiver wedged under my chin as I struggled vainly with my left arm, which seemed reluctant to free itself from my sleeve. Tara is one of my fellow waitresses at Abbe's Brasserie and although we occasionally work together, we haven't particularly struck up a rapport and have never gone out together socially. I waited for her to continue. "Is there a shift you want me to cover for you?" I finally asked presuming that was the reason for the call. "I can probably help you out."

"No. No nothing like that," she offered hesitantly. "It's just that… well… you know what a talker Ian is …"

I certainly did. My co-worker Ian or Iris as he preferred to be known (because as he was forever explaining to anyone who would listen, it was quite obvious with his impossibly long eyelashes, fabulous strut and encyclopaedic knowledge of skincare products, he should have been born a girl) was one of my best friends. He was wildly irreverent and utterly indiscreet.

I adored him. He in his turn was very fond of me and I don't think the fact that he also had size eight feet and could borrow my silver platform slingbacks for his Drag Queen act at The Jezebel Club had anything whatsoever to do with it.

"Yes," I agreed. "Once he gets started it's almost impossible to shut him up." I finally managed to yank my arm clear and sank down gratefully on to the sofa. "So, what's he been on about now?"

"It's just that he mentioned," Tara sounded a little embarrassed so I wondered what was coming next, "just in passing conversation … that you undertake Private Investigations … and so I wanted to know if you could take on a job for a friend of mine?"

Typical Ian! I'd given him the edited highlights of my recent adventures as a first-time amateur sleuth and now he was practically my agent. Well, he wouldn't be getting a commission, I thought crossly.

"Actually, what he did say," continued Tara, "was that although a highly-experienced investigator, you keep the waitressing on as a cover story."

I bit back a laugh at the absurdity of his exaggeration. I'd had one case, very nearly screwing it up. "Tara. Listen," I protested. "Ian is prone to, well to be nice let's call it sensationalism because in truth I haven't much …"

"Much time?" she misunderstood me. "That's such a shame. But what if my friend could pay more than your usual fee? Do you think you could fit her in?"

Fee? She had all of my attention now. "Well," I backtracked hastily. "Perhaps I might be able to squeeze something in. What's the story?"

"OK," Tara sounded relieved. "The thing is my friend Caroline is worried about her sister." From her delivery, she seemed to assume that this statement said it all.

"And?" I encouraged.

"Vanessa is younger than Caro and me. She's twenty-one and recently she's become involved with some people that," she cleared her throat, "well, the fact is Caroline and her family are a bit concerned about the group she's got herself mixed up with."

"So, what's the problem with them? Are they into serious drugs? Or crime?" I hazarded. "Because if so it's not me you should be talking to but someone who knows about these things…"

"No, no, nothing like that!" she cut in. "It's just that her family don't exactly approve of …"

I interrupted her impatiently. "Tara, my family have hardly ever approved of any of my friends and why on earth should they? You're telling me that this girl is over twenty-one and …"

This time it was Tara who interrupted me. "No, there's more to it than that. Look, I can't really explain over the phone. Would you agree to meet Caroline and talk it over?"

I thought a moment. "Well, OK. Sure, if you think I can help."

"Great. Thanks so much. And I'll be there too. Oh, and you'll like Caro's mother, Diana Maitland. She's a … "

"Mother?" I yelped. "Who said anything about mothers?"

Mothers, in my opinion, being one of life's natural hazards, are best avoided. They can be very tricky to deal

346

with. My own mother comes with a mental health warning, so I know what I'm talking about here.

"You don't happen to be free today, do you?" continued Tara blithely ignoring my interjection. "Because I'm seeing Caro this afternoon, at Mrs Maitland's house."

I held the receiver away and rested my head back against the sofa cushions and took a moment to deliberate. It would probably prove to be a complete waste of time but as I had nothing else planned for the next few hours, what did I have to lose by checking it out?

"Fine with me," I replied. "I'm not due at the restaurant until six. So yes, let's do it."

"Right," said Tara. "Give me five minutes and I'll call you back." And she hung up.

THE LOVE DETECTIVE
READING GROUP GUIDE

1: What did you think of the row between Clarry and Laura?

   Have you ever experienced the issue of jealousy (or at least the perception of it) with a friend?

2: Clarry loves food and is confident in her body size and shape. What are your thoughts on Body Image Activism and Body Positivity?

3: "Confidence in men so often displays itself with a sexual edge. Women instinctively recognise it and the suggestion of threat that can lie beneath its surface" thinks Clarry on meeting Simon Napier. Do you agree with this statement? What have your own observations been?

4: Clarry is reluctant to tell Laura about Simon's fuck-buddy relationship with Karen. Do you think it's right to be honest with a friend if you know her/his partner is being unfaithful? Or is it potentially too damaging to the friendship?

5: Flan is seventy years old, looks great, has bags of energy and is having an active sex life. She inspires Clarry. Do you think attitudes to ageing (particularly towards women) are changing? And do you have an older female role model?

6: Clarry embarks on a causal fling with fellow waiter, Tim. Is it ever a good idea to have a relationship with a co-worker? Or is it just too complicated?

7: "It struck me that might I, like much of society, be secretly afraid not just of poverty but of The Poor? And of what they could do if ever they grew tired of being the underdogs?" Clarry asks herself this question on meeting Dan, Maggie and Sheena. What are your thoughts on this?

8: "I noted how very ordinary they looked. You could pass them in the street or work alongside them in an office and would never know what monsters they truly were. They walk amongst us I thought. They are our fathers, our brothers, and our husbands" This is Clarry's immediate response as she watches the men at the "auction" being led away by the police. Do you think her reaction a fair one?

9: After the "auction" Clarry decides to talk out the experience and describe the fear and fury she felt. In the outpouring she finds her centre again. How important do you think speaking your emotions aloud (to yourself, your friends or a professional) is in the recovery process?

10: The Love Detective comes to a close with the following statement: "Anything can happen to us and around us. And maybe the trick is not to be afraid of whatever it is that's coming out way?"

Would you agree with this statement?